DARKMOON

BOOK 3 OF THE WITCHES OF CLEOPATRA HILL

CHRISTINE POPE

DARK VALENTINE PRESS

This is a work of fiction. Names, characters, places, and incidents are either the product of the author's imagination or are used fictitiously. Any resemblance to actual events, places, organizations, or persons, whether living or dead, is entirely coincidental.

DARKMOON

ISBN: 978-0692254547

Published by Dark Valentine Press

Cover design and book layout by Indie Author Services.

To learn more about this author, go to
www.christinepope.com.

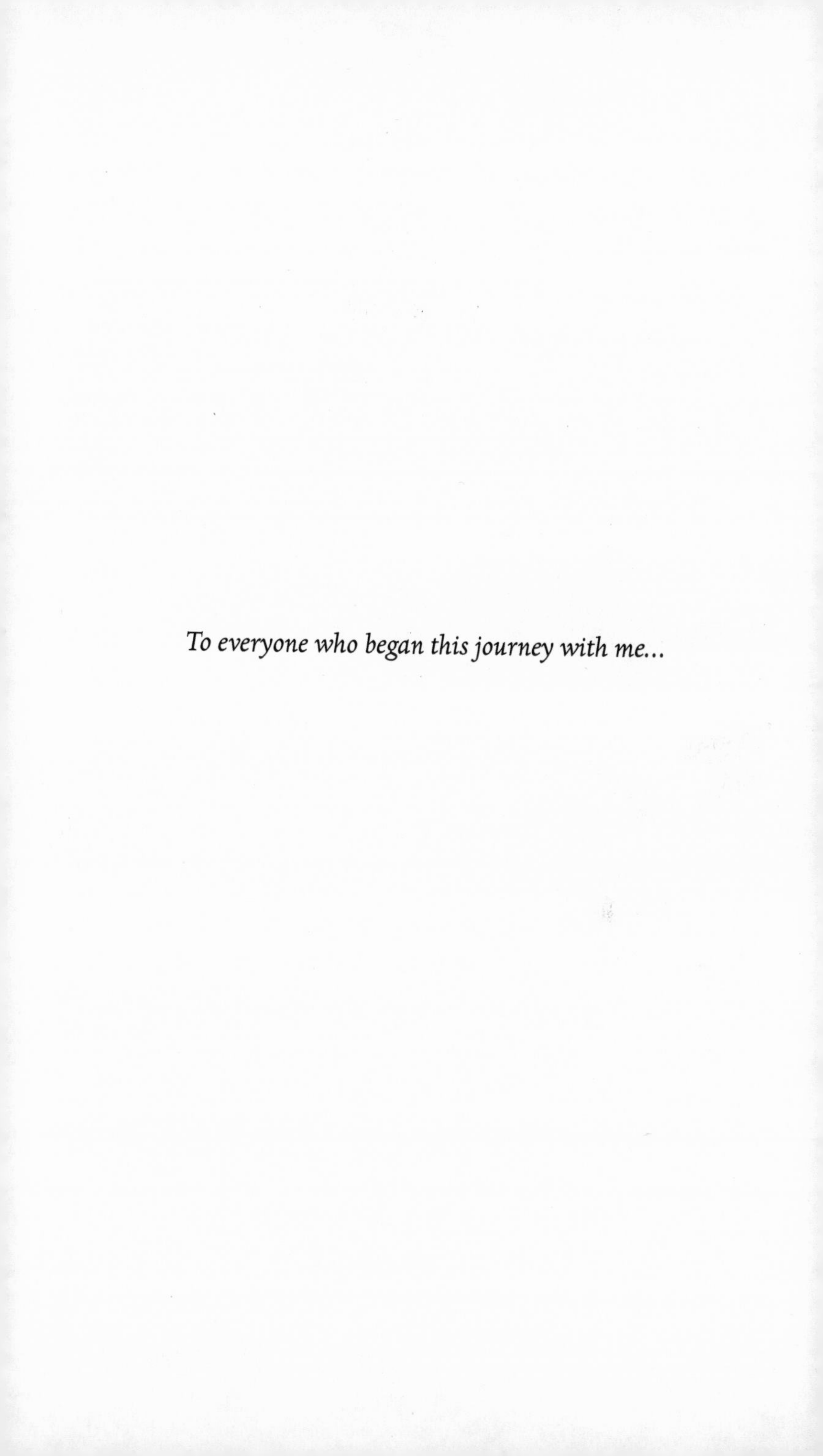

To everyone who began this journey with me...

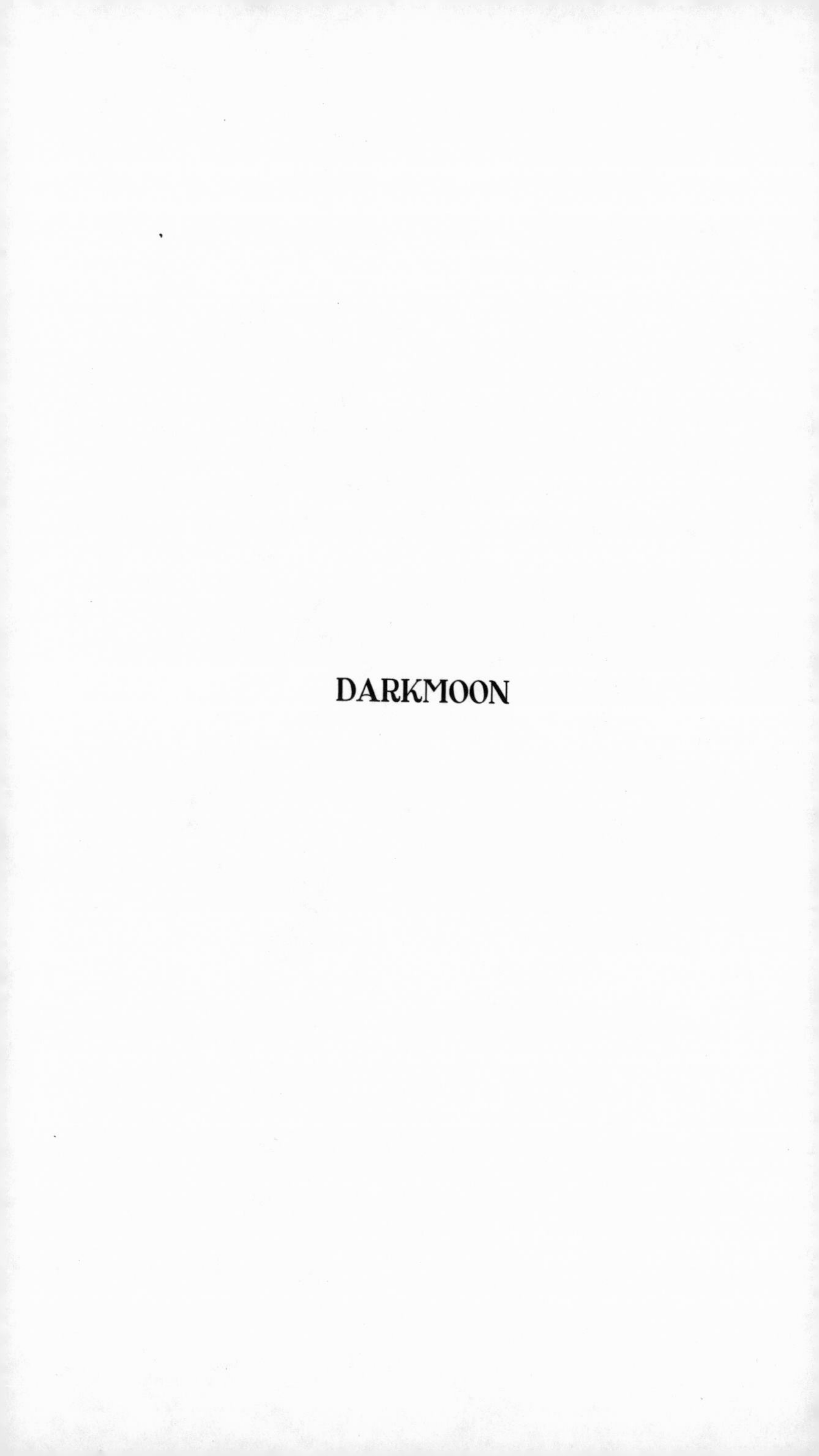

DARKMOON

CHAPTER ONE

Exile

When Sydney entered the train station, she took one look at my face and pulled me into a hug, her embrace as fierce as it was unexpected. Without saying anything, she picked up my suitcase, while I grabbed my purse and duffle bag from the bench where I'd been sitting. In silence we left the building, heading to where she'd parked her Focus in the small lot just outside. It wasn't until we were out of downtown and back on the freeway that she finally said, "You want to talk about it?"

All those unshed tears were still a logjam in my throat. I coughed, then shook my head and replied, "What's to say?"

The headlights of an oncoming car shone on her face briefly before they flicked past. I could see the tight set to her mouth, the worry in her eyes. "Angela—"

"Later," I cut in, knowing if I started talking now, I'd break down. And I really didn't want to have this conversation in her car. We could talk about it when I got home.

Home. What was home? Over the past few months I'd come to think of Connor's apartment as home, but it wasn't, not really. The rambling Victorian house waiting for me back in Jerome didn't feel much like home, either. I hadn't lived there long enough for it to have become mine yet. I realized then that I'd spent more time at Connor's place than in the house I'd inherited. No wonder it didn't exactly call out to me as a welcoming refuge.

But it was the only place I could go, so I let Sydney drive me there, the miles flashing past in silence until at last she pulled up in front of the house and parked there. We retrieved my meager luggage from the trunk and climbed the steps to the front door. It was a dark night, with barely a crescent moon, but I noticed the porch light was on. I frowned; was someone in my house?

Not bothering to hunt through my purse for the key, I laid a hand on the doorknob, willing the deadbolt to unlock itself. Which it did, the door swinging inward with a faint creak.

Sydney stared at me, mouth slightly open. "I've never seen you do that before."

"Well, my powers are a little…stronger…now." Talk about your understatements. Goddess only knows what Sydney would think if she'd seen the way I'd fought back the wolf-creature that Damon Wilcox had become.

"No kidding."

The overhead light in the entry was on, too. I scowled up at it, wondering if it had been on the whole time since I left almost three months ago. You'd think someone would have come by to check if that were the case.

But the mystery solved itself when I heard footsteps coming down the hallway toward us. Instinctively, I stepped in front of Sydney, preparing to mount a defense against the unknown intruder if necessary. Then I blinked as I saw my cousin Kirby enter the foyer.

It's hard to say who was more surprised, him or me. His gray eyes widened, even as I stammered, "K-*Kirby?*"

"Um, yeah."

"What are you doing here?"

His expression told me he was thinking exactly the same thing, but he said, "We've sort of been taking shifts watching the house. You know, turning the lights off and on, keeping the water running, making sure the pipes didn't freeze during that bad snowstorm we had back in January."

I supposed that made some sort of sense. When I left, I'd been so angry at my family and their reaction to Connor that I hadn't stopped to think what might become of the house if I left it unoccupied indefinitely. "Oh," I said after a lengthy pause. "Thanks, then."

Gaze flickering over to Sydney and back to me, he asked, "So…are you home now?"

There was a question I really didn't want to answer. But word would get out soon enough, and if I had Kirby spreading the news, I wouldn't have to worry about doing it myself. At the moment, I just wanted to hide in this house for about the next sixty or seventy years. I let out a breath. "Yes, I'm back." *For how long, I have no idea….* Since I didn't feel like going into it any more than that, I added, "But I'm really tired, so if you aren't in the middle of anything—"

"No," he said quickly. "I mean, I was going to watch a movie, maybe drink a beer, but I hadn't opened it yet. So I'll just let myself out."

Again he looked over at Sydney, almost as if he were expecting her to say something, illuminate the situation somehow, but I could tell she thought this was a family matter and therefore intended to stay out of it. So Kirby didn't exactly sigh, only went to the hall closet and got out his jacket, then shrugged into it. He paused, studying me carefully, his eyes full of questions. He must have seen that I was not in the mood to answer any of them, because he just said, "'Night, Angela." He nodded at Sydney, and she gave him a hesitant smile before he went to the door and left.

Sydney had been holding my suitcase the whole time. "Should I take this upstairs?" she asked, lifting it slightly in question.

"No, you can put it down there, at the foot of the stairs. I'll take it up later."

She did as I requested, then said, "That sounded good."

"What?"

"Kirby's beer."

"You hate beer."

"I mean, a *drink*. Don't you want one?"

Oh, yes, I did. A drink or ten. I had a feeling Syd was hoping that if she got some alcohol inside me, I'd tell her what was going on. Maybe that would work. Maybe if I blurred the lines with booze, it wouldn't hurt so much to confide in her, tell her how Connor had rejected me.

"Yeah," I said at last. "I guess we'll have to look and see if there's anything left to drink here…besides Kirby's beer, that is."

I set down my duffle bag and purse next to the suitcase, then headed toward the kitchen, Sydney a pace or two behind me. Once I got there, it looked as if the countertop wine rack had been left untouched. When I peered into the fridge, I saw Kirby's six-pack of Lumberyard IPA sitting on the bottom shelf. My throat tightened when I looked at it; the Lumberyard Brewing Company was walking distance from Connor's apartment, and we'd eaten and drunk there more than a few times over the past few months.

The contents of the refrigerator blurred, and I turned away, blinking furiously.

"Angela? You okay?"

I was incapable of speech at that moment, so I only shook my head.

She hesitated, biting her lip. "Do you still want a drink?"

I nodded.

"Okay. Just sit down, and I'll take care of everything."

Somehow I managed to blunder over to the kitchen table and fall into one of the rickety farmhouse-style chairs there. Sydney busied herself with getting out a couple of wine glasses, then selected one of the bottles from the rack. Pausing, she looked over at me and asked, "Corkscrew?"

I pointed toward the utensil drawer. Tears had begun to leak from my eyes and spill down my cheeks, and I reached up to wipe them away.

"Sweetie—" she began, taking a step toward me, but I shook my head.

"I-I'm okay. Just hurry up with that wine." As if to prove me wrong, more tears filled my eyes, forcing me to reach up with the back of my hand to try to blot them away. Streaks of black mascara and eyeliner came off on my skin; I'd put on full makeup for Damon's memorial service.

Brow puckered with worry, Sydney got out the corkscrew, then inexpertly pulled the cork out of the bottle. It came out crooked, but at least it didn't break off. After that she filled each glass almost full. She shot me a dubious glance. "When was the last time you ate?"

I shrugged. I had a dim recollection of eating a few cold cuts and some cheese at the reception following the service. The whole day had begun to take on a hazy, nightmarish quality, like something I'd experienced while suffering a high fever. I didn't want to think too hard about the service, or the reception…and especially not what had happened afterward.

"I'll see what's here," she said, correctly interpreting the shrug to mean that I hadn't eaten very much at all. To my annoyance, she left the glasses of wine sitting on the counter while she rummaged through the refrigerator. "Well, whoever's been hanging out here, they've left some good stuff behind. Here's some smoked gouda. Where would the crackers be?"

"Over there," I replied, jerking my index finger toward the pantry.

She opened the door, located a box of cracked wheat crackers, and arranged some on a plate, along with the cheese she'd found in the fridge. Finally she brought the plate over to the table, then returned with the wine.

I seized my glass and took a long swallow. It was a local red blend, and usually I found it fairly mellow and fruity. Now, though, it seemed to burn like acid when it hit my empty stomach. Although I felt as if I never wanted to eat again, I knew I'd better put some sort of a buffer in there. So I picked up a cracker, sliced off a bit of cheese, and then shoved it in my mouth.

"Better," Sydney said. She'd been smiling faintly as she watched me eat, but her expression abruptly sobered. "You ready to talk about it?"

Not really. However, I knew I couldn't hold her off indefinitely. And better that I should first relate the story to someone sympathetic, someone who didn't have any agenda where Connor was concerned.

Connor. Just the sound of his name in my thoughts was enough to send more tears welling in my eyes, and I swallowed another large gulp of wine. This time it didn't burn quite as much, instead feeling pleasantly warm. "It's bad, Syd," I said at last.

"I kind of figured." For the first time she took a sip of her own wine. "I just—what happened? You guys seemed so happy. So perfect for each other."

We were, I thought. *At least, we would have been, if it weren't for Damon.* How I'd ever begin to explain that, I didn't know. I wrapped my hands around the bowl of my wine glass, but I didn't drink. "You remember how I told you Connor's brother was the head of their clan, and that he wasn't exactly a nice person?"

"Understatement," she replied, with something very close to a snort. "Wasn't it his idea to kidnap you?"

"Yes. He wanted—he thought having me as his consort would help to break the curse."

"Curse?" she repeated, nose wrinkling.

I realized I'd never mentioned the whole Wilcox curse situation to her. Hard to say why, except I'd wanted to ignore the whole thing as much as possible. My relationship with Connor was new enough that children were way out of the picture, and if I didn't have a child of Jeremiah's line, then I wasn't in any danger. It was a pretty simple calculation.

As quickly as I could, I explained how, long ago, a Navajo witch had cursed Jeremiah Wilcox…and how that curse had affected every single woman attached to the Wilcox *primus* ever since.

"Holy shit," Sydney breathed when I was done. "So he thought your powers would destroy the curse. But how?"

"I don't know for sure. He did a lot of experimental magic, stuff no one else has tried. I'm sure he had a theory, but he didn't really confide much in Connor."

"So…." She drew out the word as she appeared to consider what I'd just told her. "I still don't get how that connects with you and Connor having a blow-out fight. I mean," she added quickly, "I'm assuming that's what happened."

"I don't think it was loud enough for a blow-out, but yeah, the end result was the same." No, that confrontation had been conducted in cold, calm tones, but it had been just as painful as if we'd been screaming at each other. "Damon got frustrated. He saw how things were with Connor and me, and—"

"He was jealous?"

It was my turn to snort. "No. That is, he never wanted me for *me,* just for what I am. But because he knew he couldn't use me to break the curse, he started exploring other kinds of magic. Dark magic."

"Darker than what he'd done before? 'Cause based on what you've told me, the guy wasn't exactly a saint to begin with."

"No, he wasn't, and yes, it was darker magic. Black, black magic." I paused, and drank some more wine. My stomach told me it needed more than just that one piece of cheese and cracker to soak up the alcohol, but I ignored it. "All those girls killed up in Flag?"

She nodded, blue eyes widening. "You're not saying—"

"It was Damon. Yeah. He'd gone…bad. Like a rabid dog, Connor's cousin said. And you know what you have to do with a rabid dog."

"Put it down." The words were barely above a whisper.

"Exactly. Problem was, no one in the clan was strong enough to do it. He was the *primus,* after all. So guess who ended up with that little job?" It was odd, but as I spoke, I could feel the tears recede. Maybe because I was relating all this in a dry tone, as if it had happened to someone else. A shrink would probably call that a distancing mechanism, but it was working for me at the moment.

This time Sydney's reply really was a whisper. "*You* had to do it?"

"Yeah. It was…awful. I don't need to go into the details. But at the end of it all, Damon was dead, and by my hand…and, as you can guess, that didn't go over so well with Connor."

"But—but he knew you had to do it, right? I mean, if you hadn't, wouldn't Damon have gone on killing?"

"Definitely. Connor knew that intellectually. But he just can't handle being around me...said every time he looks at me he thinks of how I killed his brother."

"Jesus Christ." She'd gone pale, the blush standing out on her white cheeks. "And so he just...threw you out?"

I winced. True, that was pretty much what had happened, but I still didn't like hearing it put so baldly. "Basically, yeah."

"So he said, what, 'get out'?"

Goddess, did I have to rehash the whole conversation? I could tell Sydney to stop picking at me, but I knew this was her way of trying to process what had happened. She just wanted to help. "He told me he needed to not be around me for a while."

To my surprise, she seemed to perk up a little at that. "Really? That's what he said?"

"Pretty much. True, it's a little more polite than just saying 'get the fuck out of my house,' but—"

"No," she broke in, "it's way better than that. He's upset right now. He's hurting. He didn't tell you that he never wanted to see you again—he just needs his space. You're taking a break. You're not broken up."

Oh, how I wanted to believe her. But she hadn't been there, hadn't seen the dead look in his eyes when he stared at me. True, he'd just buried his brother that day. We should have been comforting one another, though, not engaging in our own personal cold war.

But if there was even the slightest possibility that she might be right....

"Okay," I said at last. "If you want to take his words at face value, then maybe it's possible it's not totally over. It's just that right now I have a hard time believing that." And as the words left my lips, the tears followed right after, and I began to cry, body wracked as each sob tore its way out of me.

Sydney slipped out of her chair and came over, pulling me into her arms, holding me until at last the tears were spent and I couldn't cry anymore. My heart was dry as a desert.

Pulling away from me gently, she asked, "Do you want me to stay? I threw some stuff in the trunk as I was leaving, just in case. I could tell from the way you sounded on the phone that this was major."

I wiped my eyes again. No more mascara; it had long been washed away. "I love you, Syd," I said simply.

She smiled. "Love you, too. And you'll get through this. But let me go get my stuff."

In response I nodded, and she headed out to her car while I stayed in my chair and tried to pull in deep breaths. Yes, this was all really bad, but at least I wouldn't have to deal with it alone.

For now, that would have to be enough.

Sydney ended up staying with me for two days. When I asked about work, she just shrugged and said she'd called in sick, and when I gently probed about Anthony being okay with her being gone for so long, she shook her head at me and said, "He's a big boy. If he can't handle two days without me, then we're going to have to have a talk about clinginess."

After that, I let it go. I needed her there; the house felt so big and empty on the few occasions when she went out to get us food and other supplies that I knew I couldn't handle being there on my own. Not yet, anyway.

During one of those trips to Grapes to get us pizza, she was gone a fairly long time. I thought I knew why—I was in no shape to face any of my family, but I was fairly certain she'd stopped in at my Aunt Rachel's apartment to explain to her what was really going on. Maybe I should have been angry with Sydney for taking the initiative like that. I found that I didn't mind so much, though. Telling Syd had been hard enough. Having to repeat the whole story to my aunt would be even worse, because although she might refrain from saying "I told you so" out loud, she'd certainly be thinking it.

No, it was good that Sydney got that out of the way for me. Aunt Rachel would spread the word, and that meant whenever I finally felt ready to leave the house, I wouldn't have to worry about explaining myself over and over again.

On the third day, though, Syd couldn't put off work any longer. So she hugged me and told me to call if I needed her.

"No matter what," she said sternly as she paused on the porch and pulled her sunglasses out of her purse. "I mean it."

"I'm okay, Syd," I replied. It wasn't a total lie; by that point I felt as if I could get through at least an hour without feeling as if I were going to dissolve into tears.

And if I did, so what? No one would be around to see me sobbing uncontrollably, and I'd learned that I could break down, have my cry, then wipe my tears away and go on for another hour before that horrible choking sensation seized my throat and I began to weep again.

Probably not the best way to live, but I had to start somewhere.

Shifting her weight from one foot to another, she studied me for a few seconds, then nodded. "All right. I'll call you on my break."

"Sounds good," I told her, summoning a watery smile.

She didn't buy it, I could tell, but I also knew she had to leave now or be late for work. A quick hug, and then she was hurrying down the front walk to her car. She'd been parking it in front this whole time, since she claimed there was no way she was going to deal with the narrow alley that backed up to the garage, with its awkward angles and blind spots. I really couldn't blame her. Not wanting to go back into the house and face its emptiness, I sat down on the top porch step.

It was actually a beautiful day. Here in Jerome it was almost ten degrees warmer than Flagstaff, the temperatures in the upper 60s, puffy clouds scudding by. The trees were still bare, but some of them had the faintest mist of green along their branches, evidence of buds that would begin to pop any day now. And I could see down into the valley, watch the clouds trace their way over the hills and the river bottom, moving fast. My eyes seemed to be pulled northward, past the red rocks of Sedona, over the mesa....

Don't do it, I told myself. *Just look someplace else. Anyplace else.*

But somehow my gaze felt inexorably drawn to those brooding mountaintops in Flagstaff. We hadn't hiked all the way up to the top of Mt. Humphreys, since there was still too much snow for it to be safe for a beginner like me. However, Connor had promised we'd go in the late spring, saying that when you were standing up there, it felt as if you could see the whole world.

This time the pain came as a sudden knifing ache deep in my chest, as if someone had just buried a blade there. I let out a little gasp, felt the sting of tears in my eyes. Goddess, would this ever get better? Or was I destined to feel Connor's absence like a raw, gaping wound for the rest of my life?

I didn't know. I wasn't sure if anyone knew. This wasn't an ordinary breakup—or separation, if you wanted to use Sydney's more hopeful terminology. A *prima* and her consort were only supposed to be separated by death, and nothing else. I had never heard of a bonded couple like us simply…breaking up.

A shadow fell across the path, and I tore my gaze away from the faraway peaks in Flagstaff, seeing probably the last person I would have expected approaching the house.

Margot Emory.

I blinked a few times, hoping it would be enough to dispel the tears that had begun to gather. No way did I want Margot Emory catching me in a moment of weakness, however well-deserved.

She paused at the bottom of the steps and looked up at me. Her hair, dark enough for a Wilcox, was pulled back into a silvery barrette at the base of her neck, and even though the morning light was merciless, I couldn't see any lines in her pale, smooth skin. As usual, she looked perfect, minimal makeup flawless, not a hair out of place. No wonder Lucas Wilcox had been so interested in her.

But my own love life was complicated enough without worrying about Lucas' romantic woes at the same time. "Hi, Margot," I said, praying that I would sound reasonably normal and not clotty with choked-back tears.

"Good morning, Angela," she replied. Her voice was brisk and cool, just as I remembered it. "So your friend is gone?"

"Yes. She couldn't take any more time off work." I sat up a little straighter, setting my palms down against the sun-warmed wood of the porch. "What, were you just waiting for her to leave so you could come talk to me?"

A flash of irritation crossed Margot's face. "I did think it better if I could speak to you alone."

Great. So this definitely wasn't a social call. Sighing, I got to my feet and said, "Then I guess we'd better go inside."

"If you wish."

I most certainly did wish. I wasn't sure exactly what she wanted to talk to me about, but I guessed it probably wasn't the sort of thing I really wanted my neighbors overhearing. Especially since my cousin Adam's parents lived just a few doors down and often walked their dog right past my house.

So I led Margot inside. For a second or two I was tempted to take her into the dining room, make her sit in that formal room to speak her piece, but I decided that wasn't very polite. Instead, I took her back to what had been the sitting room and now was the family room, with its comfortable leather couch and matching arm chairs, and small fireplace. It wasn't really cold enough today for a fire, though, so I left that alone.

"Can I get you anything?" I asked, knowing it was probably best if I followed the forms, even if my heart wasn't in it. "Coffee? Tea? Water?"

"Nothing, thank you," she replied as she sat down in one of the chairs.

Figuring I might as well get this over with, I plopped down on the couch and crossed my arms. "So what did you want to talk to me about?"

Anyone else might have looked surprised at my lack of ceremony, but Margot merely tilted her head slightly and said, "I wanted to know if you were ready to be our *prima* now. Or do you plan to hide in this house indefinitely and only speak to your civilian friend?"

Anger flashed through me. That was fine, though. I preferred anger to the sadness that seemed to lurk behind every thought, every memory, just waiting to pounce. I snapped, "Well, I don't know, Margot. I thought the clan got along just fine the three months I was up in Flagstaff, so I figured a day or two more while I tried to get my head straight would be all right."

Her dark eyes held understanding, but no sympathy. "Do you think you're the only person to have ever loved and lost?"

Despite her even tone, I caught the edge to her words. Certainly I'd never envisioned Margot being in love, but then again, I didn't know that much about her, as she had always been a very private person. Yes, she was a clan elder, even though I knew she was about ten years younger than my Aunt Rachel. She liked to garden. Her mother was still alive, although she'd moved down the hill to a fifty-five-plus community in Clarkdale. And that was about the extent of my knowledge regarding Margot Emory.

"Of course I don't think that," I retorted. "But I'm pretty sure I'm the only prima to have ever split from her consort. Or is there something you haven't told me?"

She shook her head. "No, I'm afraid your situation seems to be unique."

Great. I was unique.

"And, despite what you might think," she continued, "we got by while you were gone, but we certainly weren't okay. The *prima* should have been here for Imbolc and Ostara, to lead the observances. We muddled through, but it's more than that. The *prima* is the touchstone for our clan, the guide. Our protection. You understand that now, don't you?"

I had to nod. Until my powers awakened, I really hadn't grasped the true strength of a *prima*. Protection. Defense. I had used that power to defeat Damon Wilcox. Fighting back a sigh, I told her, "Yes, I do. Or at least I think I do. But I'm not sure how much protection you need, now that Damon is dead. Connor certainly isn't one to follow in his brother's footsteps."

"Are you sure about that?"

"Yes," I said flatly. He might have thrown me out, might have broken my heart in a hundred thousand pieces, but I still trusted Connor to do the right thing when it came to using his magic, even if that magic wasn't precisely his anymore, but the power of a primus. "Connor is...good. I know you don't want to believe that of a Wilcox, but it's true. And so are his cousin Lucas and so many more I could name.

I won't defend Damon's actions, because they were terrible, but he's gone. We're safe."

Throughout this speech Margot had listened patiently, but I could tell by the slight furrowing of her brow that she didn't really believe me. Fine. Sooner or later she'd figure it out. Or maybe she wouldn't. I knew I didn't have the strength to keep arguing with her about it.

"Perhaps you're right about that," she said at length. "Even so, our clan still needs its *prima*. So are you going to do your duty by your clan or not?"

I knew there was only one reply I could possibly make. That destiny had been mine long before I met Connor Wilcox. My heart might be shattered, but my spirit and soul were still intact.

"Yes, Margot," I replied calmly. "I am ready to be our *prima*."

I can't say things went back to normal after that—after all, I'd barely been the *prima* for two months before Damon Wilcox kidnapped me—but it did feel as if everyone had been holding their collective breaths, waiting to see what I would do. After I realized there wasn't much I could do except try to settle back in Jerome and put Connor Wilcox from my mind, I didn't exactly stop hurting. However, I did find enough to occupy my time that those occasions when the pain welled up and threatened to overcome me gradually grew farther and farther apart.

After the first week, people stopped tiptoeing around me. I couldn't stop Adam from giving me hopeful glances, as if he was thinking that now the Connor episode was safely behind me, he might have a chance again. I knew that would never happen, that I couldn't even conceive of being with anyone except Connor, but I couldn't think of a polite way to tell Adam that. Mostly I tried to be friendly and casual, and maybe he got the hint and maybe he didn't. All I cared about was whether he'd attempt to force the issue, but he knew better than to try that. One thing about Adam; he was patient. I just didn't know how to tell him that he could wait a hundred years, and it still wouldn't change the way I felt about Connor.

It would've been easier if I could have hated him.

I distracted myself with planning the remodel of the kitchen, and consulted with Terri, the decorator who'd done the rest of the house, as well as an architect she recommended. It was going to be a massive project, since we'd decided to expand the kitchen another five feet into the side yard. I had to assure Margot and the other two elders that the exterior of the house would be restored so you'd never know the difference, and they still didn't look thrilled by the prospect. All right, Ruby had barely touched the place all the years she'd lived there, according to them, and I suppose they wanted me to follow in her footsteps. Still, it was my house, and my remodel. I'd do it the way I wanted...and hope it would be enough to distract me.

Because of ordering tile and appliances, and having to wait for the architect's preferred work crew to be available, construction wouldn't actually get started until almost the end of May. That was good, because when I roused myself from my catalogues and blueprints and paint samples, I realized more than a month had passed since I'd left Flagstaff.

See? I told myself. *You can do this.*

What Sydney thought of my latest distraction, I didn't know for sure. That is, I could tell she guessed I was over-compensating, making massive plans because that way I wouldn't have to think about Connor. Fine. I didn't have a problem with distracting myself by whatever means necessary. It wasn't as if he'd been calling or sending me pleading texts or anything like that. Not one word since that horrible night when I walked out of his apartment. Not a single word.

In fact, I'd let everything pass by in such a blur that it wasn't until I was looking at the calendar I had hanging in the library and putting a big star on May 27th—the day the contractors were going to start work—that I realized it had been more than six weeks since I'd come back to Jerome. Good, that had to mean I was healing, right? That so much time had gone by without my hardly noticing?

So much time....

And then a stray thought passed through my mind, followed by, *Oh, shit. Oh,* shit.

Six weeks, and no period. I should've gotten one at the beginning of April, and then again a week ago. I wasn't like Sydney, who was so regular you could practically set a clock by her. Sometimes I was late by a week or two, or even three, and then things would reset. But not like this. Not two months in a row, and nothing.

My hands started to shake so badly that I dropped the pen I was holding.

Get it together, I told myself. *It could just be stress. You were almost three weeks late when you were studying for your AP exams. And you've been under way worse stress than that.*

That sounded sensible enough. I didn't really believe it, though.

Only one way to find out. Drive down to Cottonwood, go to the closest drugstore—Walgreens—and get a pregnancy test. I could do that. In fact, it would be easier than ever, since a few weeks earlier I'd decided I needed to have my own transportation, and went with Syd to the local Jeep dealership, where I made the salesman go bug-eyed when I calmly wrote a check for the entire cost of a brand-new Cherokee. Actually, Syd went kind of bug-eyed, too. Yes, I'd told her that I'd come into a good sum of money when Aunt Ruby passed away, but I don't think she really got it until I paid cash for a thirty-thousand-dollar SUV.

Anyway, I'd been coming and going on my own for several weeks now, so no one would think anything of me going down the mountain for a shopping trip. And I knew I had to do it now, before I lost my nerve.

After gathering up my keys, I went out to the garage and opened the door, then got in the Cherokee and pulled out. I didn't bother to close the garage door, as I was going straight to the drugstore and then back home.

I'd been shopping at that store for years, but luck was with me, and the woman working the checkout counter was new and didn't recognize me. After I'd thrown the pregnancy test in my basket, I'd contemplated getting a few more odds and ends, just to camouflage that one portentous box, but decided against it. What was the point? Even if I'd shoved it in a plain brown paper bag, the clerk would still have had to pull it out to scan the barcode.

So I put it down on the counter as casually as possible, and she rang me up without blinking. I wondered how many women she saw buying those tests every day. A lot, I hoped. Then she wouldn't have any reason to remember the girl with the dark hair and the scared green eyes.

Once I was back home, I went upstairs to my bathroom and locked the door. Silly, because of course I was alone in the house. No one would walk in on me. Still, somehow I felt a little better after I'd made sure I wouldn't be disturbed.

I scanned the directions, but come on—peeing on a stick isn't rocket science. For the longest moment I hesitated, staring at the piece of white plastic in my hand, my heart pounding away. Then I bit my lip, went over to the toilet, and did what I had to do.

Afterward, the seconds seemed to tick by in slow motion. Was I breathing? I couldn't even say for sure.

Finally I looked down at the stick where I'd set it down on the sink, on top of a square of toilet paper. Two little pink lines.

Two.

No. Oh, no.

Blessed Brigid's charm to prevent this from happening had failed me, but in my despair, it was still Her I called on then.

Goddess, what do I do now?

What do I do?

CHAPTER TWO

Decisions

I DON'T KNOW FOR SURE HOW LONG I SAT HUDDLED ON the bathroom floor, pressed up against the clawfoot tub, shudders raking their way through my body. My heart pounded and pounded, and I kept hearing Margot Emory's words echoing through my mind.

The wives of Jeremiah's line would never live to see their children grow up.

No, I wasn't a wife…I wasn't anything to Connor, apparently. But it was his child I carried, and that meant I'd meet the same fate as all those other women, no matter what my marital status might be.

At last I pulled myself to my feet, sucked in a shaky breath, then turned the spigot and splashed some water on my face. It was icy cold, but I didn't care. Actually, it was better that way. I needed the shock of the cold water against my skin to quell the panic within me, to bring me back to earth.

Get a grip, I told myself. *It's a baby. It's not like it's the monster from* Alien *and is going to burst through your chest at any moment and kill you on the spot.*

True. But eventually I'd end up just as dead as any of the parade of actors and extras killed on-screen in those movies, albeit probably in a less gruesome fashion.

The thought tickled at the back of my mind, quiet, insidious.

Get rid of it. Connor threw you out…there's no reason for you to keep it.

There was a Planned Parenthood in Prescott. I could make an appointment, drive over….

No. It was the same deep, quiet voice I had heard in my mind before, when I'd wondered if it might have been better for Damon to have bonded with me, just to avoid all the death and destruction he'd left in his wake after it turned out that Connor was my consort instead. And in that moment I knew I could never do such a thing. Not because I believed myself to be on any particular moral high ground—I'd always believed a woman should choose what was best for herself and her future—but because Connor and I had made this baby out of love, even if that love had later withered and died. I didn't know why the contraceptive spell had failed, or what I should do next, but I couldn't destroy something that had come from such beauty.

With a sigh, I wrapped the plastic stick with its ominous pink lines in more toilet paper and then dropped it in the trash can. It had told me what I needed to know, and I didn't want to look at it anymore. I knew I should probably be calling Planned Parenthood to get a real test, for confirmation and to determine just how far along I was, but that could wait a day or two. My aunt and I saw a civilian GP down in Cottonwood when the need for something beyond over-the-counter medicine or folk cures was required, since our clan didn't currently have a healer. I knew my doctor could probably do the same thing for me as the staff at Planned Parenthood. But she knew me; there would be questions, and I just didn't know how to answer them.

I could hear my phone ringing from where I'd left it on the dresser in my bedroom. I almost let it roll over to voicemail, but then I realized it was probably Sydney calling, and she'd just keep calling back until I answered her. She'd made me promise to go to the Spirit Room with her, since Black Forest Society was playing, and although I'd tried to protest, had said I didn't want to see a band Connor liked so much, she said it was important that I go.

"Kind of like shock therapy," she told me. "You can't hide from things forever. We saw them last summer and had a good time."

All of that was true, I supposed. I couldn't block out everything that might raise the specter of a memory I'd shared with Connor. Especially now, when I had something I really couldn't hide from. Not for long, anyway.

As I went into the bedroom, I placed one hand on my stomach, which of course still felt completely flat. At least I hadn't been throwing up or anything. From time to time I had felt a little tired, but I'd just figured that was because of everything that was going on and the general ennui that had surrounded me ever since I came back to Jerome after Connor threw me out. I'd had no reason to believe I might be pregnant. Or actually, I'd had several reasons, but my grief-fogged brain had skipped right over them.

I picked up the phone. "Hi, Sydney."

She launched into a reply without even the semblance of a preamble. "So, Anthony got called in to work, which means I don't think we'll be able to make dinner, since he's not off until seven-thirty. Can we just meet you at the Spirit Room at eight?"

In a way, that was a relief. That meant less time where I'd have to pretend to act normal around them. "Sure. I'll get us some good seats."

"Great." A pause, and then she asked, "Are you okay? You sound funny."

"I'm fine," I replied, the automatic response, whether it was true or not. "Allergies, maybe. I just had a sneezing fit after doing some dusting."

"Okay," she said, but I could tell from her tone that she didn't quite believe me. Then again, she knew I'd been skirting the edges of depression for a while. It had been getting better, but that didn't mean I didn't stop suddenly from time to time and let the tears flow over me whenever I let my guard down. "Well, then, we'll see you around eight. It might be a little later, depending on how long it takes Anthony to close up."

"No worries," I told her, since I knew that was what she wanted to hear. "See ya."

"'Bye!" she chirped, falsely cheery, and I hit the "end" button and tossed my phone on the bed.

Then I looked up at the clock. A quarter after three, which meant I had about five hours to compose myself and get myself in a mental state where Sydney wouldn't notice anything was wrong.

Right.

Since it was a Tuesday night, the Spirit Room wasn't all that crowded when I got there a little before eight. I knew a lot of the crowd would start trickling in later, and in fact the band was still setting up, so I could tell they weren't going to start at eight on the dot. Moving purely by force of habit, I went to the bar, then realized I couldn't order my usual glass of wine. A pang of guilt went through me as I thought of all the wine I'd consumed over the past month or so. Not enough to get plowed every night, but still way more than anyone in the early stages of pregnancy should've been drinking. Well, I couldn't do much about that. I'd just have to quit cold turkey now and hope that would be enough.

It also didn't help that my cousin Marcus was tending bar that night. Sometimes he worked here at the Spirit Room, and sometimes up at the Asylum bar at the Grand Hotel at the top of the thill. Just my luck that he was on duty tonight, instead of one of the other two bartenders, both of whom were civilians.

"Hey, Angela," he said, and started to reach under the bar. "Glass of wine?"

"Um, no," I said quickly. "Just some"—I racked my brains; I knew I shouldn't be drinking caffeine, and I didn't like ginger ale—"just some mineral water, thanks."

He raised an eyebrow. "You feeling all right?"

"Very funny." He was about five years older than I, close enough in age that he wasn't too over-awed by my status as *prima,* and therefore didn't see a problem with giving me some shit when the situation warranted. "I just don't feel like drinking tonight, okay?"

"Hey, no worries," he replied, giving me a wink, and pulled out a glass and filled it with ice and soda water, then garnished it with a lime. After pushing it across the bar toward me, he added, "This one's on me."

"Very generous of you."

A grin, and then he turned away from me to help a couple in their early thirties who'd just approached the bar. I didn't recognize them, so I guessed they were tourists. Good; I really didn't want to deal with someone I knew commenting on my odd choice of beverage.

I took my soda water to one of the high booths at the very back of the room. That seating was more comfortable, and besides, while I wanted to hear the music, I didn't think I could handle being right up next to the stage, being that close to the band. No, I didn't know them personally, but it still felt way too intimate to be there almost in their laps, so to speak. Also, I noticed a young man around my age, maybe a little older, setting up an easel next to them, and realized that he was going to paint along with the music. I vaguely recalled Connor mentioning seeing them do something similar at a show he'd gone to before we met, but I hadn't really put two and two together. It was hard enough to be here at all without having to sit and watch someone paint…and maybe wonder what Connor would be painting if he were here instead.

Scowling, I sipped my soda water and wished I'd told Sydney that I couldn't come, that I had stomach flu or cramps from hell or something that would've gotten me out of having to be here. She always did have a knack for steamrollering over my objections, although I had a feeling that if I'd mentioned projectile vomiting, she probably would have left me alone.

Can't be helped now, I thought. At least I didn't see anyone from the local McAllister contingent in the bar, although that didn't mean they wouldn't show up later, after the band got started. Clearly, I'd revealed my inexperience by getting here right on time.

But then Sydney and Anthony came in, spotting me immediately, since I was sitting so close to the front door. "Hey," I said lamely, and Anthony gave me an equally limp "hey" in reply. I knew he was disappointed about Connor's and my breakup, since that sort of killed his "in" for possibly getting a vineyard of his own. Life sucks sometimes.

Sydney, however, chirped a cheerful "hi!" before sliding in the booth next to me. She gave my glass of mineral water the side-eye but didn't say anything except, "Hey, Anthony, can you get me a rum and Diet Coke?"

He didn't quite shudder, but I could tell what he thought of her drink choice. Not that surprising, considering he was something of a wine connoisseur. Being a wise man, though, he didn't say anything, just nodded and headed off to the bar.

"What is up with *that?*" Sydney asked as soon as he was gone, pointing a hot-pink fingernail at my glass of mineral water.

"I just didn't feel like drinking, that's all," I replied.

"Seriously? Miss 'I'm Going to Arm-Wrestle You for the Last Half Glass of Wine in That Bottle'?"

"Very funny."

"I'm not joking."

I shrugged and pretended to be absorbed in watching the artist on stage start prepping his canvas, even as the band went through their sound checks. Not that they had all that much to do, as there was only a drummer and the lead singer/guitarist. I knew on their album they had a cellist play on some tracks, but I didn't see a third person. Maybe she wasn't available for this particular gig.

"Maybe I thought I should lay off for a while. Drinking really doesn't solve anything."

"No, but it at least makes you *feel* as if you're solving something." She subsided a bit as Anthony returned, holding her rum and Diet Coke and a glass of red wine for himself. "Thanks, sweetie."

Did it make me a horrible person to think how hard it was to watch their casual intimacy? They'd definitely toned it down around me, but I could still see how close they'd gotten, how Sydney seemed to have clicked with Anthony in a way she never had with any of her other boyfriends. I was happy for her, truly, and yet it hurt to see her happiness and know that mine had been torn away from me through no fault of my own.

Well, all right, I'd made the decision to stop Damon Wilcox, keep him from hurting anyone else. I supposed I could've just walked away. But I had a feeling that would only have made matters worse. How could I have possibly known that doing the right thing would end up destroying my relationship with Connor?

"So, what up?" Sydney asked, and I blinked and glanced over at her.

"Huh?'

"Earth to Angela. What've you been up to? I haven't heard from you in a few days."

I gave a too-casual shrug. "Oh, nothing. Getting ready for the contractors. They'll be here next Tuesday, right after Memorial Day."

Anthony sipped his wine before asking, "So what are you going to do while they're working on the kitchen?"

"Eat out a lot, I guess," I said. "Although my aunt has said I can drop by for dinner whenever I want while the remodel's going on."

Yes, bless her, Aunt Rachel hadn't been quite as "I told you so" as I'd feared. Not that she could completely conceal her relief at my being back in Jerome, but I thought she also worried for me, could see that I wasn't bouncing back from this separation the way I should. How could I, though? This wasn't just a simple girlfriend/boyfriend breakup—this was a *prima* separating from her consort, something that had never happened before, at least in McAllister history.

"Mmm," Sydney put in. "Your Aunt Rachel is the *best* cook. I'd stretch out this remodel for as long as possible, if I were you."

"Considering the way most of these projects tend to go, that's probably going to happen whether or not I want it to."

She giggled and sipped at her rum and Diet Coke, then leaned her head against Anthony's shoulder. I forced in a deep breath and drank some of my mineral water, telling myself I couldn't forbid the entire world a PDA just because I'd been deprived of it myself. That sounded very sensible, even though I could feel the ache beginning in my chest, the hot sting of tears in my eyes.

This was really getting old.

Luckily, though, the band started up then, playing a song I recognized from Connor's CD. It sounded a little different now, minus the long, mournful notes of the cello moving behind the quick finger-picking on the steel-string guitar and the driving beat of the drums. Still, it was enough to recall how I had awoken that morning in Connor's apartment, hearing this music drift up below and wondering how I would be able to free myself from him.

Now I could only think about how much I wanted to be back there, to hear the mellow baritone of his voice and the flash of those green eyes in their frame of thick, sooty lashes. To lie in his arms as the sunlight poked through the blinds and lay in faint glowing lines across the brick-colored comforter that covered us.

In that moment, it all got to be too much, and I set down my glass of water, got up from the booth, and rushed out of the bar, my eyes blurring with tears. Outside, the air was cool against my fevered cheeks, and I stumbled a few paces down the side street, stopping in front of a closed jewelry shop, where the glow from the little white lights in the display window provided some faint illumination.

Goddess, I can't do this. I can't.

"Angela!"

Shit. I put up a hand to blot away my tears, noting that at least Sydney had come alone. Then again, what guy, even one as seemingly kind and enlightened as Anthony, would willingly barge in on a girl weeping alone? That was what girlfriends were for.

"I'm okay," I said, not looking at her when she stopped a pace or two away from me.

"No, you're not." Setting her hands on her hips, she watched me closely.

At least we were alone; people did hang out on the sidewalks around the Spirit Room to have a smoke or chat where they wouldn't disturb the band, but as the jewelry store and the gift shop next to it were both closed, no one had much of a reason to come this far down the dark little side street.

"Come on," Sydney said, her tone even gentler this time. "This is more than being sad about Connor. I've been paying attention these past few weeks. It seemed like you were doing better. And now a meltdown?"

"It's just—hearing that music," I finished lamely.

Silence, her blue eyes sharp on my face. I knew some people thought Sydney was kind of an airhead, but she really wasn't. She knew people.

More importantly, she knew me.

"You really expect me to believe that?" she asked, after a long pause.

No, I didn't. And we'd been friends too long for me to believe that she was going to let this go. She'd prod and she'd pry—not in a mean way, but because she knew I'd clam up if she didn't keep after me to tell her what was wrong.

And so, since I knew she'd find out eventually anyway, I blurted, "I'm pregnant."

Dead silence. She just stood there, brain clearly on overdrive as she stared at me. Finally, "Oh, shit. *Shit*." Obviously she'd recalled what I'd told her about the curse, and how this was a little more complicated than just an unplanned pregnancy.

"Shit, exactly."

Another long pause. "What are you going to do?"

I slumped up against the brick of the building and watched my blurry shadow fall against the cracked pavement. "I don't know. This wasn't supposed to happen."

"So you were…careful?"

Well, I thought *I was.* I allowed myself a bitter chuckle, then said, "I was a good little witch and performed a charm to prevent pregnancy every time Connor and I had sex. I guess it didn't work as well as I thought it would."

She pursed her lips as she appeared to work that over in her mind. Maybe she was wondering whether to inquire why I hadn't used a more conventional method of birth control. Luckily, she didn't, instead saying, "Are you…." The question trailed off, as if she didn't quite have the nerve to ask it.

That was all right. I knew exactly what she'd intended to ask. "Yes, I'm keeping it."

"But—"

"I know." *Yes, I'm keeping it...even if that means I'm sealing my own death warrant.*

Her eyes suddenly seemed too bright, even in the dim reflection from the little fairy lights in the shop window. She blinked, asking, "Okay. It's just—okay. It's your decision. You're going to tell him, right?"

"Why should I?"

"Because—it's his baby, too."

"So? Obviously he doesn't care enough to have even tried to contact me once during the past few months, so why should I bother?"

Rubbing the side of her head as if it suddenly pained her, she was quiet for a moment. Finally, she dropped her hand by her side and began, "Look, Ange, I watch a lot of reality shows—"

"And that qualifies you to give me advice here?"

"Well, yeah, it kind of does."

I crossed my arms and gave her a skeptical look.

Undeterred, she went on, "Anyway, what I was about to say was the only thing worse than telling a guy you're pregnant is *not* telling him you're pregnant. You can't hide this from Connor, Angela. You just can't. Sooner or later he'd find out, and he'd never forgive you. Or at least, he'd find it a lot harder to forgive you."

Oh, deep down I knew she was right. I just couldn't bear the thought of seeing him again…or worse, asking to see him and having him refuse to do so. What then? Would I still have the responsibility of telling him about the baby if he wouldn't even meet with me?

But that, as my aunt liked to say, was just borrowing trouble. I hadn't reached out to him, so I had no idea whether I'd get shot down unmercifully or not. I looked away from Sydney, stared up at the deep black sky, watched the stars twinkling there. I could see the Big Dipper just above the heavy shoulders of Mingus Mountain, which was a deeper black against the velvet sky.

"I know," I said at last, my voice sounding defeated even to myself. "I guess I just wanted to…I don't know…have it confirmed independently before I tried to contact him. I mean, those tests aren't foolproof."

For a few seconds she didn't say anything. Maybe she was thinking the same thing I was. True, those tests weren't completely accurate, but a ninety-eight-percent chance was still pretty good odds.

"Do you want me to go with you?" she asked then. "I mean, to your doctor or Planned Parenthood or whatever?"

"Would you?" It wasn't until she offered that I realized how much I'd been dreading going alone. With Sydney at my side, maybe it wouldn't be quite as bad.

"Absolutely," she responded immediately. "Like you even have to ask."

"Thank you," I told her. Simple words, but I could only hope she'd hear the sincerity in them, know how much this meant to me. "I'll call PP tomorrow and see when they can fit me in. I feel…weird…about going to my own doctor."

"I totally get it." She hesitated, then looked over her shoulder and up the steep street to the corner where the Spirit Room stood. "You going to come back inside?"

I shook my head. "I don't—I can't do that right now. Tell Anthony I'm sorry, okay?"

"No worries. He knows you've been through a lot. And I won't say anything else. I mean, no one will know until you're ready to let them know."

Thanking her again seemed redundant, so I gave her a quick hug before I made my way back up to Main Street, passing the open door of the bar and hearing the music drift out from within, then heading on up the hill to my house. Sydney's offer had both touched me and reminded me of something very important.

I might think I was alone in this, but I really wasn't.

Two days later we drove to Prescott to the Planned Parenthood office there. Everything was very new, clean, and modern; it seemed clear to me that the facility hadn't been open for very long. I peed in a cup and had them check my blood and all my other vitals.

"You're definitely pregnant," the doctor told me. "Looks like around nine weeks. I'd like to schedule an ultrasound in the next week or so, just to fine-tune things. Do you have a doctor closer to home you'd like to see, or do you want to come back here?"

"I—I'm not sure," I admitted. "Can I call back in a few days to set that up?"

"Of course," she replied. "Everything is looking fine, and you're in perfect health otherwise, so an extra day or two isn't going to make much of a difference."

I thanked her, and then she left me to get dressed and go back out to meet Sydney. After giving her a little nod, I went to the medical assistant at the front desk and told her I'd probably be scheduling an ultrasound, but I wasn't sure when. It seemed she was used to that sort of delay, because she just smiled and handed me a business card, and told me to contact them when I was ready.

"Are you going to call Connor now?" Sydney asked after we left the building and were headed back to Jerome.

For a minute I only watched the road passing by, the pale golden grasses blowing in the brisk breeze. "I will. But there's something else I have to do first."

She raised an eyebrow, but when she saw I wasn't going to volunteer any more information, she just shook her head and leaned forward to turn up the music. I guessed she could tell I wasn't much in the mood to talk.

Unfortunately, I knew I had a lot of talking ahead of me. It just wouldn't be with her.

Expressions quizzical, the three clan elders—Margot Emory, Bryce McAllister, and Allegra Moss—sat at my dining room table, waiting for me to explain why I'd summoned them to the house. Of course, as *prima,* I had the prerogative to do so…I just hadn't exercised it before now.

I'd realized as I left the Planned Parenthood facility that it was my responsibility to tell the elders what was going on. Anything that affected me affected the clan as well, and hiding my condition from them wouldn't do anyone any good, even if making such a confession to that trio was high on my list of extremely embarrassing situations I would rather have avoided.

"I've just…discovered something," I began, wishing I didn't sound quite so shaky and nervous. Then again, I probably had every right to be. Wishy-washy word choice, too, although I wasn't sure what the best way to approach this might be. Blurting out "I'm pregnant" didn't seem all that appealing, either. They were all adults, most of them with at least twenty years on me, although with Margot that number was probably closer to fifteen. I doubted they thought Connor and I had been spending our nights together in Flagstaff telling ghost stories and braiding each other's hair.

"What is it?" Bryce asked. There was a note of worry in his voice already, and I thought that didn't seem to be a very good sign. He was a strong warlock, gifted in magical defense, but he also had a quick temper. His reaction was the one I feared the most.

Margot and Allegra remained silent, watching me. Margot's expression was opaque, face bland and perfect as that of a mannequin, while Allegra's features seemed to show a somewhat lively curiosity. That didn't surprise me too much, as Allegra tended to be one of those people who was inquisitive about *everything*. Goddess knows her own children had never been able to get away with anything without her ferreting out the facts eventually.

I pulled in a breath, let it out, and said, "I've just found out that I'm pregnant."

Silence. Deep, hideous silence. Margot's face went even more still, if that were possible, and Bryce settled heavily against the back of his chair, as if someone had just struck him. Allegra tilted her head to one side and watched me, her mouth pursing slightly.

She was the one to break the silence. "And you need help getting rid of it?"

In a horrible way, it made sense that she'd been the one to ask the question. Her skill was with herbs and potions, and I'd heard rumors that she'd helped out a McAllister girl or two who'd found herself in my situation. Safer and quicker than the civilian equivalent of the procedure, but of course that wasn't why I'd asked to speak with the three of them. If I had made such a decision, I would have approached her quietly, and alone.

Shaking my head, I replied, "No. I'm going to keep it."

Bryce set his hands flat on the tabletop. They were strong and weathered, tanned by the harsh Arizona sun. "You're not serious."

"I am." I sounded calm and in control, the antithesis of how I felt inside. Oh, well, in this case, I figured presentation was everything.

Allegra blinked. "But—"

"But bearing a child to the Wilcox *primus* will kill me. I know." The words came out flat, without inflection, just as I'd meant them to. I couldn't let them hear the fear growing within me, growing just as surely as the baby inside my body.

"You can't really be that selfish," Margot said, tone harsh.

I glanced at her and raised my eyebrows. "'Selfish'?" I repeated. "How is that selfish?"

"Your responsibility is to your clan, not to Connor Wilcox." Her dark eyes seemed to bore into mine, and I had to force myself not to flinch under her stare. "It seems he's made it abundantly clear that he wants nothing to do with you. So why deprive the McAllisters of their *prima* just to bear a child that will bring nothing but death?"

"It's an innocent baby," I protested. "It's not as if it's going to come out twirling a mustache and plotting to take over the world. It's the curse that's the problem, not the baby."

"The child and the curse are linked," Bryce said. "You can't have one and not the other—not with the offspring of a Wilcox *primus*."

That was no more than simple fact, I supposed, and in that moment I truly understood for the first time why Damon Wilcox had fought so hard against the dark destiny to which he'd been born, through no fault of his own. "Well, then, I guess I'll just have to break the curse."

Margot let out a cold little laugh. "And that's worked out so well so far, hasn't it?"

"Not for the Wilcoxes, no," I admitted. Then my brain started to churn away as it pondered those words. True, no Wilcox had ever succeeded in undoing the curse cast so many years earlier, but technically, I wasn't a Wilcox. And, as Connor's cousin Marie had once pointed out, I wasn't just any witch. I was *prima* of the McAllisters. "So maybe it's time to apply a little McAllister ingenuity to the problem."

Bryce said, not blinking, "That's a shot in a million. You should really have Allegra help you."

Help you. There was a nice euphemism for an abortion. Not that they were probably thinking of it in those terms. All they could see was their *prima* in jeopardy, with no clear successor in sight. True, in my clan the power wasn't passed from mother to daughter, but its vessel still appeared only once in a generation, and any girl who might be the next inheritor was barely toddling at this point, far too young for her abilities to have begun to manifest themselves.

I hesitated, trying to find words to shoot him down that didn't include "fuck you, Bryce." At the same time, Allegra twisted nervous fingers around one another and said plaintively, "How did this even happen?"

Margot shot her a disbelieving look. "I'm fairly certain we all know *how* this happened, Allegra."

Color rose to the other woman's cheekbones. "That's not what I meant. Surely Rachel taught you to be careful, Angela?"

"Of course she did," I replied with some irritation. "And I was. But somehow…it just didn't work, that last time."

"'That last time,'" Margot repeated, brows drawing together, as if she'd had a sudden thought. "When was the last time you and Connor were intimate?"

Oh, Goddess. But I knew it was a legitimate question, and one I'd already answered on the questionnaire I filled out at Planned Parenthood. Anyway, the date was burned permanently in my brain, considering the events that had taken place the next day. "March nineteenth. It was—it was the night before we…confronted Damon."

"Ah," Margot responded, giving the faintest of nods. "That explains it."

"Explains what?" I demanded with some asperity. Not that I didn't want to hear her theory on the failure of the contraceptive spell, but I found it annoying that she seemed to be one step ahead of me in solving the mystery.

Her expression softened somewhat, despite my harsh tone. "The charm most likely was working just as it should, but when Damon died—when his powers passed to Connor, the only viable successor, the last of Jeremiah's line—that small charm was not strong enough to withstand the need for there to be a new Wilcox heir. It was probably that very moment when you became pregnant."

Good thing I was sitting down, because otherwise my legs probably would have given way beneath me. I'd never stopped to think about how the Wilcox line had never failed, not even with all the tragedy and untimely death that hovered around the family the way storm clouds seemed to ring Humphreys Peak as it towered over the town where the Wilcoxes lived. And even I remembered enough from biology class to know that pregnancy didn't happen at the exact moment of intercourse. No, that tricky Wilcox sperm had just been hanging out, waiting for the right opportunity to come along.

Proving…what? That I couldn't fight fate? That even though I might be the McAllister *prima,* I was no match for the manifest destiny of the Wilcox clan?

No, I refused to believe that. It wasn't fate, precisely, but I did believe that everything happened for a reason. Connor and me. Damon's death. This child. All of it.

After a long pause, I said, "That does make sense, Margot."

She seemed vaguely surprised that I hadn't argued with her, but then inclined her head, as if acknowledging my acceptance.

"Anyway," I went on, "I wanted you all to know. I'll speak to Rachel, and I suppose the word will get out from there. It's very early—I'm not quite three months along—so we have plenty of time to plan contingencies. But there won't be any more talk of my getting rid of the baby. Understood?"

With some reluctance, Bryce nodded, and a few seconds later, Allegra did the same. Margot's lips compressed, and then she said, "That is your decision, Angela. Just remember that it will affect everyone in this clan, and not only you."

"I know that," I said wearily. *And maybe if I were as cold-blooded as you, I would get rid of it. But I can't.* Not wanting to hear any more comments about my "selfishness," I went on, "But now I'm a little tired, so—"

"We'll go," Allegra said at once. At least she'd had three children, so she could sympathize with the symptoms of early pregnancy, even if Margot and Bryce couldn't. "Thank you for feeling you could confide in us."

After that the other two had to murmur their thanks as well, even if they didn't truly believe them, and then all three of them left, leaving me alone in the house, which felt very big and empty. I knew I could call Sydney and ask her to come up, but I told myself if I were really going to be a mother—if even for a short time—then I needed to put on my big-girl panties and learn how to handle things on my own. I couldn't keep calling Syd every time I had the blues.

So I got some rocky road ice cream out of the freezer, went to the family room, and switched on the TV. I could do this. I could.

Unfortunately, I knew a far worse confrontation than the one I'd just survived still lay ahead of me.

CHAPTER THREE

By the Banks of Oak Creek

Aunt Rachel had reacted in horror when I told her the news, pretty much as I'd expected. Luckily, though, Tobias had been there when I went over to tell her what was going on. I didn't see his presence as an intrusion, but rather a welcome buffer. He at least seemed hopeful when I said I'd do whatever I could to bring this curse to an end, even as Rachel shook her head and said that no one had ever been able to break the Wilcox curse.

Which was true. But, as they say, there's a first time for everything.

With that unwelcome task out of the way, I went home, then sat upstairs on my bed for the longest time as I stared at the phone I held and wondered what on earth I could possibly say. Would Connor hear the fear and the nerves in my voice and demand to know what was wrong? Or would he see my number on the caller I.D. and not even bother to pick up?

In the end, I took the coward's way out. I went to my contacts, selected Connor's number, and then sent a brief text. *We need to talk. It's important. Can you meet me in Sedona?*

I hit "send" before I could lose my nerve. A minute ticked by…then another. I set the phone down on the bed and went to the window, staring out at the terraced streets of Jerome and the golden hills beyond. The cottonwoods following the line of the Verde River blazed a brilliant emerald, foliage still fresh and new. Another minute passed. My eyes began to burn, but I wouldn't let myself cry. If he wanted to ignore me, fine.

But then my phone pinged, and I hurried over to the bed and picked it up with shaking fingers.

Okay. When and where in Sedona?

I still wanted to cry, although this time more from relief…and possibly nerves. Damn hormones. Blinking, I typed, *Tomorrow at ten? Down by Oak Creek behind Los Abrigados?*

This time the answer came back quickly, as if he'd been waiting for my reply. Maybe he'd just been away from his phone the first time. *Okay. See you then.*

And that was it. Nothing else, no words of love or reassurance or anything else, but at least he hadn't said no. That was something. It *had* to mean something.

Or so I told myself.

The next morning was bright and beautiful, a typical May day that promised warmth but not real heat. I spent about twenty minutes agonizing over what to wear and finally settled on my favorite pair of jeans and an embroidered peasant top, along with some jeweled flip-flops Sydney had talked me into. They showed off the pedicure I'd gotten the week before—before my entire world had changed. My toes gleamed hot pink, matching the embroidery on the blouse I wore. In the mirror, I looked fresh and relaxed, ready for summer. Connor had never seen me like this, and I wondered if he would appreciate the change in my appearance. But at least he'd always liked me in jeans, and I figured I might as well squeeze myself into them while I still could.

Then I was out the door and heading down the hill, through Clarkdale and Cottonwood and on into Sedona. The resort town was halfway between Jerome and Flagstaff, more or less, and neutral territory, so I figured it was the best place to meet. Finding someplace private had required a bit more thought, as this wasn't the sort of discussion I really wanted to have in a restaurant in front of a bunch of other people. But then I remembered the quiet park-like area between the Los Abrigados resort and the shopping area at Tlaquepaque. Yes, people went down there sometimes to feed the ducks or simply watch the water flow past. Even so, it was far more secluded than anyplace else I could think of, especially on a weekday morning. Or so I hoped.

Since I arrived a little before ten, before the shops were open, there was plenty of parking. I chose a spot close to my destination but one that wasn't designated for resort guests only. A quick scan of the parking lot told me Connor wasn't there yet, so I went ahead and walked down toward the creek.

As I'd expected, it was very quiet. There were a couple of bored-looking teenagers poking around the ornamental maze set up between the parking lot and the creek, but they didn't even give me so much as a second glance as I passed them by and continued on to the water's edge. Here, the grass was green and fresh, the trees overhead thick, with leaves equally as green. Sunlight glinted off the surface of the water as it moved between its wide banks. The water level was fairly high; snow must still be melting up in Flagstaff and making its way here.

As if thinking of Flagstaff had somehow summoned him, I caught a glimpse of movement in the corner of my eye, then turned to see Connor approaching me. My breath caught in my throat. Yes, I'd been thinking of him, dreaming of him, for the past few months, but none of that could compare to seeing him before me now. I'd forgotten how tall he really was, how broad his shoulders, how strong and fine the bones of his face.

It looked like he hadn't cut his hair since the last time, just a day before Damon's funeral. Now a lock of it fell over Connor's forehead, and he had it pushed back behind his ears. He wore a dark gray button-down shirt with the sleeves rolled up to his elbows, showing tanned forearms. Apparently he hadn't been wasting away in his studio, mooning over me. Then again, even in the depths of winter, his skin tone had always been warm, quite a bit darker than mine.

Mouth dry, I somehow managed to say, "Hi, Connor."

"Hi, Angela." Calm, casual…just the way he'd been when I first woke up in his apartment. Back then, I hadn't known quite what to make of such behavior.

Now I knew it was his way of covering up what he was really feeling.

"Thanks for coming." Oh, Goddess, that sounded terrible. I might as well have been thanking him for showing up at a business meeting.

The tiniest lift of his shoulders. "Since I hadn't heard anything from you before this, I figured it must be important."

Hadn't heard anything from you before this. Well, that was rich. Since he was the one who'd thrown me out, I sort of thought he should be the one making the conciliatory gestures. But this was going to be hard enough without me tossing accusations around. "I—I was trying to give you your space," I replied.

Another shrug. That green gaze seemed to slide past me, toward the water. "Thanks," he said at last.

I'd known this was going to be hard, but somehow I hadn't thought it would be quite this hard. Even though I knew Connor had a tendency to clam up when he was upset or nervous, in that moment I felt as if I were talking to a brick wall. But now that I had him here, I knew I had to go through with this, even though I found myself wishing I'd never sent him the text to meet me.

Just get it over with, I thought. *Tell him. No matter how he reacts, it can't be any worse than this.*

Lifting my chin, I looked up into his face, practically forcing him with my gaze to meet my eyes. At last he did, and without flinching. Good. That was better.

"I asked you to meet me because, well"—I pulled in a breath, forced the words out—"I'm pregnant."

Immediately the cool mask was gone. I saw fear, true fear, flare in his eyes. "Oh, God," he murmured. Then he shook his head. "You can't keep it, Angela. It'll kill you."

How he'd known what my decision had been, I couldn't guess, except that he knew me. We were bonded, even if he'd tried to ignore that bond. Or maybe he thought that if I'd decided to quietly get rid of the baby, there would be no need to ever say anything to him.

"That's what everyone's been telling me," I replied, actually relieved to see the worry and dismay in his eyes. If he truly didn't care about me anymore, would he be reacting this way? "But this child is ours, Connor. I want it to be born, no matter what happens."

He didn't reply at first, only continued to stare down at me as if he'd never seen me before. Finally, "You'd really do that? Even knowing what's going to happen?"

"I don't know what's going to happen," I told him. "Neither do you. Not for certain. But I'll tell you what I told my clan elders—I *will* find some way to break this curse. I want to see this child grow up. And—" For the first time I faltered, because my next words weren't about our unborn baby, but about us, and that felt like much more dangerous ground. "—And I really hope we can experience that together."

I'd been expecting a dismissal, or at most another one of those infuriating shrugs. What I hadn't expected was for him to reach out and pull me against him, to feel his arms go around me in an embrace so fierce it almost suffocated me. Not that I minded, of course. What was a little missing breath when the man you thought you'd lost forever takes you in his arms like that?

His lips brushed the top of my hair. "I want that, too," he murmured. "I want that more than anything."

Even as my heart leapt at those words, I couldn't help pulling away slightly so I could cast a quizzical glance up at him. "Not that I'm not totally thrilled to hear that, Connor, but if that's the case, why the radio silence? I've spent the last few months thinking you never wanted to see me again."

He did look shamefaced at that remark. "I know, I know. It's been killing me."

I raised an eyebrow.

"I mean it, Angela." A pause, and he added, "That is, I did feel that way for the first week. I was furious with you—and with myself—thinking there must have been another solution, some way to save Damon. And I was having to deal with that while finding myself suddenly *primus* of my clan, and settling Damon's affairs, which weren't trivial, either, and—well, I was in a bad place."

"I'm sorry," I said softly. All that time I'd been agonizing over losing him, and I'd barely spared a thought for what he must be going through on his end. He'd never thought he would be *primus*, never thought he'd have to do anything except live quietly in his brother's shadow. And while I certainly didn't claim to know much about wills and trusts and all that, I could only imagine that managing the disposition of Damon's estate probably hadn't been terribly easy.

A hint of surprise flitted over his features, and then he shook his head. "You don't need to be. I mean, after my head cleared, I realized there really wasn't anything else any of us could have done. In clearing out the house and getting it ready for sale—"

"You didn't keep it?" I asked, surprised despite myself. For some reason I'd thought Connor would hold on to the house, if only for a while longer.

"How could I? My brother died there. Jessica was murdered there. He left it to me, but I sure as hell didn't want it. So I sold the whole place—furniture and everything—for a price that Lucas told me was criminally low. But I didn't care."

I supposed I could see that. After all, I was used to talking to ghosts, and even I wouldn't have felt all that comfortable living in a house where two people had died. After I nodded, Connor continued,

"Anyway, when I was clearing out the house, I came across some of Damon's papers, his writing. Most of it was theoretical stuff I couldn't make much sense of, but it wasn't until I read what he'd written that I understood how insanely obsessed he was with you, with using your powers to break the curse. I guess I'd realized it on some level, but seeing it written down really brought it home to me." Connor reached out and took my hands in his, and I wanted to weep at feeling those familiar strong fingers wrap around mine, comforting, *real*. "He doomed himself, Angela—and he did so knowingly, and willingly. I still haven't forgiven him for that." Green eyes searched my face, urgent, pleading. "But I did forgive you. There really was nothing else you could have done."

Oh, how I'd longed to hear him say that! Even so, I asked, "Then why didn't you call me? I've been dying a little every day I haven't heard from you. All this time we could have been together—"

"I know," he said, the guilt clear in his voice. "And I was going to, I swear it. But then Marie told me to wait."

"What?"

"She did. I told her about ten days after I sent you back to Jerome that this was crazy, that I was going to call you and tell you I was an idiot, that I'd made a horrible mistake—and she said I needed to wait, that she'd seen you would contact me at a critical moment, and that it was very important I not say anything to you until then."

Marie. I'd never liked her, but in that moment I hated her, hated that she'd kept Connor and me apart for no apparent reason. "That's just stupid," I snapped. "What, did she say it was another of her goddamn visions or something?"

"Well, yeah, more or less."

That did stop me. Despite my dislike for the woman, I couldn't deny that her visions were true ones, her instincts stronger than those of anyone else I'd met. "What else did she say?"

"That's all." He paused, then added, "Well, that I needed to wait, and then when we did reconcile, that we needed to speak to her immediately."

The last thing I wanted was to go talk to Marie. What I wanted was to drag Connor to the nearest hotel room for some make-up sex. But ignoring the seer when she obviously had something important to say was probably not that good an idea.

"So, what, you want me to go with you to Flagstaff to meet with Marie right now?"

A glint I knew all too well entered his eyes. "Well, what I want is to head over there"—he jerked a thumb toward the Los Abrigados resort—"and see if they have any rooms available, and forget about anything else for a while. But since Marie was pretty adamant about seeing her, I think we probably should do as she asks."

I found myself smiling, despite everything, because of the way Connor's thoughts had run almost exactly parallel to mine. "Rain check on that hotel room?"

The grin he sent me in reply was positively ferocious. "Damn straight."

I decided to follow him up to Flagstaff in my own vehicle, not because I thought I needed an escape plan, but because I didn't feel comfortable leaving my brand-new Cherokee for an unknown amount of time in the Tlaquepaque shopping center parking lot. Connor's eyes widened a bit when I went to the car and unlocked it.

"That new?" he inquired.

"Yeah," I said casually. "What, did you think I was going to keep borrowing my aunt's Jeep indefinitely?"

"Guess not," he replied, with another one of those grins. "I'll call Marie from the road, and you can follow me over to her place."

That sounded workable; I'd walked to her house before but hadn't driven there, and it was probably better to have Connor guide me in. And there was definitely more street parking at her place than at Connor's.

The last time I'd been in Flagstaff, spring hadn't truly arrived, no matter what the calendar might have said. But today I could see only a few small patches of snow lingering on Mt. Humphreys' north face, and while the wildflowers were sparse compared to what grew around Sedona and Jerome, the aspens and oaks and sycamores had leafed out, making the landscape a bit lusher than what I was accustomed to.

Irises bloomed along the front walk of Marie's house, not the usual purple-blue, but deep crimson and yellow and some that were almost black. I parked behind Connor's FJ and got out, feeling the cool breeze catch at my hair. As usual, it was a good ten degrees cooler in Flag than it had been back in Sedona, but now the air just seemed refreshing rather than biting.

"I take it you got a hold of her," I said as I joined Connor where Marie's walkway met the sidewalk.

"Yeah. It was almost like she was waiting for my call." He shrugged. "With anyone else I'd say it was a coincidence, but—"

"But in this case it probably wasn't."

"Probably not."

I reflected then that the McAllisters' current lack of a seer wasn't necessarily all bad. Having someone around who knew what was going to happen before it actually did happen could be a bit disconcerting.

Connor rang the doorbell, and, as before, Marie opened the door almost at once. Yes, he'd called her on the way up, but still….

Too bad she wasn't a poker player, because her usual impassive expression would have stood her in good stead on the pro circuit. As it was, I gave her a half-hearted smile as we entered the living room. The last time I had been here was when we were planning Damon's death, and what a grim, cold meeting it had been. Today she had the windows cracked open, letting in a fresh-smelling breeze, and a slim vase of ruby-colored glass held a bouquet of irises from the garden. There was even a pitcher of water and three glasses sitting on the low coffee table in front of the couch.

I shot a sideways glance at Connor, and he offered the smallest lift of his shoulders. Apparently he didn't have any more idea than I did why Marie would provide us such hospitality this time when she certainly hadn't ever before.

"It's good to see you, Angela," she said, and I almost tripped over the rug as I made my way toward the couch.

"Um…thank you," I faltered. "It's good to see you, too."

Marie's gaze shifted to Connor, and he said, "So…things are better. A lot better. But Angela and I have some news we'd like to share."

His remark didn't surprise me; we'd agreed that Marie needed to know about the baby. It seemed only fair, since my clan's elders had been informed of my condition. The Wilcoxes didn't have clan elders, not in the same way we McAllisters did, but Marie—and, to a lesser extent, Lucas—seemed to have something of the same capacity in their family.

Then again, it was entirely possible that Marie already knew….

"Connor and I are going to have a baby," I said, even if making such a proclamation turned out to be unnecessary.

Her expression didn't change. "Ah. So it has come at last."

"What has come at last?"

For the first time since I'd met her, Marie appeared almost nervous. She reached for the pitcher of water and poured some in each glass, then handed one to me. "The joining of the Wilcox and McAllister clans."

She made it sound as if it were something she'd been expecting for some time. "And so…that's a good thing, right?" I ventured. "So Damon was right? This will break the curse?"

Even as a look of relief began to spread across Connor's face, she shook her head. "No. That is, the two lines being commingled in such a way is not enough to end the curse. But it is the reason you must make the attempt."

I should have known it wouldn't be that easy. "Making an attempt isn't good enough. Damon tried—Jasper tried, too, from what I've heard. So how is this any different?"

Marie picked up her own glass of water and took a sip, and after a brief hesitation, Connor did so as well. From the tight set of his shoulders, I gathered he'd drunk the water to keep himself from telling Marie she was being no help at all. Goddess knows I felt like saying more or less the same thing.

"Because it will not be a *primus* seeking to break the curse, but *a* prima. The energy involved is completely different."

That made some sense, I supposed. Maybe. "So what do I have to do?"

Her eyes shut. I noticed how long and thick and black her eyelashes were, just like Connor's…and those of most of the Wiloxes I'd met. The blood ran strong and true in this family, no matter what it was mixed with, apparently. Then she opened her eyes and, rather than looking at me, seemed to stare through me, as if her gaze was intended to pierce something that no one but she could see.

"It is not my place to tell you everything. You must make the journey yourself. But I can tell you that sometimes you must go back to the beginning to see your way through to the end."

Well, that was helpful. Any more vague, and she could have pulled that pronouncement out of a fortune cookie. "Um…do you want to give me any more details?"

She blinked, and suddenly the faraway gaze was gone, replaced by a stern and not all that approving look. "As I said, you must make the journey for yourself. Just because I sensed this coming, and knew you would play a key role, does not mean I know everything. I've told you what you need to do."

No, you haven't, I thought. *So I have to make a journey. Never mind that I have no idea where.*

Connor spoke for the first time. "It might help to know a little more, Marie. Unless you want us to fail the same way Damon did."

Her mouth tightened. "It's not that I want you to fail, Connor. It's simply that there are some matters it's not my place to speak of. This is Angela's story—and yours as well, to a lesser extent. You are the *primus* of this clan, true, but we've already learned that the *primus* does not have the power to make a difference here."

Frowning, he glanced over at me. I didn't really like the sound of that, and I guessed he didn't, either.

It could have been that I was misreading her statement, but it almost sounded as if she was saying Connor couldn't possibly hope to prevail when his own brother, a much stronger warlock, hadn't managed to do so. Thanks for the no-confidence vote, Marie.

But since I'd already come to the realization that it was a *prima*'s turn to sort out this mess, I couldn't be too angry with Marie for having her own doubts. It would have been nice if she could've given me a smidge more information, although I'd already figured out that wasn't exactly her style. Maybe that was just standard seer practice; if you didn't get too specific, later on you couldn't be blamed for seeing things incorrectly if events didn't turn out as expected.

"Well, sounds like we need to get our thinking caps on," I said in a too-bright tone that made Connor raise an eyebrow. "Thanks for the insight, Marie. We'll let you know if we come up with something. Connor, let's talk about all this over lunch. I'm starving…eating for two, you know."

And with that I got up from the couch, grasping the strap of my purse as I did so, and he rose a second or two later. Actually, I wasn't all that hungry, but it seemed as good an excuse to get out of there as anything else I could think of.

If Marie saw through my little subterfuge, she didn't show any sign of it…not that I really expected her to. She stood up as well, saying, "I know you wanted more from me, but this is the best advice I can give. Don't allow what you think you know to get in the way of what you need to know."

"Thanks, Marie," Connor said, obviously realizing that I was about to utter a few pithy words about his cousin and her "advice."

I sent her a smile that probably wouldn't have fooled anyone, let alone Marie Wilcox, and then Connor and I were headed out the front door and back to our cars.

"Don't say it," he told me, just as I opened my mouth to speak. "I get it. I really get it. Let's just go back to the apartment and regroup, okay?"

"All right," I said with some reluctance.

"You take the spot behind the building. I'll park my car on the street."

"Connor, you don't have to do that—"

Rather than argue, he bent down and kissed me, smothering my protests. Not that I minded; the kiss ignited all the fire I had forcibly banked down the past few months, and right then I didn't care who parked where as long as we were together at his apartment. Soon.

I followed him back downtown, then turned in at the alleyway that led to the rear of his building. He disappeared around a corner, apparently in search of a parking space—no easy feat in the historic section of town on a bright and breezy May afternoon. Since I didn't have a key, had taken the one he'd given me this past winter and shoved it into a compartment in my jewelry box, all I could do was wait at the back entrance to the building until he returned a few minutes later, over-long hair flying in the wind.

"Turning into a hippie?" I asked, lifting a hand to push the heavy dark strands away from his face.

"Just didn't care, these past few months."

My heart twinged, and I reached out and touched his hand, not saying anything. He gripped my fingers for a few seconds before letting them go so he could open the door.

Nothing seemed to have changed since the last time I entered the hallway. It still smelled of mildew and damp, still looked as if someone needed to get into the corners with a good stiff brush and some heavy-duty cleaner. In silence we climbed the stairs to the second floor. Connor opened the door to the apartment, and I held my breath. It felt like years since I'd been here, and I didn't know what to expect. Maybe he'd let the place go after I left. Maybe it would be a total disaster.

But as I entered the familiar short hallway and glanced around, it seemed as if nothing much had changed. Everything looked neat and clean, nothing out of place except the usual collection of finished paintings stacked up against the walls in various spots. Some of them I didn't recognize, which meant he'd kept working after I was gone. Good. I hated to think that our separation might have affected his art. I remembered then that he'd had another gallery show scheduled for the end of April, and wondered if he'd gone through with it, or whether he'd canceled the whole thing. Since quite a few paintings I remembered seemed to be gone, it looked as if he'd had the show after all.

"Connor—" I began, but didn't get much further than that, as he'd reached out and pulled me against him, brought his mouth against mine, pushing my lips open with his tongue, tasting me.

The purse fell from my suddenly nerveless fingers and dropped with a heavy thud against the wooden floor. At the same time, Connor scooped me up in his arms and headed for the stairs, moving up them so quickly that I didn't have time to think about anything except the strength of his embrace and the thudding of my heart in my chest.

And then we were in his bedroom, and his hands were on my blouse, pulling it over my head, and his fingers were working the front clasp of my bra before he slid the straps down my shoulders and pulled the whole thing away from my body, tossing it onto the chair under the window. His hands cupped my breasts, and I moaned, needing his touch, needing the magic of flesh against flesh, his lips and tongue caressing me even as he undid the button and zipper of my jeans and pushed them down. I kicked off my flip-flops and did the same with my jeans, and then his hand was sliding down over my backside, cupping it as he pulled me against him, lifting his head from my nipple so he could kiss me again.

I went to work on his shirt buttons, undoing them one by one until his beautiful chest and stomach were revealed. Slipping my hands over him, I caressed my way down his torso until I came to his jeans and undid those as well.

Oh, he was so ready, so thick and hard it looked almost painful. A groan wrenched its way out of his throat as I moved my hand up and down his shaft. "Not too much," he warned me. "It's been a while."

"So you don't want me to do this?" I teased, lowering my head so I could take him in my mouth, taste the familiar salt of his skin, run my tongue over the silky yet rock-hard flesh.

"No—yes—Angela—"

I took pity on him then, pulling him against me as we sank down onto the bed. His fingers brushed their way up the inside of my thigh, feather-light and yet awakening more fire, more heat, before they reached my core, stroking me, caressing me. I cried out, knowing I was close, so close, because it had been so long. An eternity without him.

But now he was here, and I was here, and it was the most natural thing in the world for him to slip into me, to fill the aching emptiness that had been a painful void ever since he sent me away from him. Two into one again, not Wilcox and McAllister, not *prima* and *primus*, not even Connor and Angela, but simply two souls merging into a perfect, ineffable one. There was no need for me to say the charm, because we had already kindled a life between us.

In that moment, I refused to believe any evil could come from such joy.

CHAPTER FOUR

Beginnings

WE DOZED IN EACH OTHER'S ARMS AFTERWARD, MAYBE FOR only five or ten minutes, maybe as much as half an hour. Neither one of us was paying much attention, but eventually Connor stirred and said, "So did that work up an appetite?"

I realized it had. By then it was past one, and my stomach was telling me that I had better put something in it. "I think it just might have."

With a groan, he rolled over, then bent to retrieve his discarded underwear. I did the same, afterward going to the bathroom to clean up as best I could. It wasn't like before; I didn't have a change of clothes here with me. Still, I straightened my hair and patted some cool water on my flushed cheeks before returning to the bedroom for the rest of my clothes.

"I guess you'd been saving that up for a while," I teased.

Connor slipped into his shirt and began to button it up. "Well, I think it was the toes that did it."

Arching an eyebrow at him, I glanced down at my pink toenail polish. "What, are you telling me you have a foot fetish or something?"

"Or something," he said with a grin.

I shook my head and retrieved my own top. After slipping it over my head, I climbed back into my jeans. I'd just finished fastening them shut when I looked up to see Connor standing in front of the dresser, holding the concho belt he'd given me for my birthday.

"I hated that you left this behind," he said quietly. "Will you take it back now?"

Something in the simple request made my throat tighten. "Yes, Connor," I said. "Oh, yes, I want it back."

We both knew I was talking about a lot more than just the belt.

He came to me and fastened it around my hips. I felt the heavy weight settle against me and smiled. "I might as well wear it as much as I can now," I joked. "In a few more months I'm going to be as big as a house."

"And you'll be beautiful," he said, bending to kiss me gently on the cheek. "And when that happens, we'll just put it in a drawer until you can wear it again."

The smile slipped from my lips, and I stared up into his face, wondering how I could have ever lived a whole two months without him. "I love you, Connor."

"I love you, Angela," he said solemnly, seeming to understand that we needed to say it to one another, to re-bind us to each other. "There's something I want to show you, and then we can go eat."

I wondered what that something was. Since he was looking very serious, I attempted to lighten the mood a bit. "I thought you already showed me *that*," I replied, flashing him a grin, but he didn't smile, only took my hand and led me out of the bedroom.

We went downstairs. I let go of his hand, then bent down and retrieved my purse from the spot where I'd dropped it. Afterward, he wrapped his fingers around mine before leading me across the landing to the apartment he used as his studio. He paused there, saying, "Just promise you won't freak out."

"Wow, Connor, real reassuring."

I thought maybe he'd grin at my response, but his expression remained somber as he pushed open the door. "I mean it."

And when I walked into the studio, I realized why he'd made that request.

All around me was…me.

That is, paintings of me. Large ones, all the way down to tiny pieces you could hold in the palm of your hand. Obviously all done from memory—a painting of me standing in the snow, ponderosa pines dark and stately in the background. Sitting in the chair by his bedroom window, with the winter light streaming in and wakening reddish tones in my dark hair. The largest one, still on the easel, a stylized portrait of me with my hands outstretched, my face raised to the sky. It was a pose I'd used often during our seasonal observances back in Jerome, but of course Connor couldn't have possibly seen me doing such a thing.

In all of them he'd painted me as looking far more beautiful than I thought I was in real life. But then I realized he'd been painting me as he saw me, and not as the world did.

It was overwhelming. I had no idea what to say. I only stood there, staring, for the longest moment. Finally I managed, "And here I thought you only did landscapes."

Then we did burst out laughing, more to break the tension than anything else. Connor sobered abruptly, however, and said, "I couldn't get you out of my mind. Every time I closed my eyes, you were there. Every time I turned around, I thought I could hear the sound of your voice. It was as if you'd become a ghost, too, and were haunting me. But if I could paint you, think of your face that way, it helped. A little."

"They're—" I broke off, not sure of how to put it. If I said they were beautiful, was I praising his art, or my own features? It just felt…strange. "They're incredible."

"So you're not freaking out?"

Was I? No, not really. Everyone handles pain in their own way, and if painting me over and over again helped Connor come out on the other side of his grief, who was I to say that was wrong? "No, Connor, I'm not freaking out. I won't say it's not overwhelming, but it's not freak-out worthy." I smiled up at him. "I mean, I've got people coming next week to knock out the walls in my kitchen. I needed something to focus on, and I figured remodeling the kitchen was as good a distraction as any."

He tilted his head to one side, seeming to consider me. "We really are a pair, aren't we?"

"Yes, we are," I told him. "Now buy me some lunch before I pass out. As I told Marie, I'm eating for two."

"Angela McAllister, I would love to buy you lunch."

We ended up at the Lumberyard Brewery, partly because it was walkable, and partly because by then

I really was starving, craving something heftier than tapas or a sandwich.

"You sure you're okay with eating at a brewery?" Connor asked after the waitress had handed us our menus and left to fetch us some water. "I mean—"

"It's okay," I cut in. "I was never much of a lunch drinker anyway. As for the rest…." I shrugged. Thank the Goddess that I really hadn't drunk excessively after I got back to Jerome, except for that first night. Part of me had wanted to, had wanted to down bottle after bottle in an attempt to erase Connor from my mind. That wouldn't have solved anything, though, and I'd told myself I wasn't going to let him affect me that way. Even so, I'd had more than I should. I could only hope a glass here and there hadn't hurt the baby, but there wasn't much I could do about it now. "I'm not such a lush that I can't give it up for a while. What worries me is that I think I heard somewhere that you're not supposed to eat chocolate when you're pregnant. Now, *that* would be a hardship."

Connor grinned and shook his head. The waitress came by then with our waters and asked if we wanted anything else, but we both demurred. I had a feeling Connor could have used a beer at that point, even though it seemed he was planning to abstain right along with me. We both ordered burgers, and I asked for a side of mac and cheese in addition to my cheeseburger. After the waitress left, he remarked,

"You weren't kidding about eating for two."

"Nope," I replied, swirling the straw around in my glass, watching as the lemon slice bobbed up and down between a couple of ice cubes.

"Have you seen a doctor?"

I looked up from my water to see Connor gazing at me intently. It seemed pretty clear that he wanted a lot more detail than what I'd already provided. Fair enough. "Yes. I went to Planned Parenthood, because at that point I really didn't want to see my own doctor. I'm around ten weeks, and they want to have me come in for an ultrasound if I'm not going to get my own doctor in Cottonwood. But otherwise they said everything looks fine and I'm totally healthy, and it's really not a big deal."

"It *is* a big deal," he said, his tone quiet. "And we both know that."

He was right, of course. To the doctor at Planned Parenthood, mine was just another in a long line of pregnancies she'd encountered, and since I was young and healthy and everything looked normal, she couldn't possibly understand what this baby meant in terms of my personal survival.

"You should come with me to see our healer," he continued. "I mean, if you're not going to your own doctor."

That suggestion gave me pause. True, that was the way we witches usually dealt with such matters; a healer's gifts were often far more reliable than modern medicine. And I'd met the Wilcox healer when the Damon-wolf had bitten my leg. She seemed pleasant enough, an attractive woman in her late forties or early fifties. What was her name? Eleanor?

Even so, I hesitated. Going to see the Wilcox healer seemed so…final. As if I were choosing sides. And we'd had enough of that.

"I don't know, Connor," I said at last. "I think I'd rather just go to a doctor. I mean, I don't even know where—" Breaking off, I hesitated. I'd been about to say, I *don't even know where we're going to end up.* It seemed that Connor and I had reconciled, and that was wonderful, but there were still some logistical issues we needed to work out. After all, my clan needed me, and his needed him. Settling down permanently in either location was going to leave one family or another out in the cold.

He seemed to understand, and nodded. "It's something we'll have to figure out eventually, I know. So do you want to see a doctor near Jerome, or would you be open to choosing one here in Flag?"

It would actually make more sense to find someone in Flagstaff, just because it was a much bigger city and had some very good medical facilities. "Do you know anyone?"

"I can get some recommendations. Eleanor has a lot of experience, but I know a couple of my cousins went ahead and got their own ob-gyns. I'll get the information from them."

That sounded good, and refreshingly normal. That was probably what most expecting couples did—ask their friends and family who was best equipped to take on such an enormous responsibility.

The waitress came by with our food then, and conversation ceased for a few minutes as we made some serious inroads on the plates piled with food in front of us. After I'd demolished about half my burger, though, I stopped and said, "But I guess all that is moot if we don't figure out what Marie was talking about."

"Well, you need to see a doctor no matter what—" He stopped himself there, but I knew what he'd been about to say. Curse or no curse, we needed to make sure everything was all right with the baby, although I had a feeling it was fine. In general, it wasn't until *after* the Wilcox heirs made their appearance in the world that their mothers needed to start worrying.

"I know," I said. "And I will. But if she wants us to go back to the beginning…." I stopped, picking up a french fry and dipping it in some ketchup. After taking a bite, I chewed thoughtfully for a minute. She'd said there were things I needed to find out for myself, things she couldn't tell me. That made me think she must be referring to my own beginnings, which were mostly shrouded in mystery. I knew I'd been born in California and that my mother had brought me back to Jerome when I was barely two months old, but I knew nothing beyond that. I'd never even seen my birth certificate; Aunt Rachel had taken care of the paperwork when I got my driver's license.

"What is it?" Connor asked, setting down the last bit of his burger. "You look like your brain's going a mile a minute."

"The beginning," I said slowly. "My beginning. There has to be something…something important. Maybe it's something I need to figure out in order to break the curse."

His eyes begin to gleam. "That makes sense. You really don't know all that much, do you?"

"Hardly anything. I tried asking a few questions when I was younger, but my aunt said she really didn't have that much to tell me, that my mother had barely said a word about what she'd been doing in California." Talking about it now, I realized how strange that was, how little Aunt Rachel had claimed to know.

"So what's the plan?"

"Finish lunch," I replied, pulling the dish of mac and cheese toward me now that I'd thoroughly killed my burger and fries. "Then I think we need to go back to Jerome."

We took my car, and Connor packed his beat-up old Northern Pines athletic bag with some toiletries and a couple changes of clothing, just in case. As I drove us back to the highway, he called Lucas and let him know where he was going. I could tell Lucas was more than pleased about the reconciliation, but Connor ended the call before his cousin could wax too effusive.

"I think he's ready to start planning the wedding now," Connor remarked, slipping his iPhone back into his pocket.

"He'd probably have to arm-wrestle Sydney for the privilege."

Out of the corner of my eye I saw Connor's mouth turn up in a grin, but then it faded. "I want that, too," he said quietly. "I want to make this official."

Something in my chest seemed to turn over. Maybe it was just that everything seemed to be happening so fast. Then again, Connor and I were meant to be together. We'd hit a bump in the road—a little parting gift from Damon, I supposed—but we were back on track now. Marriage was just the next step, a practically foregone conclusion.

"I do, too," I told him. "But I think we need to focus on—on making sure that we'll *have* a real future. You and me and the baby. The wedding can come later."

Talk about your role reversals. Usually it was the woman charging gung-ho into wedding planning and choosing flowers and menus and bridesmaids dresses and all that, but as much as I wanted to be married to Connor, I also wanted to make sure our marriage would last. And that meant breaking the curse so it would no longer be a threat to us…or to our child's spouse, or any more of the Wilcox wives.

"You're right, of course." He turned to look out the window, at the ranks of ponderosa pines flashing past. Here there weren't many wildflowers yet, but grass gleamed green between the dark pine trees.

Spring. A time for beginnings…including my own.

It was not quite four o'clock by the time we pulled into my garage. I'd left the house just six hours earlier, and yet it felt as if everything had changed in those few short hours. Then again, I supposed it had.

The house was quiet and still, the only sound the hum of the refrigerator as we came in through the back door. In less than a week this stillness would be effectively destroyed by the arrival of the contractors and all their equipment, and I was glad that the start of the remodel had been delayed until after Memorial

Day. It would have been awful to come back here with Connor, only to have a bunch of workmen knocking out walls and tearing out countertops.

"I'll call my aunt," I said as Connor dropped his bag on the kitchen floor. "She's working, but since it's Tuesday, she'll be closing up at five. Then we can go over and talk to her."

"Is she going to be okay with that?" he asked, expression dubious. "I mean, I have a feeling she wasn't too sad about my being out of the picture these last few months."

"Well, she'll have to be okay with it, because you and I are together, and that's not changing ever again." I paused, considering. He'd been right when he said Rachel wasn't all that broken up about the separation. She'd been as comforting as she could manage, but even with that I could tell that she thought the universe had righted itself, with me back here in Jerome and Connor in Flagstaff, and a safe span of miles between us. The news that he and I were back together would not be exactly welcome.

"No, it's not changing," he agreed, coming over to me and pushing my hair away from my neck so he could place his lips on the sensitive skin there.

That welcome fire licked through my veins, and I thought longingly of the king-size bed up in my room, and how much I'd like to be lying on it with Connor. But we'd made love only a few hours earlier, and we had business to take care of. The bed would have to wait…but not for too long, I hoped.

I went to the old rotary-dial phone that hung on the wall next to the refrigerator, bit my lip, and dialed Aunt Rachel's number.

As I'd expected, she welcomed Connor's return with about the same enthusiasm the residents of Hamelin must have greeted their town's infestation of rats. Still, she did agree to let us come over around five-thirty, which was about all I could ask for. And when we arrived at the apartment, I saw that, being Rachel, she'd set out a pitcher of iced herbal tea and scones she'd baked that morning, along with a bowl of strawberries.

"Thanks for all this," I said, putting a scone and a strawberry on one of the small dessert plates she'd put on the coffee table with the rest of the refreshments.

She shrugged, but I couldn't help but notice the way her expression softened as Connor bit into one of the scones, chewed in apparent ecstasy, and said, "Wow, Angela, now I really understand how you turned out to be such a good cook. You definitely learned from the best."

Even so, she made a dismissive gesture with one hand. "We do what we can. Anyway, I don't really know how much I can help you. You've asked me so many times before, and all I can give you is the same answer. Sonya never told me anything when she came home all those years ago, and believe me, it wasn't because I didn't keep asking."

That I could believe. My aunt was pretty good at the whole third-degree thing. "How in the world did she explain me?" I asked after breaking off a third of the scone and trying to eat it in small, decorous bites rather than wolfing it down. Rachel did make the best scones.

"She didn't." My aunt leaned forward and poured herself some of the tea, although I noticed she ignored the scones. "That is, all she told me was that she'd met somebody, which was sort of obvious. I mean, we're witches, but we don't really believe in immaculate conceptions."

Next to me, Connor made a noise that sounded like a cough but was probably a suppressed chuckle. Ignoring him, I said, "So she never gave a name? A place? Anything?"

"No names." She set down her glass of iced tea. "I have your birth certificate, but it didn't have anything in the field where the father's name is supposed to be."

"Can I see it?" I asked.

The briefest of hesitations, and then she nodded. "Sure. You should probably keep it now anyway, along with your other important papers. Just give me a minute to dig it out."

She got up from her chair and went upstairs, presumably to her room. I knew she had a small chest on a shelf in her closet where she kept her own paperwork—the deed to the building, insurance papers, passport, that sort of thing. What she wanted with a passport when she'd never even left the state, I had no idea, but I supposed it was a good piece of identification, if nothing else.

For some reason I felt uneasy, although I couldn't quite think why. Maybe it was simply that I'd never seen my birth certificate. To distract myself, I turned toward Connor where he sat beside me on the couch and commented, "That was smooth, complimenting my cooking…which is about the same thing as complimenting hers. Keep that up, and she may actually start to like you in about five years or so."

"That soon? She must be a real pushover."

I couldn't help grinning as I reached for a second scone. Hard to believe I was still hungry, after everything I'd eaten at lunch, but suddenly I felt ravenous. Maybe it was the make-up sex.

Connor must have felt the same way, because he gave that scone the side-eye and asked, "Are you sure you're just eating for two? Because I don't think even I could keep up with you at the rate you're going."

Somehow I managed to resist sticking my tongue out at him, which was just as well, because Rachel returned in that very moment, holding a piece of paper in one hand. It was faintly yellowed around the edges, which I supposed made sense, considering that it was more than twenty years old.

Well, twenty-two, to be precise.

"Here it is," she said, handing to me. I took it from her with fingers that shook only a little. "I'm not sure how much it's going to help, but...."

"Thank you," I told her. "It's still more than I had."

She resumed her seat in the armchair and picked up her neglected tea. "I suppose I should be glad that Sonya at least brought the birth certificate with her. It would have been just like her to not even have that."

The condemnation was clear in her tone, and I couldn't really blame her. To have your sister who'd disappeared almost a year earlier show up out of the blue, bringing a newborn with her—well, on the scale of life disruptions, that had to be close to an eight or nine. I didn't know very much about my mother, but it was pretty clear to me that she hadn't been the most responsible person in the world.

An awkward silence fell. Connor reached out to get another scone, probably just for something to do rather than because he was at all hungry. I smoothed the birth certificate out on my knee, scanning the little boxes for the pertinent information. Aunt Rachel hadn't been entirely accurate about the "father of child" fields—they weren't entirely blank, but instead had "UNKNOWN" typed in all of them. But at least I could see that I'd been born at Hoag Hospital, in Newport Beach, at 11:30 p.m. on December 21st. Also, I was able to see from the "mother of child" fields that she'd been living at 822 Oceanfront Drive, also in Newport Beach. There wasn't an apartment or suite number, so I assumed it must have been a house.

So my mother had fled Jerome—and the responsibility of being the next *prima*—to live in a house in Newport Beach, California, where she'd met… someone. Was he a tanned, blond surfer type? There weren't many of those in northern Arizona, that was for sure. But that didn't make much sense, since from what I'd seen in pictures of her, my mother's hair was much lighter than mine, a warm pale brown with a lot of red in it. If my father had been blond, wouldn't my own hair be at least as light as my mother's, rather than the near-black it actually was?

Like every McAllister, she had access to a good chunk of money that was her own, so the house could've been hers, or it could have belonged to my father. Or maybe she hadn't lived there at all, had spent all her time in Southern California crashing at various hotels, and gave a made-up address at the hospital when they asked for her information. I had no idea, and obviously neither did my aunt.

Finally I looked up from the birth certificate to see both Connor and Rachel watching me. "Sorry," I said. "I guess I kind of got lost in this."

"It's okay," Connor said. "Do you think it will help?"

"Maybe," I replied, my mind working furiously. He and I needed to talk…alone. Not that I thought Aunt Rachel would attempt to interfere, but there were some things I would rather not discuss in front of her. I shifted away from him so I faced my aunt and added, "Thanks again, Rachel. I really do appreciate…all of this."

To my surprise, she smiled and nodded. "I probably should have given it to you a long time ago. I suppose I thought there wasn't much point in focusing on the past. Now, though…." Her gaze slid somewhere toward my midsection, and I knew she was thinking about the baby—the child she was sure would kill me.

"Now, it could really help." I carefully folded up the birth certificate and tucked it inside my purse, then got to my feet. Connor rose as well, saying,

"Thanks for the scones and the tea."

"You're welcome," she said stiffly, and I thought I saw the glitter of sudden tears in her eyes. "Just—just take care of her, Connor."

Clearly startled, he replied, "I will. I promise."

She nodded, and he and I murmured a few awkward goodbyes before we let ourselves out. In silence we walked back up the hill to the house, Connor's hand in mine, while my free hand clung tightly to the strap of my purse with its precious piece of paper inside.

It wasn't until we were back at the house that he spoke again. "So what's next? Does having the birth certificate help at all?"

Hard to say, but I knew there was only one way to find out for sure. "It might." I paused, then went on, "I'm glad you packed stuff for a few days. Because it looks like we're about to take a road trip."

CHAPTER FIVE

Going to California

It wasn't quite as simple as that, of course. Southern California was the territory of the Santiago clan, and if Maya de la Paz hadn't interceded on our behalf, I don't know if we would have even been allowed to go. After all, even a clan as large as the Santiagos might be less than thrilled at having the *prima* and the *primus* of two different witch families descend upon them. But after I explained the situation to Maya, and she passed on a carefully edited version of our reasons for needing to travel to Newport Beach, we were given grudging permission to travel there, as long as we promised not to stay for more than a few days, and to only go to and from Newport.

That seemed fair enough, so I agreed to those conditions. After all, we weren't going to California to visit Disneyland or see the Hollywood Walk of Fame or watch a Dodgers game. Newport Beach was the only place we probably needed to go. I could only hope that our business wouldn't take more time than the mandated two or three days.

I knew I didn't have time for a lengthy phone conversation with Sydney about everything that had happened, but I also knew she'd never let me hear the end of it if I left her completely in the dark. So after I ended my call to Maya, I sent a quick text to Syd. *Connor & I worked it out. We're going to California for a few days.*

She must have been home, because the reply came back almost immediately. *OMG, really? I need all the deets!*

I'll tell you everything when I get back.

Why California?

It's where I was born. I need answers.

OK. Have a safe trip. I'm jealous. :-P

She always had wanted to go to the beach. Unfortunately, this wasn't really a pleasure trip, more a fact-finding mission. I kind of doubted I'd be hanging out on the sand and working on my nonexistent tan.

Don't be jealous. Sand is highly overrated.

:-D

I couldn't help grinning as I locked down my phone and set it on the nightstand.

Since by the time everything was all arranged it was too late to head out—unless we wanted to show up in Southern California at roughly three in the morning—Connor and I spent the night at the house, where we did get to break in that king bed all over again. And then we were up early the next morning, grabbing breakfast in Cottonwood before we made the big push toward Phoenix and then on across the desert and into California.

Through all this he'd been seemingly content to let me plan and make the decisions. Maybe he was remembering what Marie had said about this being my journey, and how he would only be playing a secondary role. It wasn't until we were heading south on I-17 and were about an hour outside Phoenix that he asked, "So what is it you think you're going to find?"

"I'm not sure. Something. I have an address. That's where I'll start."

"An address where your mother lived more than twenty years ago," he said. His tone was gentle, though; I could tell he wasn't trying to make trouble, but only helping me to see more clearly what I was doing. "Southern California isn't like Jerome, you know. People generally don't live in the same places for years and years. I doubt you'll find anyone who remembers your mother."

"I know," I replied. Then I shot a quick glance over at him before returning my attention to the road. "What makes you such an expert on California? Have you been there?"

"No, but I went to college with a few people who grew up there." He frowned, drumming his fingers on a jean-clad knee. I could tell he wasn't used to being chauffeured around. Or maybe something else was bothering him.

"What is it?" I asked. "If my driving makes you that nervous, I can pull over at the next rest stop, and we can switch."

Immediately, he shook his head. "No, that's not it…although you may want to let me drive once we get into the more populated areas of SoCal. I doubt you're used to that kind of traffic."

"And you are?"

"At least I spent four years in Phoenix."

"True."

He was quiet for a bit, watching the scrubby desert landscape flash past outside the window. "It's California. I wish we didn't have to go there."

"What, you're not into swimming pools and movie stars?"

"Not particularly, but that's not what I meant." Frowning a little, he shifted in the passenger seat so he was more or less facing toward me. "People might think we're the wild west here in Arizona, but it's really California that's wild. Or Southern California, at least. Yes, the Santiagos are the clan in charge, but they've had some challenges to their authority."

"Really?" I asked, surprised. Not that I'd paid much attention to what was going on with the clans outside my immediate area—the Wilcoxes had generally been enough to occupy my mind—but this was the first that I'd heard of any of this. "Like what?"

We'd bought some bottled water at the Safeway in Cottonwood, and Connor took a swig of his before replying. "About six years ago—just when I was working on transferring from Northern Pines to ASU—there was some trouble in California. It's a big population, new people coming in, trying to integrate. It's the same with the witch clans, I guess, although in this case it was more smaller subgroups, not whole clans. They were moving into Santiago territory, and there was a lot of friction. I think Maya de la Paz actually took a few in. There were even a couple who wanted to come up to Wilcox territory." He frowned, putting his bottle of water back in the cup holder in the center console. "They weren't too reputable, and I guess they thought they could come up to Flagstaff and do whatever they wanted. Damon disabused them of that notion pretty quickly, and that was the end of it, because even they weren't prepared to go up against Damon. I'm not sure where they eventually ended up, but it wasn't anywhere around here."

This was disturbing news. I'd always been raised on the idea that clans and clan territories were immutable, that once you were born in one, you pretty much stayed put. True, tiny Jerome couldn't handle the entire McAllister contingent, and so we spilled over into Cottonwood and Clarkdale and even Camp Verde, just as there were Wilcoxes outside Flagstaff in Williams and Winslow and points even farther east, all the way to the New Mexico border. But that was understood to be their land. It wasn't as if they'd decided to pick up stakes and move into a whole other clan's territory.

"So should I be offended that no one asked to move onto McAllister turf?" I inquired, smiling so he wouldn't take my question seriously.

But that's exactly what he did. "The McAllisters don't control a lot of space, when it comes right down to it. You barely have room for your own people. We've got a lot of space up and down I-40, and of course Maya's territory is huge. Some of them were okay, and I suppose it's good that Maya took them in. But in general, you should count yourself lucky that they didn't try to move in on your land."

I could tell from the quiet, intense tone of his voice that he wasn't joking. Even though this had happened more than five years ago, obviously it had made an impression. And while it probably was something that had been discussed by my clan's elders and most likely a good number of the McAllister adults in general, it wasn't a topic my aunt would have wanted to share with me, especially since I would have been sixteen at the time and embroiled in school. As I'd learned over and over again, the people around me in Jerome had been pretty damn good at keeping secrets.

"So anyway," he continued, "that's why I'm not all that thrilled about going to California. It'll probably be fine—I mean, we're going straight to Newport Beach, and we're not going to be hanging around all that long. But I'll be a lot happier when we're on our way home, and crossing the border into Arizona and back into Maya's jurisdiction."

Well, in light of what he'd just told me, I couldn't really argue with that. "Hey," I said lightly, "we McAllisters are great at flying low and avoiding the radar. It'll be fine."

He nodded absently, his thoughts clearly elsewhere. I had to keep my attention on the road, as we were just now entering the outer bands of the greater Phoenix area, and the traffic had begun to thicken. Just as I was cutting over to get on the 101 Loop so we could avoid driving through the downtown area, Connor's phone rang.

Looking a little surprised, he pulled his cell out of his pocket, glanced at the display, then put it to his ear. "Hi, Lucas."

I raised an eyebrow but remained silent, maneuvering through traffic as we began to climb up the overpass.

"No, we found a place online last night, but—really? That sounds great." A pause, and then he said, "Can you text me the address? I don't have anything to write with." Another short silence while Lucas apparently was speaking, and Connor replied, "We will. Thanks again." Then he ended the call and looked over at me, his expression far more cheerful than it had been a few minutes earlier.

"What did Lucas want?" I asked.

"He was calling to let us know that a golf buddy of his has a timeshare in Newport, and he said we could use it since the guy and his wife are going to Scottsdale this week instead."

"'Golf buddy'?" I repeated. "Since when does Lucas play golf?"

"Since…forever, I guess. Remember, you met him in the dead of winter. Not exactly golf weather in Flagstaff."

"True." I couldn't help chuckling a little. "I guess I just can't get used to how…mainstream…so many of you Wilcoxes are."

"Yeah, we're not a bunch of hippies like the McAllisters," he agreed, but I could tell from the quirk at the corner of his mouth that he was teasing me. "But yeah, Lucas fits in with that crowd pretty well. As far as I can tell, they're a bunch of rich guys who play a lot of golf and don't seem to do much else. I have no idea where they get their money."

"I'm sure they probably think the same thing about Lucas."

"Probably."

After that we slipped into a companionable silence as we pushed on through the Valley sprawl, driving through all those bedroom communities of Phoenix: Peoria, Glendale, Avondale, Goodyear. We stopped in Goodyear and grabbed some burgers at the In-N-Out just off the freeway, since there probably wouldn't be much else until we hit Quartszite, a few miles from the border. After that we got back on Interstate 10 and began to head out into the vast, desolate desert that stretched between Phoenix and L.A.

It was certainly the farthest I'd ever driven in my life, and I had to force myself to keep my attention on the road rather than keep looking around me. Not that this particular stretch of desert had that much to recommend it, although some late wildflowers were still clinging to their blooms at the side of the road.

"Just let me know when you want to switch places," Connor said, breaking the silence somewhere outside a wide spot on the road called Tonopah.

"How about in Blythe?" I'd looked up our route online the night before, just to familiarize myself with the waypoints. I knew Blythe was right at the Arizona / California border, and it seemed as good a place as any.

"Sounds good," he replied, adjusting his seat slightly so he could lean back a little more. He didn't exactly close his eyes and go to sleep, but I could tell he wasn't in a chatty mood. Just as well; I adjusted the volume on the stereo, glad that I'd decided to pay a little extra for satellite radio, and let the Foo Fighters serenade us across the desert.

Even though I'd glanced at Google maps so I'd know where I was going, they didn't give much of a sense of scale. I felt as if we were driving forever, unending mile after unending mile flashing past as I let our speed drift up past eighty. No big deal, as the speed limit was seventy-five, but even so I felt as if we were standing still. Finally, though, we reached Blythe, made a pit stop at a fast food place there, and got some iced teas to perk us up. We switched places after we filled up the Cherokee, Connor getting into the driver's seat as I gladly reclined in the passenger seat. Four hours of driving was enough for me.

But if the Arizona desert had seemed interminable, it was even worse on the California side. It seemed to stretch out forever, and oddly, the landscape was far more desolate, a real wasteland. At least in Arizona there had been wild grass and cactus and scattered wildflowers. Here I saw only widely spaced scrubby bushes, and in some places not even that. If I hadn't known better, I would have thought we were driving across the surface of the moon.

At last, though, we hit Indio, then Palm Springs, and after that we began to drop down into Southern California's immense suburban sprawl. I thought I'd gotten a sense for what that was like in Phoenix, but this was far more than that, mile after mile of houses and industrial parks and big-box stores and chain restaurants. I turned and looked at Connor, wide-eyed.

"There's just so…much of it."

"I know." He didn't look as appalled as I felt, but I could tell he didn't care for our surroundings all that much, either.

And it went on, and on, until at last we dropped down from Interstate 10 to I-15, and from there to another freeway whose number I didn't catch, and then another, still with the overwhelming spread of suburbia on every side, rows of houses that looked the same, shopping centers that looked the same… cars and people that looked the same. I knew that wasn't true, not really, but in that moment I was very glad that I'd grown up in wacky little Jerome, where everyone knew each other and every house was a little different, and there wasn't a perfect right angle to be found.

All the while, though, we were heading steadily south and west—well, steadily until we came to an abrupt standstill on the 55 Freeway, in someplace called Orange. I glanced at the clock; it was a little past three-thirty, which seemed early for rush hour to me. Then again, "rush hour" in Jerome was waiting for a tourist to get the nerve to make a left onto 89A.

"How much farther?" I asked, attempting to stretch. The Cherokee's seats were comfortable enough, but after more than seven hours cooped up in the SUV, I just wanted to get out. Thank the Goddess I wasn't at that stage of pregnancy where you had to pee all the time.

"Miles or minutes?" Connor asked with a grin.

"Minutes."

"Hard to say. I was kind of hoping we'd be getting in early enough that we'd miss some of the traffic, but…." After letting the words trail off, he gave an eloquent lift of his shoulders. "I think it's still about twenty miles to Newport Beach, but if it stays this backed up, that could take us more than an hour."

"Crap," I said.

"Normally I'd say we could pull off, go get a snack somewhere and wait for it to die down, but from what I've heard, this probably isn't going to clear up until at least seven."

"Great." I shook my head, wondering why people would put up with this sort of congestion when there were so many other places they could live. "No, let's just keep going. I suppose we'll get there eventually."

"And we have a five-star timeshare waiting for us at the end of it instead of a Motel 6."

"True." That made me perk up a little, and so I tried to tell myself to be patient as we inched along. Things did get marginally better once we passed a minor fender-bender, and so we were able to rocket to a full twenty miles an hour instead of doing that horrible stop-and-go thing.

At last we were pulling off the freeway and onto a major road, which, while also congested, still moved a bit faster, and we came to the crest of a hill before dropping down toward Pacific Coast Highway.

"Wow," I said, since I couldn't think of anything remotely appropriate.

The Pacific Ocean sparkled ahead of us, deep blue, whitecaps catching the lowering sun and sparkling as if someone had tossed a bag of diamonds on the water's surface. It seemed to stretch on forever, the horizon so much farther away than I had ever seen it, I in my world bounded by hills and mountains on every side.

"Yeah, that's...." He let the words fade away, then shook his head as we coasted down the hill toward our destination.

Here everything was clean and perfect and manicured, from the carefully clipped trees to the smooth green lawns. I'd never seen so much grass in my life. We turned into the timeshare property, slowing down to accommodate the speed bumps, and eventually pulled up under a *porte cóchère*. I found myself wishing we'd borrowed Lucas' Porsche, because even though my Cherokee was brand-new and shiny, it couldn't really compete with the Mercedes and Beemers and other luxury cars I saw around us.

"What's that?" I asked, pointing at a low-slung convertible parked off to one side. I'd never seen anything like it.

"Tesla. It's electric...and expensive."

I'd never really been into cars, but that convertible was something else. And electric? Cool, I supposed, and maybe practical here in Southern California, but I wondered what its range was. We had a lot of wide-open spaces in northern Arizona.

We got out of the Cherokee, and a cool breeze touched my skin. It felt damp and heavy compared to the dry air I was used to. The breeze carried with it a strong, almost wild scent, one I'd never smelled before but knew had to be sea salt. In that moment, I didn't just feel as if I was in another state...I felt as if I'd somehow landed on a different planet.

And yet I'd been born here.

Connor opened the hatch, and we retrieved our meager luggage. Right then I sort of wished we'd gone to the Motel 6. I wouldn't have felt quite so out of place.

But the people at the front desk were very friendly, and gave us a map of the compound—it was probably bigger than all of Jerome—and told us where we could park. We got back in the car, drove slowly through the winding streets of the complex, and eventually ended at the unit that was our destination.

When Connor unlocked the door, I said "wow" for the second time in the space of an hour, and for good reason. This wasn't a dinky hotel room, but an entire apartment, with a separate living room and dining room, not to mention a full kitchen. Best of all, it had sliding glass doors that opened to a balcony, and that balcony offered a breathtaking ocean view.

"Feeling better?" Connor asked as I stood there, mesmerized.

"I—this is amazing, Connor. I had no idea."

"Neither did I, but I suppose I should have known. Lucas doesn't exactly hang out with the low-rent crowd."

"Guess not," I said shakily.

He glanced up at the clock. "So…it's after five. What do you want to do?"

Good question. It wasn't that late, but I was feeling wiped out after that drive. Maybe it would be better to take the rest of the evening to unwind, to relax and be tourists, and then get a fresh start the next morning.

"Freshen up a little, and then walk on the beach."

"No food?" he asked, teasing me.

"Oh, that, too. But I think I want to watch the sun set over the ocean."

"They're on Daylight Savings Time here. That sun may be setting later than you think."

"And there are no restaurants here with ocean views?"

"Touché. I'm sure we can find something." He held out a hand to me, and I went to him, let him fold me against him, felt the warmth of his body on mine. We stood like that for a long moment, and then he relaxed his embrace somewhat. "Okay," he said, "let's go sightseeing."

All my weariness seemed to drop away with the touch of that fresh ocean breeze, the feel of the cool sand beneath my toes. It was colder than I'd expected, chilly enough that I wished I'd brought a sweater with me. Even so, I saw people all around me in shorts and tank tops, or girls in bikinis catching their last few rays for the day.

To his credit, Connor didn't seem to be openly gawking at any of them—so much so that I said, "It's okay to look, you know. I'm guessing there aren't a lot of opportunities for bikini-wearing in Flagstaff."

"You might be surprised. We do have a lot of hot tubs up there." Then he shook his head. "Why should I be looking at those girls? You'd look just as good in a bikini."

I sort of doubted that, but it was gallant of him to say so. "Well, for the next month or so, anyway. After that I'm going to start looking like a beached whale."

"You don't know that. With one of my cousins, you could hardly tell she was even pregnant. Lucas used to tease her that she must be carrying the baby in her shoe."

Somehow I doubted I would be that lucky, but I only shrugged and said, "Maybe."

We walked for a while, and then my stomach growled, causing Connor to grin and comment that maybe it was time to get something to eat. Of course we knew nothing about the area, but a few minutes on Yelp helped direct us to a nearby restaurant. Again, I felt woefully underdressed, even though I'd changed into a fresh top and jeans before we left the hotel. Once I started eating, though, I stopped worrying about my style—or lack thereof—and just concentrated on the amazing sea bass and twice-baked potato. I did regret not being able to have a glass of wine with my meal, but it wasn't enough to keep me from enjoying myself.

It was easy to forget why we were really here, our true reason for coming to California. Connor and I might have been just another young couple enjoying a night on the town. Looking at us, no one would be able to guess that we possessed powers far beyond the ordinary, or that we were suffering under a curse cast many, many years earlier, in a time and place so far removed from where we were now that they could have been something out of a fairytale… albeit a Grimm one.

But I knew it wasn't a fairytale, but my life. Connor and I needed this time together, I knew, to return to one another, to be a couple. We'd have our meal, and then we'd go back to that luxurious little apartment Lucas had so thoughtfully procured for us. And then Connor and I would make love with the sound of the waves in the background, and we'd fall asleep in one another's arms, dreaming only of each other, keeping tomorrow for tomorrow.

And that is exactly what we did.

CHAPTER SIX

Unburying the Past

We took our time the next morning, sharing the shower, luxuriating in one another's company. There was a restaurant on the resort's grounds, so we wandered over there to fortify ourselves for the day. By the time we were done, it was past ten o'clock, and I knew I couldn't delay any longer.

"So...." Connor said as we climbed back into the Cherokee. By tacit agreement, he got into the driver's seat. "Hospital or house?"

"House," I replied. I'd briefly toyed with the idea of going to Hoag Hospital to see if there was any more information I could dig up, but realized that was a dead end. There might be the remotest chance that there were nurses or doctors still on staff who'd been there when they delivered me, but I kind of doubted it. Twenty-two years was a long time. At least at the house, even if no one was around who remembered Sonya McAllister, there was a slim chance that she might have left something behind, something that could have been kept, just in case.

All right, a very slim chance. But I didn't have much else to go on.

It turned out that 822 Oceanfront Drive was at almost the opposite end of Newport Beach from the resort where we were staying. We inched our way up Pacific Coast Highway, drove past the Porsche dealerships and yacht dealerships and restaurants, passed the turn-off for the hospital where I'd been born, and then turned left into a development that was built right up against the beach. The houses were all on the large side, vaguely Cape Cod in style with their clapboard siding in various shades of brown and cream and deep gray-blue. I didn't know a lot about real estate, but I knew anyplace built this close to the ocean had to be extremely expensive. And yet this was where my mother had lived during her time here, had probably conceived me? I couldn't quite wrap my head around that.

"Maybe it'll turn out that your father is some long-lost millionaire or something," Connor suggested, although I noticed he gave me a quick glance to make sure I hadn't taken the quip the wrong way.

"Maybe," I allowed. I knew that my mother had told Rachel before she left that she wanted to see the ocean, but this seemed to be taking that idea to the extreme.

Parking was horrendous, of course, but then Connor spotted a convertible Beetle pulling out of a space just ahead of us, and he hit the brakes, waiting for the car to get out of the way. Then he somehow managed to jigger the Cherokee into the too-small spot while I held my breath and hoped he wouldn't hit the Mercedes in front of us or the Land Rover behind us. Somehow he managed it, though, and we both got out, feeling once again the wind in our hair and tasting salt on the breeze.

"Which way?" he asked.

I looked up at the street signs, trying to calculate which way the house numbers ran. "Up there," I said, pointing to my left.

In this development, the garages faced out on the street, while the front yards were actually on the ocean side of the houses, their gates opening directly onto the sand. After a few steps, I decided to take off my flip-flops and walked along barefoot, although Connor didn't seem too eager to abandon his hiking shoes. We progressed slowly, reading the house numbers.

And then there was 822.

It was one of the smaller houses on the block, but still impressive-looking, freshly painted, with a balcony that ran along the entire façade and what looked like a staircase that led up to the roof, probably for more ocean viewing. I'd seen a few houses in Sedona built like that, too. What I didn't see were any real signs of occupation, like patio furniture or potted plants—unlike the house directly next door, which had a riotous collection of fuchsias and orchids and other tropical flowers I didn't recognize blooming in the small fenced-in yard.

"What do you think?" Connor murmured, standing close and reaching out to give my hand a reassuring squeeze.

Frankly, I didn't know what to think. The last thing I'd expected was to come all the way out here and find a house that didn't look like anyone lived in it. I supposed it could be a vacation home. In fact, that made sense, if it turned out that my mother or her mysterious lover had rented it all those years ago.

In that moment the front door to the house next to it, the one with all the flowers, opened. A trim-looking older woman with expertly highlighted hair came out, holding a water can. She seemed to notice Connor and me right away, and smiled. "Are you looking for someone?"

Well, of course I was, but I couldn't think of a good way to explain that to her. "Um…sort of," I confessed. "I think my mother lived here a long time ago. At least, this is the address she put down on the birth certificate."

The woman peered at me intently, and her eyes widened. After setting the watering can down on a glass-topped accent table, she came to the gate, her gaze never leaving my face. "I don't believe it! You—you're Sonya's baby?"

Oh, Goddess. Was it possible? "I'm Angela McAllister, yes."

"Sonya McAllister," the woman said, and shook her head. "Such a pretty girl she was. You look a good deal like her—and you must be about the same age, too."

"I'm twenty-two."

"Yes, that's right. Twenty-one, twenty-two, somewhere in there."

I felt Connor's fingers tighten around mine. "So you knew her? You've lived here all this time?" he asked. He sounded a bit incredulous, and I couldn't really blame him. There went his theory that people in California moved all the time.

She smiled. "Yes. I'm Linda Sanderson. My husband and I bought the house about two years before Sonya came here. That house was a rental property—still is, actually. The new tenants are coming this weekend and will be here all summer." Then she seemed to shake her head at herself and said, "Why don't you both come in, Angela and—" She gave Connor an expectant look, and he seemed to recover himself, saying,

"I'm Connor Wilcox, Angela's fiancé."

It was the first time he'd ever referred to himself that way, and his use of the word made me feel as if I'd been lit up from the inside. It seemed to please Linda as well, because her smile broadened and she said, "Very nice to meet you, Connor. Please, come inside. I'd love to hear all about Sonya and what happened to her."

Oh, boy. That wasn't a very pleasant story. But I wouldn't lie—not about that, anyway. Obviously I couldn't tell this Linda Sanderson that my mother and I were from a clan of witches, or that Connor, my handsome fiancé, just happened to be a warlock.

Slipping my flip-flops back on, I followed Linda inside, Connor a few paces behind me. The interior of the house was casual and elegant at the same time, much like its owner. She gestured for us to sit on a couch covered in a soft, nubby beige fabric, with beautifully embroidered pillows. All around were more orchids, and a glass bowl filled with shells and sand dollars sat on the glass and blond-wood coffee table.

"Iced tea?" she asked.

"Just water, thank you," I responded. I didn't want to ask whether the tea was caffeinated and then have to go into the whole caffeine-avoidance pregnancy thing.

"Sure thing," she said. "And you, Connor?"

"Tea sounds great, thank you."

She went and busied herself in the kitchen for a few minutes, then came back with tall green-hued glasses filled with water for me and tea for Connor. After she sat down on the love seat facing the couch where Connor and I had seated ourselves, she asked, "So, what brings you here after all these years? Your family is from Arizona, isn't it?"

"Yes," I replied. "Northern Arizona. A little town called Jerome." And how far away it felt from this serene beachfront house and the woman who sat across from me, with her perfectly bobbed hair and smooth, tanned skin. I had a feeling she had to be in her late fifties or early sixties, but she looked amazing. Botox, maybe? It seemed a Newport Beach sort of thing to do.

"And how is your mother?"

I swallowed. "Well, that is—she passed away a long time ago, not too long after she came back to Jerome. A motorcycle accident. I don't even remember her."

An expression of dismay passed over Linda's regular features. "Oh, I'm so very sorry to hear that. She was a lovely girl."

"She was?" That didn't seem to jibe with most of Aunt Rachel's remarks about her sister, which generally centered on her heedlessness and lack of responsibility. "I mean," I added quickly, as I saw Linda's eyebrows lift in surprise, "I don't really know anything about her. My aunt—her sister—doesn't like to talk much about it."

"Ah." She nodded in apparent understanding. "Well, Sonya didn't tell me all that much about her family, only said she was from Arizona and that both her parents had passed away. When she came here with Andre—"

"Andre?" I asked.

"Her fiancé," Linda replied, looking puzzled. "Your father. You didn't know about him?"

"No," I said. I felt Connor's fingers reach out to touch mine, give them a reassuring squeeze. "That is, my mother didn't talk about him. On the birth certificate, it just says 'unknown' where the father's name should be."

For a few seconds Linda didn't say anything, just lifted her own glass of tea and sipped at it. Now I could see the worry line between her brows deepen, and I supposed Botox couldn't erase everything. At length she said, "Well, I suppose I can partly understand that. They had a terrible fight only a few days before you were born."

"They did?" Connor's fingers tightened around mine, offering his strength, and I asked, "What was the fight about?"

"I don't know for sure. They were shouting, and their windows were open, but ours weren't." She gave a grim little smile. "I suppose they thought it was still fairly warm, although it was sweater weather for the rest of us SoCal natives. Anyway, there was shouting, and then Andre—your father—drove off in his Jeep. He never came back."

And because of that argument...whatever it had actually been about...my mother had made sure I'd never know who my father really was. "Do you remember his last name?"

"Williams, I think. He seemed like a very nice young man, so I couldn't figure out what on earth it might have been that would make him and Sonya argue like that. So handsome, too." Her gaze flicked toward Connor, and I saw the little line appear between her brows again. "It's funny, but you remind me a little of him. Not exactly, but there's something...." She shook her head. "Maybe it's just that you're both tall and dark-haired. I think I remember him saying once that he was part Native American. Navajo, maybe."

Suddenly the room felt a little chillier. "Navajo? You're sure?"

"I think so."

I risked a quick sidelong glance at Connor. He was sitting motionless, his hand still holding mine, but I thought I saw a tremor in the muscles along his jaw line, as if he'd had a sudden thought but wanted to keep it to himself. "That's interesting," I managed to say. "I don't suppose you remember if they told you how they met?"

"Actually, I do. Andre was out running to the store or something, and my husband was at work, so Sonya and I were having some tea and chatting, just watching the beach. I remember asking her what had brought her and Andre here to Newport Beach, and she said that was the funny thing, that she'd actually met him here, even though they were both from Arizona."

"They were?" I asked, my voice sounding strangled. "Do you remember where?"

"Hmm…somewhere around the Phoenix area, I think. Scottsdale or Tempe. Or was it Mesa?" Linda gave an apologetic shrug. "Sorry, that was a long time ago. I'm surprised I'm remembering as much as I am, but maybe it's seeing you, seeing how much you look like Sonya, although your hair is much darker."

"It's all right," I replied quickly. I didn't want her to think I was upset with her; after all, she'd already given me more information about my parents than I'd previously heard in my entire life. "And—and can you tell me what happened? Why she left?"

"Well, the two of them had come here in late April, and she left in the middle of February, so she still had a few months left on her lease. Even so, the owner of the house told me she paid everything that was owed before she moved out. I always wondered how a young couple like that could have afforded the house in the first place, but obviously money wasn't an issue." Another lift of her shoulders, and she continued, "Anyway, she just said she didn't want to stay here alone with the baby, so she was going back to Arizona to be with her family. And she packed up her things and left. I worried about her driving all that way with a newborn, and asked her if she couldn't have someone from her family come here to get her, but she said that wasn't possible. So she drove off one morning with you in a car seat, Angela, and that was the last I saw of her. I've often wondered what happened to her…and to Andre."

Andre Williams. Andre wasn't that common a name, but Williams sure was. I didn't know how I'd begin to track him down. Hire a private investigator, maybe? There had to be records of some sort, starting with the lease on the house next door.

More than anything, though, I wanted to talk to Connor alone, find out why he'd reacted the way he did when Linda revealed that my long-lost father had possibly been part Navajo. Was it only the Wilcox connection with that tribe…or maybe something else?

Since I'd already let too much time elapse before I replied to her speech, I said quickly, "Thank you, Linda. That's a big help. At least now I know who my father was." Well, sort of, anyway. I had a name, and the possibility of him being part Navajo. Maybe he was listed in the tribal registry or something. I wasn't really sure how those things worked.

She smiled at me, although something about her expression looked a little sad, as if she was recalling the young woman she'd known so many years ago and having to mentally adjust to the thought that she'd never lived to see her daughter grow up. "I wish I could tell you more, but that's really all I can remember."

"No, it's fine. I really can't begin to thank you for this." I looked over at Connor and gave him the slightest of nods, signaling that I was ready to go. "We've really taken up enough of your time, though, so we'd better get going."

It seemed as if she was about to demur, to say it was fine if we wanted to stay longer, but then she appeared to get a good look at my face, and nodded. "It's no trouble. I'm very glad I was able to meet you. Well, meet you again, I mean."

And what a span of years filled the space between those two meetings. Of course I didn't remember this place at all, just as I had no recollection of my mother, but I'd come home from the hospital to the house next door, had no doubt cost Linda some sleep with my crying. Or maybe I'd been a quiet baby. I didn't know; Aunt Rachel never shared even the tiniest detail about my earliest days.

"And I'm very glad I was able to meet you. Thank you again for everything."

I rose from the couch then, and Connor followed suit. Linda saw us to the door, then said, "Would you like to give me your phone number? Just in case I remember anything else?"

That sounded like a wonderful idea, so I rattled off the number to her while she wrote it down on a pad next to her phone, which was sitting on a side table. Then Connor and I both made our final goodbyes to her, and headed out into the bright sunshine.

I really didn't want to go back to the car. Not yet, anyway. I needed some time to think. The beach was occupied but not crowded, so it seemed as good a place as any to talk. Slipping off my flip-flops once again, I made my way to the water's edge, to a spot where the closest people were a good ten yards away. As the cool water rushed over my toes, I asked Connor, "Do you want to tell me what that was about?"

"What was what about?"

Maybe it was just the glare from the water that made him narrow his eyes and glance away, but somehow I doubted it. "I saw you. When Linda said my father was part Navajo, you looked like, I don't know, like you'd just thought of something. So what was it?"

"It could be nothing...."

"Or it couldn't." I turned away from the water, away from that endless expanse of glittering blue, shifting so we faced one another. "Connor, we have to be honest with each other, no matter what. No more hiding things. No more lies."

He was quiet for a few seconds, chest rising and falling as he took in breaths of the wild salt-laden air. "Okay. You probably heard through the family grapevine—also known as Mason and Carla—that Marie was engaged once, and that her fiancé just up and disappeared?"

"Yeah, they told me about it when I asked why Marie always seemed so hostile. What about it?"

"Her fiancé's name was Andre. Andre Wilcox."

The air felt as if it had been sucked out of my lungs. I stared at Connor, trying to draw breath, trying to make sense of what he'd just told me. "What are you saying? That my father and this Andre are the same person?" A horrible thought occurred to me. "That you and I are *related?*"

"Only distantly," he hurried to say. "If it's really the same person. He was, I don't know, descended from Jeremiah's middle brother, I think. We're way more distant cousins than you and your cousin Adam are." He stopped there, mouth tightening as if he'd meant to say more and decided against it.

I could imagine what he'd been thinking, though. Adam and I were third or fourth cousins, perfectly legal even outside the Ozarks, and there had been many more generations and far more intermarriages separating whatever distant relationship Connor and I might or might not have. If this Andre Williams really was Andre Wilcox.

"What else do you know about it?" I demanded.

"Jesus, Angela, not much." He crossed his arms and didn't quite glare at me, but I could tell he was annoyed by my tone. "I mean, I was probably five when all that went down. Did you pay attention to the love lives of your relatives when you were five years old?"

"No, of course not, except for going to weddings, which were fun because there was cake."

"Exactly. I mean, it's been part of the family gossip ever since, but I don't pay attention to that kind of crap. I leave it for my cousin Leah—Carla's mother—to keep spreading it around."

"And the Navajo thing?" I asked. I still couldn't quite wrap my head around that part of the story. "Marie's mother was Navajo...was Andre's mother, too?"

"Grandmother, I think. Like I said, I don't pay a huge amount of attention. There are people in the family who keep track of all the genealogy, but I'm not one of them."

"But after what Jeremiah did—"

"More than a hundred years ago, Angela." He sighed and turned his head into the wind, too-long hair whipping in the brisk breeze, gleaming like the wings of the ravens that made northern Arizona their home. In that moment, I wondered what he would look like if he let his hair grow all the way out, let it be straight and silky and free, like that of his own long-ago Navajo forebears. "There's bad blood, no doubt about it, but the Navajo aren't one huge monolithic tribe. They all have their own hopes and dreams and fears. Maybe a pretty girl looked at her future on the reservation and decided being with a Wilcox wasn't so bad. After all, if you're not married to the *primus*, you'll probably have a pretty good life. Also, if that girl has any kind of magical gifts, she's better off away from the res. The Navajo don't have the same view of witchcraft that we do, and shun it, apart from the powers of their shamans. Whereas we'd welcome someone like that. Why do you think Marie is so powerful? It's not all Wilcox blood."

For a minute I didn't say anything, just stood there and let the cool water lap at my feet and the wind pull at my own hair. My thoughts were as chaotic and complex as the patterns of the waves breaking a few yards away from us. "Did he ever come back?" I asked abruptly.

"Who? Andre? No. He just…disappeared."

Twenty-two years was a long time to be disappeared. Maybe he'd met the same fate as my mother, wiped out on a highway in a traffic accident. Or maybe he'd just picked up stakes and moved across the country, although that wasn't as easy for someone with witch blood as it was for the world's civilian population. You had to find someone willing to take you in.

Willing to take you in…. I blinked, thinking of what Connor had told me on the drive here, of how Maya de la Paz had allowed some of the refugees from Southern California to settle in her territory. Maybe my long-lost father's lie had become truth. Maybe Andre Wilcox had never gone back to Flagstaff because he'd ended up in Scottsdale or Tempe or Mesa, somewhere on de la Paz land.

"Do you think he could have gone to take refuge with the de la Paz clan?"

"I have no idea." Connor frowned at me, obviously attempting to follow my logic. "What makes you think that?"

"Because you said a while ago Maya had taken in some of the Southern California witches. Why not my father?"

"Aside from the fact that he's a Wilcox?" A shake of the head, followed by, "Maya's a generous soul, but I think she might have drawn the line there."

"Well, it's worth asking, isn't it? We'll be going through Phoenix on the way home, so what could it hurt to go see her and ask?"

I could tell by his expression that Connor wasn't buying it but didn't want to get into an argument with me. "I suppose it couldn't hurt. Just—just don't get your hopes up, okay?"

Too late for that. True, there were many other places he could have gone, but it seemed logical to start with the closest and easiest first. Well, relatively close, anyway. It was still a good five hours or more to Phoenix, depending on the traffic.

"I won't," I told him. "But we'd better get back to the hotel and get packed up. I don't know when rush hour starts around here, but the sooner we're on the road, the better chance we have of avoiding it."

"And that's it?" he asked. "We haven't even been here twenty-four hours. Isn't there anything else you want to do, anyone else you might want to see?"

"No," I said firmly, staring across the beach to Linda Sanderson's house. "I've found out everything I needed to know."

CHAPTER SEVEN

Rocky Road

LUCAS HAD MADE OUR RESERVATION FOR THREE NIGHTS, SO the clerk at the front desk looked a little puzzled when we appeared and said we wanted to check out. "Is there anything wrong with the accommodations?" she inquired, a worried little frown pulling at her expertly plucked brows.

"No, not at all," I said at once. "The room was perfect. I hope we can come back someday. But we just had some urgent family business come up, so—"

"Oh," she replied, expression clearing. "Of course. Let me take care of this. We can only refund one night because we need twenty-four-hour notice, but—"

Oops. I hadn't thought of that. I certainly didn't want Lucas (or his friend with the timeshare…I wasn't exactly sure who had financed the room) losing out on hundreds of dollars, and I bit my lip, not sure what I should do.

Luckily, Connor cut in then, saying smoothly, "That's not a problem. We're sorry about the inconvenience."

"Oh, it's no inconvenience, sir," she said, with a quick bat of her eyelashes. Despite her professional appearance, I could tell she was a little smitten with Connor.

Then again, who wouldn't be?

She typed away on her computer, then said, "You're all set. Just let me get a copy of your paperwork." Moving away from us, she went to a printer a few feet away, picked up a few sheets of paper, and handed them over to Connor. "Thank you for staying with us, and I hope you can make it back here in the near future."

I somehow doubted that was going to happen, but I didn't reply, only gave her a smile and a nod as Connor folded the papers and then shoved them into the Northern Pines bag he was carrying. He thanked her, and then we were headed out the door, going to where we'd left the Cherokee waiting under the *porte cochère*.

And a few minutes after that we were winding our way out of Newport, heading back to the freeway. I glanced at the clock. One o'clock. Normally that would be lunchtime, but we'd eaten breakfast so late that I wasn't really hungry yet. Anyway, I could feel the urgency building in me, the need to get out of here as early as possible before traffic created an impenetrable wall that would only delay our arrival in Phoenix.

Connor must have noticed my nervous survey of the time, because he reached out with his right hand and brushed a stray strand of hair off my cheek. "It's okay. We'll get out of Orange County and head east on the 10, and then maybe we can stop for a late lunch in Palm Springs or Indio or something. We'll be fine."

His words did reassure me somewhat…or maybe it was just the thrill I felt from that brief brush of his fingers against my skin, a touch that seemed to right the world again. Whichever it might be, I could feel my heartbeat calm somewhat as we drove north and east, especially since we didn't encounter much in the way of traffic jams. We slowed here and there, and there were far more cars around us than I'd seen even in Phoenix, but everything more or less flowed until we were away from most of the SoCal crush, passing through towns like Redlands and Banning and Beaumont, cresting a hill and then dropping down into the low desert, into a landscape that grew sere with almost shocking suddenness.

"Which do you want, Indio or Palm Springs?" Connor asked as we passed a sprawling outlet mall.

"Palm Springs is nicer, but it's off the main highway, so we'll lose a little more time."

"Indio," I said automatically. My stomach was telling me I needed to eat, that the lovely frittatta I'd had for breakfast was long gone, but I didn't want to waste any time. I was fine with grabbing a burger somewhere and then getting back on the road.

"Indio it is. It's still about fifteen miles up the road. Can you check your Yelp app and find someplace that looks like it might be halfway decent?"

Here I still had a decent signal, unlike parts of the desert we'd driven through on the outward journey. I pulled up the app, scrolled through a few choices, and asked, "What do you want? Mexican? Burgers? Doesn't look like there's much else."

"Either one. Maybe Mexican. Flagstaff's Mexican food is kind of meh. I probably got spoiled living all those years down in Tempe."

I nodded, chose a restaurant based on the reviews, and then told Connor which exit we should use to get off the interstate. Even though I'd tried to streamline things, we still had to drive a couple of miles to get to our destination, as it seemed as if most of the businesses in town were clustered away from the freeway.

Since we were coming in at the tail end of traditional lunch, at almost two o'clock, the place was busy, but not so much that we had to wait long for a table. In just a few minutes we were seated and had been served what tasted like freshly made chips and salsa, which I attacked as if it had been a day since I'd last eaten rather than four hours.

Connor must have gotten used to my pregnancy appetite, because he just gave a small shake of his head before he pulled his phone out of his pocket. "I thought it might be a good idea to call Maya, let her know we were dropping in."

"You have her number?" I asked, after taking a swallow of water to wash down the chips.

"Lucas gave it to me."

"Lucas?"

My tone must have been disbelieving, because Connor smiled a little and replied, "Well, I guess they do have their ways of keeping in touch in case of emergency or something. I know my brother had it, since he was the one who patched the call through to Maya when I was trying to transfer to ASU." At the mention of his brother, Connor's smile disappeared as quickly as it had come. We'd deliberately danced around the issue, had hardly mentioned Damon to one another. I didn't know if that was the best way to handle it, but I also didn't want to reopen any barely healed wounds. Better to allow Connor to decide what he wanted to say…or not say. "Anyway, when I told Lucas what our plans were, he gave me Maya's number, said it was a good idea to have it with me, since we were going to be traveling through her territory."

"I guess that makes sense," I said, my tone neutral.

He had to wait to make the call, though, because then the waiter came by to ask what we wanted. I'd barely glanced at the menu, but made a quick choice and ordered a chimichanga, while Connor got fajitas. That should be enough to hold us on the drive across the desert. After the waiter left, Connor picked up his phone again, scrolled through his contacts, and selected Maya's number. After waiting a few seconds, he said, "Maya? Hi, it's Connor—fine, we're fine.... No, we're already on our way back home. But we're going to be in Phoenix in about four hours or so, depending on how long lunch takes, and Angela would really like to stop by and talk to you, if that's okay.... Sure, we'll call again when we get into town...hang on, let me write down the address." He made a frantic writing gesture with his free hand, and I scrabbled in my purse for a pen. Luckily, I actually had one, and I gave it to him, then watched him write down an address on his napkin. "Okay, thanks, Maya." He ended the call and shoved the phone back in his pocket, then said, "We're set. She's actually in Scottsdale, not Phoenix proper."

"Well, that makes sense," I said. "I mean, the *prima* of the de la Pazes should live in the high-rent district."

I'd meant it halfway as a joke, but Connor appeared to take my words seriously, asking, "And what about the *prima* of the McAllisters?"

"Well, Paradise Lane *is* the high-rent district in Jerome," I pointed out.

"That's not what I meant," he said. "Lucas is already pressuring me to look for a different place. He says I'm the head of the family now and shouldn't be living in a loft apartment above a storefront."

"I *like* your apartment." How could I not like it? It was where we'd fallen in love, where we'd made love for the first time. Even more than that, it *felt* like Connor. I really couldn't imagine him anywhere else…although of course I'd had daydreams where he'd come to share the big Victorian in Jerome with me. But that was before Damon died, before the unwanted *primus* powers had passed to Connor. There was no way he could relocate permanently to the house on Cleopatra Hill.

"I like it, too." He lifted his eyes to meet mine, and once again I was struck by the layered shades of green in those depths, sage and moss and dark, dark emerald, all fringed in black lashes so thick they almost didn't seem real. "But Angela…it's no place to raise a child."

Almost unconsciously my hand went to my belly, to the secret hidden there. I still hadn't begun to show at all, so sometimes I felt like I could almost pretend I wasn't even pregnant. But of course I was…and that child was the reason we'd come to California in the first place. "So you're going to move?"

"Eventually. To get Lucas off my back, I told him he could start looking around for me. He was thrilled, of course. The only thing he likes better than spending his own money is spending someone else's."

I laughed at that, albeit a little stiffly. "And so… how is this going to work? I want to be with you, but…."

"I know. I feel the same way. I like that big creaky Victorian of yours…well, except for that bathtub… but there's no way the Wilcoxes would ever let their *primus* live in McAllister territory."

"And of course the McAllisters feel the same way about Wilcox territory." I sighed and tucked a strand of hair behind my ear. "Too bad we can't just elope and, I don't know, go live in Wyoming or something. I've heard it's really beautiful."

"What, you didn't like the beach?"

Wrinkling my nose, I shook my head. "Not really. That is, I liked the beach itself just fine, but I couldn't handle having that many people around me all the time. I'm too used to wide-open spaces."

"I can't really argue with that."

And so we shared some idle chitchat about Southern California and the hotel, leaving behind the subject of our future residence. After all, it was all going to be pretty academic if we couldn't figure out a way to break the curse. And what would happen if I was gone, and left the baby behind? A morbid thought, but one I had to make myself think about, considering the track record of all those former Wilcox wives. I supposed if it was a boy he would go to live with the Wilcoxes and be the next primus after Connor, and if the baby was a girl, she'd go to the McAllisters. All very neat and sensible. I had a feeling the reality would end up being a little messier than that, as I doubted Connor would ever willingly hand over a child of his to my relatives to raise, thus abdicating any responsibility.

"Chimichanga," the waiter said, startling me out of my reverie as he set my meal in front of me. "Very hot plate, miss."

I nodded, forcing my dark thoughts away, and watched as he set down a sizzling plate of fajitas next to Connor, along with one of those little plastic warmers for the tortillas. After the waiter asked if we needed anything else and we both murmured that we were fine, Connor sent an inquiring glance in my direction.

"You didn't look like you were thinking very happy thoughts."

"I wasn't," I admitted. Not that I really wanted to tell him what had been on my mind, but I'd admonished him earlier that there could be no secrets, no lies between us, and I'd be a hypocrite if I didn't follow my own rules. "I was just thinking about what would happen to the baby after—I mean, if we can't—"

"Don't say it," he cut in. "We will figure out a way to make this work. We *will*."

He looked so determined that I could only nod and say, "You're right, of course. Well, let's eat so we can get back on the road."

And that's what we did, plowing into our food and concentrating on the here and now, and not what might be in the future. That chimichanga restored my faith in humanity, and Connor seemed to be having a similar reaction to his fajitas, so I was glad I chose this place, even if it was a little off the beaten track. After we were done, the waiter asked if we wanted anything else, but we both just shook our heads. Even I couldn't have fit anything else in my stomach, not even some homemade flan.

"Just the check," Connor said, and shortly thereafter we settled up and made our way back outside.

The restaurant was located in a small strip mall with inadequate parking, so we'd had to leave the

Cherokee around the corner on the street. I wasn't that thrilled about the area, but the car had a security system and of course was insured up to the hilt, so I'd told myself not to worry about it. As we approached the SUV, it looked fine—no windows broken in or anything like that. My feeling of relief quickly began to fade, however, when I saw a group of five young men begin to approach us from down an alley across the street.

"Connor," I murmured.

"I know," he said, his jaw tense. "Just keep walking."

But it wasn't just any gang of toughs out to car-jack what they thought was an easy mark. As they got closer, I could feel the power coming from them, the same pulsing energy all witches and warlocks shared. My eyes widened, even as Connor sent a quick worried look down at me. Clearly, he'd sensed it, too.

The young men paused about ten feet away from us, blocking access to the car. The leader, a young Hispanic man who looked like he was around Connor's age, flashed us a sardonic grin. "So, what are you doing here, *witches?*"

"Just passing through," Connor said calmly. "We don't want any trouble."

"Ah, well, I guess it's not a question of whether you want it, *ese*." The four other warlocks came up to flank their leader. They were all in their twenties, muscled builds shown off by tight-fitting T-shirts or wife-beaters. I wouldn't have wanted to come up against them even if they didn't also happen to have magical powers.

"Really, we're just heading back to Arizona—" I began, and the leader let his dark gaze rake up and down my body before he laughed and said,

"Don't worry, *chica*, we'll have some fun with you after we take care of pretty-boy here. As for Arizona"—he spat on the ground—"we got no use for that shitty state, or the *pinche puta* who thinks she runs things over there. Deciding who can come in and who has to stay in this rathole!"

I realized then that these must be some of those rogue warlocks Connor had told me about on the drive here to California, the ones who had been turned away from relocating in the Phoenix area. Obviously they had no love lost for Maya de la Paz. And although there had been a few other cars parked here when we got out to head into the restaurant, they all seemed to have disappeared. There was no one around to intervene.

Then again, Connor and I weren't exactly helpless. After all, we'd defeated a skin-walker.

"I really think you'd better step aside," I said, making sure my voice sounded cool, confident. "I don't think you know who you're dealing with here." Even as I spoke, I could feel the *prima* energy beginning to uncoil in me, warmth without heat, the power flowing through every limb.

And somehow Connor seemed able to sense it, too. He reached out to take my hand, and it was as if a spark ignited between us, one that had nothing to do with passion and everything to do with power. Never before had a *prima* and a *primus* been able to work together in harmony, and I wasn't sure what that meant.

I had a feeling we were all about to find out, though.

The lead warlock laughed. "Yeah? And who are you, *puta?*"

"No one you want to fuck with," Connor said. His fingers tightened on mine, and the power flared in me, searing without burning, coiled, ready… eager.

"Fuck that shit," the warlock said, raising his own hand.

Of course I had no idea what his power might be, and I wasn't going to wait to find out. An unspoken signal passed between us, and Connor and I lifted our hands, fingers still intertwined. The energy crackled all through my body, surging through my arm, moving away from me.

A wall of white light seemed to blast outward from where Connor and I stood. It hit the group of young men, crashing into them like a tidal wave into a pier. They were all knocked backward a good five yards or more, and went sprawling on the sidewalk, their bodies limp and unmoving.

Heart pounding, I looked up at Connor. "Are they…?"

"I don't know," he said with grim indifference. "And I don't much care. Let's get to the car before anyone comes to find out."

I decided I didn't really want to argue. After all, they were the ones who'd initiated the confrontation. We hurried to the Cherokee, which appeared completely unaffected by that magical shockwave, and climbed in, Connor gunning the engine and peeling away from the curb before I even had a chance to fasten my seatbelt.

It wasn't until we were moving up the main street that would take us back to the interstate that I turned to him.

"What," I asked, "the hell was *that?*"

He could only lift his shoulders in reply.

We pulled into Scottsdale a little after six. The place was still baking—the thermometer on the dashboard indicated it was a hundred and three degrees outside—and I stared moodily out the window as we wound our way along wide streets planted with cactus in the dividers. Palm trees loomed overhead. Everything was extremely manicured, very neat. Not the sort of place you'd expect to find the head of the local witch clan, but then again, I was coming to realize that perhaps the bohemian McAllisters weren't the norm in the witching world.

Connor took out his phone and made a brief call, saying we'd be there in about five more minutes. "She's expecting us."

Of course she was. I wondered what she might have to say about Connor's and my latest display of power. "Are we going to tell her?"

"Tell her what?"

"About Indio."

For a few seconds he didn't say anything, only kept his gaze fixed on the street, eyes hidden behind his sunglasses. "Should we?"

"I think—I think yeah, we should. Maybe she'll have some insights."

"Or maybe it's better that she not know the extent of our powers."

"Now you sound like a Wilcox," I said, annoyed.

The barb hit home, I could tell. His gaze flickered toward me briefly before returning to the road. "What's that supposed to mean?"

"Just that you tend to be a little paranoid. I meant that as the general 'you,'" I added, when I saw his lips begin to compress. "Maya de la Paz has been nothing but helpful, and you know it. She has her own kingdom down here, so to speak. She certainly doesn't have any designs on McAllister or Wilcox territory. So why not take advantage of her age and experience and see if she has any advice to offer?"

At those words, his expression relaxed somewhat. After a brief pause, he replied, "You're right, of course. Sorry. All those years with Damon...." He let the words die away, but I thought I knew what he meant. Growing up with Damon Wilcox as your older brother would make even the saintliest person suspicious of everyone's motives.

I nodded but didn't say anything else. Just as well, because we pulled over then, coming to a stop in front of a sprawling Santa Fe–style adobe house with stately saguaro cacti planted in the front yard, along with several varieties of lower, more sprawling succulents blooming in vivid hues of yellow and hot pink. I undid my seatbelt and got out, glad of the chance to stretch my legs at last.

The heat hit me like a wall, though, feeling almost like a physical weight on my chest. True, I'd been to the Phoenix area several times before, but those McAllister expeditions always happened sometime between November and March, either after the endless scorching summer or before it had a chance to begin. Not that we didn't get hot in Jerome in the summer, but not like this.

Connor seemed singularly unaffected by the heat, though, moving smoothly around the rear of the SUV to join me on the sidewalk.

"How come you're not even breaking a sweat, Flagstaff boy?" I asked as we headed up the front walk.

"I lived down here for four years, remember? I'm used to it." He paused and amended, "Well, used to be used to it. I'll admit that I don't miss the heat too much, now that I'm back in Flag, but I can live with it."

I didn't know why anyone would want to, but I just shrugged, reaching out to push the doorbell. About a minute later, a tall young man around Connor's age appeared at the door.

"Come on in," he said. "She's expecting you."

The enormous door of carefully aged wood, banded in black iron, didn't open onto an entryway as I'd expected, but rather a large courtyard laid with red sandstone flags. A fountain splashed into the hot, still air, and vivid flowers bloomed from hanging containers of brightly painted Mexican pottery.

We followed the young man—who I thought I recognized as one of the "bodyguards" Maya had brought with her to Connor's gallery opening in Sedona—through the courtyard and on through a second, equally enormous door into a high-ceilinged foyer. In here the air was cool and friendly, obviously the product of a very hard-working air-conditioning system. From the entry, we went into a large living room decorated with heavy hacienda-style furniture. Faded Persian rugs covered the red-tiled floor.

Maya rose from one of the leather couches and came toward us, hands outstretched. "Connor, Angela, so good to see you…together."

From her emphasis on the last word, I gathered that she'd known about our separation. Who exactly had been her informant, I didn't know, although I had a feeling it was probably someone in the McAllister camp and not the Wilcox clan. "Thank you for letting us stop by," I said, not wanting to jump right into Connor's and my relationship status.

"It's no problem, and not too much out of the way for you, I hope."

"No, not at all," Connor said. "We'll just get on the 101 Loop and head home from here."

"Ah," she replied, dark eyes twinkling. "And where exactly *is* home for you two?"

Trust Maya de la Paz to get right to the heart of the matter. But I wasn't going to let her distract me from the true reason for our visit. "Jerome, Flagstaff," I said shortly. "You know. Actually, though, Maya, I wanted to ask you something."

"And it must be important, or you could've simply asked on the phone, rather than driving all the way here. Ah, here are the refreshments," she put in, smiling as the young man returned with a silver tray laden with a pitcher of lemonade and three heavy hand-blown glasses, rims tinted cobalt blue. "I thought you might be thirsty after your long drive."

"Thanks, Maya," Connor said, reaching out for one of the glasses and handing it to me, then taking one for himself.

"It's nothing. I'd invite you to stay for supper as well, but I can tell from the look in Angela's eye that she's on a mission, and will want to be on the road once your business here is finished." Her dark gaze sharpened, even as she took a sip of her lemonade. Setting the glass down on a sandstone coaster, she asked, "And did you find what you were looking for in California?"

"Sort of," I hedged. Yes, I'd lectured Connor about being truthful and not hiding things, but now, with Maya's shrewd eyes studying my face, I wondered how much I should really tell her. After all, this was Wilcox and McAllister business. The de la Paz clan really had no stake in this game. Then again, we probably wouldn't have even been able to go to California if Maya hadn't put in a word for us with the Santiago family there. Beside me, I could feel Connor shift, hear the leather squeak faintly under his weight, and I could tell he was waiting, too, wondering how much I planned to reveal.

Well, nothing for it. The story would get out sooner or later.

"I found out my father is a Wilcox," I said boldly.

That did seem to surprise her; she blinked, and the strong black brows—unmarked by gray—lifted slightly before she replied, "Indeed? Well, that does put a different…perspective…on things."

"Just a little," I remarked, my tone wry. "And I was thinking—well, hoping, I guess—that you might know what happened to him."

"Why on earth would I know that?"

She'd replied coolly, with only a hint of question in her voice, and so it was difficult for me to gauge whether she really didn't know anything or whether she was stalling me for some reason. "Well, Connor told me on the drive that a while back you'd taken in some refugee witches and warlocks from California, and so I thought maybe…." I let the words trail off as she continued to stare at me blankly. Then her mouth, still full and pretty, twitched a little.

"Oh, my dear, that was only a few years ago."

"I know, but—"

"That was the first time I allowed anything like that," she cut in, the interruption so gentle that I couldn't really be upset by it. "And—no offense to you, Connor—while I did allow Connor to have a residence here for a few years while he was going to school, there is no way I would allow a Wilcox to live in my territory permanently."

"Maybe you wouldn't have even known he was a Wilcox," I said, desperation beginning to seep into my voice. "He was using the last name of Williams at the time. Andre Williams."

She shook her head. "My dear, I would have known he was a Wilcox at once. I've been *prima* of this clan for more than thirty years. There isn't much that gets past me."

No, I supposed there wasn't.

Connor laid a hand on mine. Just that gentle pressure made me feel a little better, even though it couldn't erase all my frustration. "And would you know if a Wilcox passed through your territory, even if he didn't stop and ask to stay?" he inquired.

"Of course. I could sense when you were here in the valley, although your presence was not at all disruptive. It was more like…a small blip on a radar screen, I suppose. And much stronger when your brother came here last November." She paused then, a small frown tugging at her brows. "Now that I think of it, there might have been something, many, many years ago."

"Long enough ago that I would have still been a baby?" I asked eagerly. If Maya had sensed my father moving through her territory, at least it would tell me that he had come back to Arizona after leaving California.

"It might have been around then." Another hesitation, one she attempted to mask by picking up her lemonade and drinking some more of it. Then she went on, "I reached out to some of my clan members, our defenders, to investigate, but whoever it was, they were gone from our territory before we could catch up with them. And since pursuing someone beyond the borders of our clan lands is not something we would ever do, we let the matter go."

Maybe it had been Andre—my father—driving through Phoenix and its bordering communities as quickly as he could, knowing he didn't have a lot of time before the de la Paz contingent figured out he was there. A speeding ticket would probably be preferable to getting caught by a group of hostile witches and warlocks. In my mind I saw him racketing down the highway in a beat-up Jeep, black hair blowing in the wind. Silly, I supposed; that Jeep of his could have been brand new back then, and of course I had no idea whether he cut his hair short or wore it long.

"Heading north?" I asked.

"I don't recall. Probably." She set down her tea and made an odd little wave with her hand—a gesture of frustration, maybe. "At the time I was just glad that I did not have to force a confrontation. Your brother, Connor, was difficult enough to deal with, but your father…no."

Of course. This had been so long ago that Jackson Wilcox would have still been in charge of that clan. Damon would have only been a kid in junior high.

But I didn't like to think about that, because pondering Damon's past only made me realize he'd been a boy once, full of his own hopes and dreams for the future, before the dark fate hanging over his clan had twisted him into the man he became. A man who should have been in the prime of his life, and was now dead.

Something very like the first beginnings of tears seemed to tighten my throat, and I swallowed. I couldn't possibly be weeping over Damon Wilcox, could I? I could blame my emotions on pregnancy hormones, but I thought there was more to it than that.

Maybe I was just worried about what would happen to Connor if he lost me to the curse. Would he pick up his life and move on, focus on raising his child, or would he succumb to the same black plotting that had taken over Damon's life?

Connor seemed to sense something of my roiling emotions, because his fingers slipped around mine, intertwining, bringing with them that sense of warm strength I always got from him. "Are you all right?" he murmured.

Managing a nod, I raised my chin and tried to meet Maya's gaze. "Well, I knew it was a long shot. I just figured I would ask."

Somewhat to my surprise, she reached out and gave me a sympathetic pat on the knee. "I can only imagine how difficult it must have been for you to never know your own mother. And then to learn something of your father, but not know where he is, or what happened to him?" Her gaze sharpened, and I knew she must have seen something of the beginnings of those earlier tears in my eyes, although I had a feeling she couldn't begin to understand their true cause. "I would be more surprised if you hadn't asked. But truly, I know nothing else beyond what I've told you."

I nodded, then said, "And there's something else…."

"I had a feeling there might be."

Now it was my turn to hesitate, and once again I felt Connor squeeze my hand gently, telling me it was all right to go ahead and relate the story of what happened in Indio.

So I did, speaking quickly, just giving the straight facts of what had transpired, not embellishing anything. When I was done, Maya sat quietly for a long moment, clearly weighing what she intended to say next.

"There are many bad elements over there now," she said at last, her tone heavy with worry. "Some are good people, of course, merely displaced and looking for somewhere to call their own. This is why I took in those whom Connor mentioned to you. But there are many troublemakers, and I fear Simón Santiago is not quite as in control of things as he believes. There is little I can do, though, save protect my own. And this other thing...."

"Have you heard of anything like that?" Connor asked, clearly hoping that Maya, with her far greater experience of the witching world, might be able to offer some insight, some advice.

"No." She lifted her shoulders, and although I knew she was not a young woman, had to be in her early sixties at least, this was the first time she looked old to me, old and tired, as if for the first time in a very long while she had been confronted by something she didn't understand. "You realize that what you have now—the joining of a *primus* and a *prima*—this has never happened before, at least in no history that I have ever read, or had told to me by she who was *prima* before me. So it is not so surprising that you would be exploring new strengths, new powers, that no one else has yet seen."

"But what are we supposed to do with them?" I asked.

Another shrug, not of indifference, but of uncertainty. "That, I suppose, is up to you."

CHAPTER EIGHT

Double Jeopardy

We drove out of Phoenix with the lowering sun blazing strong and hot orange, casting long shadows from the saguaro and ocotillo cacti on the side of the road. After we left Maya's house, neither Connor nor I said anything, only got in the Cherokee and headed back to the freeway. My thoughts kept darting this way and that, and as the suburbs of the various valley communities flashed by, I couldn't help wondering if my father had taken this same route so many years ago. Where had he been heading? Where had he gone?

I didn't know, and I was feeling the beginnings of a headache. The heat, probably, and it frustrated me that I couldn't ask Connor to pull off at a drive-through so I could get a Coke. That had always worked for me in the past, and a glass of wine would have been even better, but I knew that I had to watch the caffeine consumption, and alcohol was really out of the question.

It wasn't until we were almost completely out of the Phoenix sprawl, passing by the outlet stores at Anthem, that Connor finally spoke. "You doing okay?"

"I guess so. Just tired, probably."

He looked over at me quickly, then returned his attention to the road. "Should we have stopped to get something to eat?"

"No, it's not that." Well, maybe it was, in a way. I could feel the beginnings of hunger pangs starting, and I knew there wasn't much between Phoenix and our turn-off on the 260. On the other hand, I really didn't want to delay getting home. There were a few places in Cottonwood that stayed open past nine. We could stop there if we needed to. Fidgeting with the cap of the water bottle that sat in the cup holder next to me, I said, "It just seems like every time we go asking questions, I end up with about a million more."

"Such as?"

"Well, the whole Wilcox thing, for one. I'm not saying my mother was a strong enough witch to sniff out a Wilcox the way Maya can, but she should have known my father was a warlock."

"Maybe she did. It's not exactly the sort of thing they would've been discussing around Linda Sanderson, after all."

He had a point. Even so, I felt like I should press on. "But if my mother had known he was a warlock, wouldn't she have wanted to know more about his family? I mean, part of the whole witch thing is your clan affiliation and all that."

"Maybe he lied and said he was with the Santiagos or something."

"Maybe," I repeated, my tone dubious. Of course, I had no idea what my father had really looked like, except he was tall and dark-haired, so maybe he could've passed for one of the Santiagos. As I mulled that over, another thought struck me. "That could have been what their fight was about."

"That she found out he was lying?"

"Yes, especially if she somehow discovered he was a Wilcox. I can't think of too many other things that would make someone so angry that they'd kick out the father of their baby only a few days before the child was due."

Connor didn't reply immediately, but instead tapped his fingers on the steering wheel, apparently considering what I'd just said. "That makes sense, I suppose."

"And it also explains why she would never say anything to my aunt about who my father was. I mean, if he really had been a Santiago or just some beach bum she'd picked up in Newport, then it wouldn't have been so important to conceal his identity."

No arguing from Connor on that one. He only gave a grim little nod, as if acknowledging his clan's poor reputation. Now I knew it wasn't that clear-cut, that there were people in the Wilcox family who were just as honorable as any McAllister, but twenty years ago the lines had been pretty clearly drawn. East was east and west was west, and all that. Those twain definitely didn't meet...until my mother and Andre got together.

Would Aunt Rachel have agreed to take me in, raised me, if she'd known I was half Wilcox?

I wasn't sure I wanted to think about that. I tried to tell myself of course she would, that she would never abandon her sister's child...but I just didn't know for sure. And maybe my mother had known, or at least guessed, and so made sure to keep her mouth shut.

Right then I almost wished her ghost had taken to haunting that tricky curve partway down the mountain. Then at least I could have gone to her and demanded some real information. But apparently she'd seen no reason to stick around. Her spirit was long gone, and I'd have to find my own answers.

"Another thing," I began, and the setting sun flashed off Connor's teeth as he grinned.

"Just one?"

"Well, I figured I'd start with this one."

He gave a slight nod of acknowledgment, so I went on,

"I'm also trying to figure out what his game was."

"Game?"

I shifted in my seat and glanced up at him, wondering if he was being disingenuous. "Come on, Connor—think about it. Supposedly he was engaged to Marie, and yet he dumped her for some unknown reason, went to California, and just magically met the runaway McAllister who was supposed to be the next *prima*...before she chickened out and disappeared."

"Okay, if you put it that way...." Even so, he shrugged, then pushed the visor up and out of the way. The sun was low enough now that the visor wasn't doing him much good. "Maybe things weren't working out with Marie, so he took off."

"Do people in your family have a history of taking off and going to California?"

"Well, no."

"It's almost as if he knew who my mother was, even if the reverse wasn't true."

"I think that may be stretching it a bit."

I wasn't so sure. After all, what were the odds that two members of warring witch clans would meet so far from home? Pretty high, even if witches had a way of sensing others with similar powers. "And what about Marie?" I asked.

"What about her?"

"Do you think she'll talk to us about Andre?"

At that question he did look away from the road and over at me, frowning slightly. The last reddish light of the sun painted the outline of his profile, making him look like some god who'd condescended to share a ride with me. His next words, however, were far from godlike. "Oh, yeah, I'm sure she'll be plenty happy to tell us everything about the guy who dumped her more than twenty years ago."

"I'm not asking as if she'd be *happy*—I'm asking if she would do it."

For a long moment he didn't say anything. Then, finally, "I honestly don't know."

We didn't talk much the rest of the way, each of us absorbed in our thoughts as the long dusk finally gave way to night and a thin yellow crescent moon rose above the mesa to our right. By the time we pulled off at the 260 and began heading toward Cottonwood, I could feel my stomach protesting its current empty state. We stopped at the Denny's in town because there wasn't much else open at that hour, and ordered some burgers. After that it was back up the winding road to Jerome, back to the quiet Victorian house waiting for us on the hill.

By then I was completely exhausted, and it seemed that Connor was, too, because we fell into bed and only held each other, too tired for anything else. My sleep was heavy, deep and dark, quiet, until I heard a keening sound and realized it was the sound of gulls. Below that came the deep rhythmic murmur of the ocean crashing against the shore.

Well, I'd just come from the beach, so I supposed it wasn't so odd that it had invaded my dreams as well. The image in my mind brightened, almost as if the sun was coming up over the water. But no, that had to be wrong, because in Newport the sun set over the ocean, not the other way around.

Not that dreams had to make any sense, of course.

Someone was walking down the beach, her loose hair whipping in the wind. As she got closer, I saw that she was slender, although her belly was rounded, in the later stages of pregnancy.

My mother.

I'd often wished I would dream of her. When I was younger, I used to sit and stare at the one picture of her my aunt kept on her desk, thinking that if I looked at my mother's face long enough, memorizing her features and how they were similar to mine, then she'd have to appear in my dreams. She would come and talk to me, tell me she missed me and loved me. That never happened, though.

But she was here now. As she stopped a few feet away from me, I realized our eyes were nearly level. So I was dreaming this as my now-self, and not the wistful little girl I used to be.

"I've been waiting for you a long time," I said.

"I know." Her hand dropped to the curve of her belly, and she smiled. She was wearing a loose jumper-style dress with a T-shirt underneath it, and Mary Jane–style Doc Martens. Looking at her, I realized she was exactly the same age I was now.

In a way, it was eerie to watch her, to see in her face my own straight little nose and arched brows, the rather wide mouth. My hair was darker, my eyes brilliant emerald where hers were bright blue, but anyone seeing us in that moment would have thought we were sisters.

"Why did you come here?" I asked.

"Here?" she asked vaguely, looking around.

"California."

"We're not really in California, you know."

I'd had these sorts of circular conversations in dreams before, so I knew the best thing to do was press on. "It looks like California. Close enough."

"I wanted to see the ocean."

"And that's the only reason?'

Her dreamy expression cleared, and the look she gave me was almost sharp. "You of all people should know why I wanted to get out of Jerome."

"I should?"

"Are you happy, being *prima?*"

The question took me aback. I hadn't ever really stopped to think about it that way. Not that I'd had much of a chance to stop and think about anything, what with how crazy my life had been for the past six months. I was certainly happy with Connor, but that happiness wasn't dependent on my being *prima*. In fact, things would have been a lot less complicated if I had just turned out to be your ordinary garden-variety witch.

"I don't think it's a question of being happy," I said slowly. "It's what I was born for, so…I guess I'm settling into it."

"Rachel trained you well," she remarked. "Making sure you were raised to be a good little *prima*. That wasn't me."

I didn't bother to hide the bitterness in my voice. "Apparently not, since you took off at the first opportunity."

"As I said, it wasn't me. Their expectations were crushing me."

"So you just left? And what about me? Having a baby was just something you did for kicks, like going to look at the ocean?"

In real life, she probably would have taken offense. In my dream, though, she only looked away from me, at the sun rising in the wrong place. "No. I wanted you. Or at least I thought I wanted you. Until…."

"Until you found out my father was really a Wilcox, and not whatever he told you?" A far braver question than I would have asked if she'd really been standing there in front of me. But I guessed that my subconscious understood this wasn't real, and had decided to go for broke.

"Would you want a child of a Wilcox?" she asked frankly, blue eyes wide with guileless curiosity.

"I'm having the child of a Wilcox," I pointed out. As I replied, I suddenly felt heavy, oddly off-balance, and I looked down to see that my belly was nearly as rounded as my mother's.

"Unfortunately," she said, laying a hand on my swollen midsection. Then, almost off-handedly, she added, "You might want to get that looked at."

Then she was gone, disappearing as neatly as the ghostly Maisie or Mary Mullen ever had. I stood there on the beach, feeling the unaccustomed heaviness of late pregnancy. Something about that odd west-rising sun compelled me, and I began to walk into the water, hardly seeming to notice as it came up to my knees, then my waist, then my chest, and finally my mouth. Cool black surrounded me, and suffocated me, and I drifted away with the tide, letting it take me.

An urgent hand on my arm. "Angela. Angela!" Connor's voice.

I blinked, taking in the blackness of the space around me, my eyes gradually adjusting to see the faint glow of moonlight coming in from the window across the room. "Wha?" I said groggily.

"You were breathing really hard, gasping, almost like something was choking you." He was turned toward me, leaning on one elbow as he watched me with worried eyes. "Bad dream?"

"Sort of," I replied. My face felt oddly chilled, so I reached up to touch my cheek, only to find both it and my mouth wet, as if someone had splashed water on me. What the…? I wiped the moisture away, telling myself it could've been saliva. But I'd never been much of a drooler, and my skin was wet enough that it would've required a Great Dane to create that much slobber.

Walking into the black water, letting it rise up and over my head….

I shivered, and at once Connor was reaching out to me, taking me in his arms and holding me close. "Jesus, you're freezing," he said. "It's not even cold."

And it wasn't. Late May and June were some of the warmest months in these parts, until the monsoon rains came with their blessed moisture and much-welcomed cloud cover. We almost always got a cool breeze at night in Jerome, but even so, the temperature in the room was probably in the low 70s.

"I dreamed," I began, then shook my head. "It's silly."

"What?" When I didn't answer, he brushed his lips against my hair and said quietly, "Angela, you're the *prima* here. Even if you're not a seer, even if you don't necessarily have visions, your dreams still can be important."

What he said was true, but I wasn't sure I really wanted to acknowledge that fact. It would mean that in my dream I'd slipped into the astral plane, had left my body to walk in that otherworld. Events that happened there could affect one's corporeal body, or so I'd been told. Until now, though, I'd never experienced that kind of psychic travel. What did it mean?

"And your hair is damp," he added, sounding quite matter-of-fact, as if these sorts of things happened every day. Maybe they did in the Wilcox family. He'd never given me a great deal of detail on how Marie's second sight really worked.

"I dreamed that I was talking to my mother, and she was pregnant with me. Then she left, and I walked into the ocean. Just walked straight into it, like I *wanted* to drown."

For a few seconds he was silent, apparently processing this latest revelation. "And you woke up all damp, as if you really had gotten wet."

"Yes." Despite the warmth of his embrace, my teeth began to chatter, and I realized the tank top I wore was sticking wetly to my body. True, that could've been sweat, but it wasn't quite warm enough in there for me to have been perspiring that much. "I need to get out of this top," I told him.

He let go at once. I pushed off the covers and slid out of bed, then went to the dresser and got a clean top. As I pulled it on and tugged it down to mostly cover my underwear, my hand slid against my belly. Maybe the slightest roundness there, which could have had just as much to do with the enormous burger I'd eaten too soon before going to bed than the baby, which still couldn't be much bigger than a fingernail at this point.

My mother's words came back to me. *You might want to get that looked at.*

After locating a hair elastic on the dresser's top and tugging my damp hair back into it, I turned to Connor. "I think we need to get that doctor's appointment lined up as soon as possible."

Whether any magical strings were pulled, I didn't know for sure, but that Friday I was in Flagstaff at the office of Dr. Ruiz, the ob-gyn several of Connor's cousins had recommended. I decided to leave aside the improbability of getting an appointment at all on the Friday before a long weekend, let alone with a highly in-demand doctor, and just be glad that I wouldn't be left to stew over the holiday as to whether my baby was okay or not.

The medical assistant asked if I wanted Connor in the room with me while they did the ultrasound, and of course I said yes. This was the part that scared me the most—logically I knew it was just a baby and that everything should be fine at this point—but damn straight I was going to have Connor at my side as I got the first true confirmation that the baby was real. Okay, yes, I'd done the home pregnancy test, and had it confirmed at Planned Parenthood, but that wasn't the same thing as hearing your baby's heartbeat for the first time.

Dr. Ruiz was probably in her early forties, with her dark hair cut in the kind of sleek bob I envied because I knew I could never get my own half wavy/half curly hair to do anything that controlled. She also seemed always calm, always unhurried, even though her waiting room was full and she had to be chomping at the bit to get out of there and start her own long weekend…most likely praying that none of her patients would go into labor while she was attending a barbecue.

Probably because mine was a very low-risk pregnancy, she'd decided a transvaginal ultrasound wasn't necessary at this stage. I lay there in a pink paper examination robe while she poured cold goo on my stomach and then began the procedure. Connor stood next to me, holding my hand.

"Okay," she said, peering at the monitor as she moved the ultrasound wand slowly over my belly, "the baby looks good, just about the right size and in the right position. And there's the heartbeat. Nice and strong." But then she paused, a line appearing between her brows as she frowned.

"What is it?" I asked, worry pulsing like ice through my veins. "Is something wrong?" Connor's fingers tightened around mine, but he didn't say anything, just stood there, waiting.

"Just a sec...." She was moving the sensor back and forth over my belly, her dark eyes intent on the screen. "Wait...got it!"

"Got what?" I asked, thinking, *Are there any congenital birth defects in the Wilcox family? No, that's crazy...I've met most of them...they're all fine....*

Sometimes it would be really nice if I could just get my brain to shut up.

The worry line disappeared, and she smiled at us. "Well, you two are going to have your hands full. It looks like you're carrying twins, Angela."

"Twins?" I said blankly.

"Yes. One is mostly hidden by the other, so it's hard to see right now. But look there." She pointed at a blot on the ultrasound screen. To me it just looked like a paler blip against an amorphous darkness, with the faintest little trace of…something…behind it.

"That's our baby…our babies?" I asked, reflecting it was a good thing I'd never had a burning desire to be an ultrasound technician. I had a feeling I wouldn't have been very good at it.

"Yes. They look about the same size, which is good. And this explains why some of your blood test results came back so high. The hormones in your bloodstream are elevated because you're carrying two babies, not one."

"But everything else is okay?" Connor asked. His expression was, in a word, gobsmacked. Not that I could blame him. One baby was enough to handle, but twins?

"Perfectly okay," Dr. Ruiz assured him. "They're a good size, and their heartbeats are strong, in the 116 to 118 range. No reason why they shouldn't be—Angela is a very healthy young woman." Her gaze flicked back to me. "But because you're carrying twins, you need to make sure you're eating enough to properly nourish both of them—"

"That's not a problem," Connor remarked with a grin. "She's been eating her weight lately."

I shot him a mock-severe glare, but Dr. Ruiz merely said, "That's good to hear, although you should be putting on more weight than you are. Worry about losing the baby weight after you have the babies."

Babies. Plural. It was such an alien concept that I still wasn't sure exactly how to process it.

"I'll do my best," I told her. "But Connor's right. I've been eating just about anything that isn't nailed down. I've always had a fast metabolism, though."

"Okay, we'll keep an eye on it." She turned to the medical assistant, who'd been hovering in the background during the procedure. "Lora, let's have Angela back here in three weeks."

That sounded like an awfully long time to go between appointments. I must have looked dubious, because the doctor went on, "Everything's going well, so I don't see any need to make you come in before that. However, if anything feels off to you, if you have any bleeding or severe nausea or cramps—any of that—call us immediately. Okay?"

I nodded, not liking the sound of that very much. But things did go wrong sometimes, and better to know someone was standing by, ready to dive in, so to speak, in case the unthinkable happened.

After that everyone went out, leaving me alone in the exam room so I could get dressed. As I did so, I tried to keep myself from panicking. Twins. Two babies. Two tiny little people growing inside me. I had no idea how that happened. Twins did not run in the McAllister family. Yes, my cousin Brady and his wife just had twins, but she was the daughter of a twin, and it sounded like they did pop up about every other generation in her family.

I slung my purse over my shoulder and went out to see the receptionist. My next appointment was set for June 12th, and Connor and I walked out of the office into the bright sunshine, both of us a little unsteady on our feet.

It wasn't until we were on Route 66 and headed toward his apartment that he spoke. "Before you ask, no, twins don't run in the Wilcox family. I mean, I'm the anomaly because I was born at all, since all the other heirs in Jeremiah's line were only children. But we really don't have any twins in the extended family, either."

"Same with the McAllisters," I said. Twisting in my seat so I could see him better, I added, "So what do you think it means?"

"I have no idea," he confessed. "This is where I really wish Marie would get back to me."

We'd come up to Flagstaff the night before, and Connor had tried calling her, saying he wanted to talk. She hadn't responded, which, according to him, was strange. Usually she got back to him within the hour when he called.

"Maybe she went away for the long weekend?" I suggested, and he'd only shaken his head and said that he'd never heard of Marie going away on vacation. Ever.

"Why did you want to ask her about this particularly?" I asked now. "Hoping for a vision?"

I'd been teasing him, just a little, but he didn't smile. "Marie sort of acts as the unofficial family historian—keeps all the genealogical files, that kind of thing. So she'd know if there were some Wilcox twins out there that I hadn't heard of."

"Hmm," I said, considering. It did seem kind of strange that Marie was out of contact, but I wasn't going to let myself worry about it too much. "I'm sure she'll call you back soon. It hasn't even been a full day yet."

He tilted his head slightly but didn't say anything.

"Are you…okay with this? I mean, one baby is a big enough deal, but two…."

The distant look disappeared from his eyes immediately, and he reached over and laid a hand on my thigh, gave it a reassuring squeeze. "Of course I'm okay with it. Although it does figure that Angela McAllister the overachiever would be the first McAllister *prima* to ever have twins."

"Bite me," I replied blithely, and then we both started to laugh. The tension that had filled the interior of the car seemed to evaporate at the sound of our laughter, and I knew then that we were going to be okay.

Because of my appointment with the ob-gyn—and because it was supposed to be almost ninety in Jerome, compared to the upper seventies in Flagstaff—we'd already decided to stay at Connor's place for the long weekend. Besides, I figured it would give me a chance to do some shopping in town and start putting together a wardrobe to accommodate my waistline, which I guessed was going to start expanding any day now.

Between shopping and going out to eat so I could keep the twins properly supplied with nutrients, I didn't stop to think much about Marie's disappearance, even though I knew Connor kept trying to get in touch with her. Several times I'd been tempted to call Sydney and tell her about the twins, but Connor and I had made a sort of unspoken agreement not to tell anyone quite yet. At any rate, she wasn't all that available, as she'd gone to the Colorado River with Anthony and a bunch of his friends. Cell reception there was horrible, although she did manage to squeeze out a text or two, mostly to say they were having fun and wished Connor and I could have come along. *Maybe next yr* was her final comment. I didn't bother to respond to that. If I were still around a year from now, I'd have my hands full with not one but two newborns, and playing in the Colorado River would be pretty far down my priority list.

Finally, on Sunday afternoon, Connor turned to me and said, "I'm going to call Lucas. Maybe he knows what's going on with Marie."

"Sure," I told him. Although part of me wanted to ask what was really fueling his obsession over talking to Marie, on some level I thought I understood. Connor had spent his whole life thinking Damon would be running things, and that he'd be able to go on quietly living his life without a lot of interference. But with Damon gone, Connor found himself the head of the clan, in a position of authority he'd never anticipated. It was probably natural of him to go to Marie for guidance, since she'd apparently offered counsel to Damon during most of his tenure as *primus*.

So Connor pulled out his phone and called Lucas, who did pick up, luckily. I listened with half an ear as Connor asked after Marie. Of course I couldn't hear Lucas's reply, but from the growing frown on Connor's face, it appeared his cousin hadn't spoken with her, either.

"Okay, thanks," Connor said. "We'll just keep checking—no, we really hadn't talked about that." A long pause, and I looked up from my iPad to see him frown and push his overgrown hair back off his forehead. "I don't think—well, okay, I'll talk to Angela about it and let you know. I doubt we could do anything before Tuesday because of the holiday. Yeah, okay. 'Bye."

He ended the call and shoved the phone back in his pocket. Sensing I wasn't going to be getting any more reading done today, I closed the Kindle app on the iPad and set the device down on the coffee table.

"What was that about?" I inquired.

"Lucas hasn't heard anything from Marie, either." He was frowning, reaching up to rub his brow as if his head hurt.

"I sort of gathered that." Since he continued to scowl, I got up from the couch and went over to him, then put my arms around his waist. "But what did he want you to talk to me about?"

Connor folded me in his arms, pulling me close. "Oh, you know Lucas. He's got the bit between his teeth on this house thing, says he was talking to one of his golf buddies, someone who's going through a nasty divorce. Anyway, the guy wants to sell their second home—or maybe it was their third home—the one here in Flag. He's selling it fully furnished and is ready to deal, mostly because he just wants to get out from under it."

In a way that sounded great, as long as Connor and I both liked the furniture. It would save us a lot of work. Then I wanted to shake my head at myself.

I couldn't live in Flagstaff. My home was in Jerome, high up on Cleopatra Hill. But because I didn't know what was going to happen, and had to make myself realize that Connor might be raising two babies on his own, I had to recognize that this apartment was going to be woefully inadequate in a few short months. If Connor could slide into something that was basically turn-key, it would take a lot of the pressure off.

"Okay," I said. "It sounds like it could be a possibility. What's he asking for it?"

"A hair under a mil."

I pushed myself away from him and gazed up into his face, looking for the joke and not seeing it. "A—a *million?*" I finally managed.

"Ange, I got more than that from the sale of Damon's house. If we like this place, we can get it for cash."

Since I didn't know what else to say, I had to settle for a weak "wow" before going back to the couch so I could sit down. Suddenly my legs felt just a little shaky. I had to hope that someday I'd get used to the casual way the Wilcox family threw large chunks of money around. "And he wants us to look at it."

"Sooner rather than later. Maybe Tuesday."

"That won't work," I said immediately. "I've got to be back in Jerome. The contractors are coming to get started on the kitchen."

He grimaced before coming to sit next to me on the couch. "Damn. I'd forgotten about that." A pause as he seemed to study my expression. "Are you really going through with the remodel? It just seems so…disruptive."

"It will be," I replied. "But I can't cancel the whole thing. It's way too late for that. And it wouldn't be fair to all those people counting on the income from the project."

"You're right, of course. And that sounds like something a *prima* would say." To my surprise, he bent forward and kissed me, very gently, on the lips. "So okay, maybe Wednesday or Thursday."

"Thursday," I told him. "I need to be back in Jerome for more than just one day. Partly because I should be around for the contractors, and partly because I know no one's thrilled about me disappearing up here for the weekend. They didn't *say* anything, of course, but you could practically see the disapproval radiating off the elders when I told them I wouldn't be around for a few days."

"They need to watch it…especially Margot. She has no idea that I could unleash Lucas on her at any time."

The thought was so incongruous that I had to laugh. "I dare you. Seriously."

"Well, if Lucas sells us on this house, he's going to need something to occupy his time…."

The glint in Connor's eye as he said this as so devilish that all I could do was pull him to me and kiss him, kiss him hard. His mouth opened to mine, and we tasted one another, the fire of our bond licking along our veins. In short order I was in Connor's arms and being carried upstairs, where we spent the rest of the afternoon losing ourselves in one another, forgetting about houses and disapproving elders and the mystery of Marie's radio silence.

Even then, though, I knew they wouldn't be forgotten forever.

CHAPTER NINE

Gone

As I'd expected, the next morning Connor tried calling Marie again, still with no response. He set his phone down on the counter that separated the kitchen from the dining area and let out a brief gust of breath. "Okay, that's it," he announced. "We're going over there."

I put down my cup of green tea. Even though I'd been trying to avoid coffee anyway, over the weekend I seemed to have developed a sudden aversion to its smell. Poor Connor had tried to make himself some French roast, and I nearly vomited at the aroma. Strange, because otherwise I really wasn't experiencing any morning sickness. But now—at least for the time being—if he wanted to get his caffeine fix, he'd have to go to the coffee house down the street and drink his venti before he came home.

"Do you think that's such a good idea?" I asked in dubious tones. "For all we know, Marie's not answering the phone because she's shacked up with the pool boy or something."

Connor didn't crack a smile. "She doesn't have a pool. And I've never heard of her being with anyone, let alone a pool boy, so there goes that theory."

"Oh, now I've figured it out," I said. "Her main problem is that she just needs to get laid. She'd be so much more relaxed." *Then again, probably the real reason she always acts hostile around me is that I'm the child of the man she wanted to marry....*

Not bothering to respond to my remark, he went on, "Do you think you can be ready to leave by eleven?"

It was ten-thirty now, and although I'd showered, I was still roaming around in yoga pants and a tank top, with no makeup on. "No problem," I said blithely. Thank goodness my "beautifying" routine was pretty basic.

And, sure enough, we were out the door at five after eleven. I'd eschewed my jeans, which were starting to feel a little tight, for one of my flowing sequined skirts—thank the Goddess for elastic waistbands—and a camisole. It wasn't even that hot in Flagstaff, but I thought the outfit was a good kick-off for the start of summer.

As before, we walked the few blocks to Marie's house, letting the mild breeze be our companion. Connor and I didn't talk much; I could tell he was still brooding over her silence, and attempting to figure out the reason behind it. Well, we should know in a few minutes, one way or another.

Her house didn't look much different from the last time we'd seen it, only a few days earlier. The irises still bloomed, although they were starting to look a little dry around the edges, as was the lawn. Well, maybe she was big into water conservation.

Connor went to the front door and rang the bell. We waited, the breeze picking up and pulling at my spangled skirts, causing a brief swirl of reflections around the front stoop, like a drift of falling stars.

Nothing.

"She could be out shopping or something," I suggested. "I mean, even Marie has to replace the toilet paper sometime."

A brief twist of his mouth, and Connor shook his head before ringing the doorbell once again. We could hear it echoing in the house, but there were no answering footsteps, no Marie coming to the door and giving us that look of quiet disapproval she'd mastered so well.

"I'm going to open it," Connor said, after we'd waited another minute.

"I don't think she'd be too happy about us breaking and entering."

"I don't care. I'm the *primus* of this clan—what's she going to do about it?"

To that I had no answer, so I merely lifted my shoulders and watched as he laid his hand on the latch. A pale glow seemed to drift from his fingers, surrounding the dark metal piece, and then he pushed down, and the door swung inward.

"Wow," he said, lifting his hand and staring at it as if he'd never seen it before. "She had it warded, but I just pushed with the power—the *primus* power—and the wards...disappeared."

"You haven't used it very much," I said. It was not a question.

"No. Except that time in Indio, with you. It sort of...well, it scares me a little. I saw what it did to Damon, and I don't want to be anything like that."

Again I couldn't really find the words to reply, to reassure him that he would never be anything like Damon. Instead, I slipped my fingers in his, pulling him gently into the foyer. After all, if he'd gone to the trouble of using the *primus* powers to unlock the door, then we might as well go inside and see what's what.

Everything was neat and clean, everything in its place. Well, almost everything. As we moved from the entryway into the combined living room/dining room space, I noticed a cream-colored envelope, the kind that you might put a birthday card in, leaning up against the Navajo basket filled with dried gourds that sat in the center of the dining table. One word was written on that envelope, in handwriting so elegant that it looked almost like calligraphy.

Connor.

Mystified, the two of us exchanged a glance before he stepped forward and lifted the envelope, turning it over in his hand. Nothing else had been written on it.

Connor stood there for so long, staring down at the envelope, that I felt compelled to ask, "Aren't you going to open it?"

"I guess so. Yes. It's just…I don't know. I can't imagine she would've left a note unless it was bad news."

A weird prickling sense of unease told me the same thing, but I shook it off, saying, "Even if it's bad news, we need to know what it is."

"I know…you're right." A final hesitation, and then he ran his thumb under the flap of the envelope, tearing it open. Inside was a single piece of paper, also cream, thick and heavy. That surprised me; Marie seemed like the last person in the world to care about nice stationery, although I knew I should probably stop trying to understand all the quirks of the individual Wilcoxes.

As Connor unfolded the paper, I saw that it contained only a few words written in that same flowing handwriting. Peering over his shoulder, I could just make out what they said.

I thought I could do this, but I can't. You'll need to discover your own path to the solution.

"What the hell?" Connor exclaimed, turning the paper over, almost as if he expected more words to magically appear on the reverse of the note. Well, it had been written by a witch, so I supposed that expectation wasn't entirely unwarranted, but even so, the paper's surface remained smooth and blank.

"So…she's gone?" I asked.

"Sure looks that way."

And even though the house was clearly empty, he still went from room to room, with me trailing in his wake, as if Marie might be discovered hiding in a broom closet or something. Like the main rooms downstairs, the bedrooms and bathroom on the second story were clean and neat, nothing out of place. One bedroom was clearly a guest room, with a daybed and small dresser and not much else, and the other seemed to be her office, although the desk that must have once held her computer was now empty. There was a table opposite it that she seemed to have used for some kind of mosaic work; the surface was covered with a plastic sheet, and there were still jars of glass tiles sitting there, and a half-finished piece showing a jagged mountain range and a stylized sunburst behind it.

"It's beautiful," I said. "I didn't know Marie was an artist, too."

He gave a shrug, clearly not interested in Marie's artistic pursuits at the moment. "Yeah, she's been doing that stuff for as long as I can remember. Sells it to the local shops, has an online business, too, I think."

My knowledge of Marie had just doubled in the last five minutes. "It looks as if she didn't care much about taking it with her."

"Well, it's not quite as portable as knitting, I guess."

Moving out of the office, he went down the hall to the master bedroom. The door stood ajar, so it wasn't as if she'd locked it behind her, but I still felt strange going in there. My aunt's bedroom, which was about my only frame of reference for an adult woman's private space, was a cheerful jumble of antiques and knickknacks and decorative frames filled with various photos of family members. This chamber was almost the exact opposite, spare Shaker-style furniture and a queen-size bed with a white-on-white quilt laid across it. No pictures, no decorations at all except a couple of Navajo rugs hanging on the walls, just as in the living room downstairs.

Well, there was one thing out of place.

Lying in the middle of the bed, glaringly obvious against all that white, was a small 4x6 photo. Connor went to it at once and lifted it up, again turning it over to see if anything was written on the back. But the reverse of the photo was blank, except for the faint watermark of the photographic paper.

As he flipped it back over, I saw it was a picture of a young couple, the woman clearly Native American, the man also dark-haired, but his skin was lighter, and his eyes hazel. They were standing in front of what looked like the gate to a corral; in the background I could just make out the dark brown shape of what was probably a horse.

"Who is it?" I asked.

"I think that's Marie."

"Marie?" I asked incredulously, reaching for the photo. Connor surrendered it, and I stared down at the picture of the couple, attempting to see the cold and distant Marie I knew in the laughing face of the girl in the image. She was probably barely twenty in the photo, her face not as sharply angled as it was now, the chin rounder. But I recognized the dark, arched brows and the thin nose and the long, long lashes. Somehow, though, this girl was beautiful, whereas I'd never thought of Marie that way. Striking, yes, but sharp and almost hawklike, as if the passage of years had worn away all that youthful prettiness. "Okay," I allowed at last. Then my heart seemed to drop a beat or two as I focused on the young man more closely. Was that…? "And the guy?" I asked, my voice casual. Too casual, I knew.

Connor's gaze flickered up at me, and his eyes narrowed as he seemed to take in my expression. Then he said, "I don't recognize him, but I think that's your father. He's around the right age, and Marie's looking pretty friendly with him."

That was true—she was leaning into the young man's shoulder, a flirtatious glint in her eyes. And even though I'd been waiting all my life to know what my father looked like, now that the time had come, it was harder than I had thought it would be to stare down at that photo, make myself really study his face.

He was handsome, with sooty hair almost as dark as Marie's, and fine high cheekbones and a nice strong chin. I could see why my mother had fallen for him. But that still didn't explain why he had left Marie and gone to California, apparently intent on seducing the wayward McAllister daughter who had gone there to escape the heavy expectations of her family.

"I can see it a little," Connor said, glancing from the photo to me and back again. "Something in the shape of your face. And your hair color is almost exactly the same."

I wasn't sure I wanted to dwell on those similarities, because I had a feeling I'd start obsessing about which feature I'd gotten from which parent, and we really didn't have time for that. Turning to the matter at hand, I asked, "But why would she leave it here?"

"I don't know. Maybe for you to find? Obviously the whole thing is still painful to her, or she wouldn't have treated you the way she did. Does. Whatever." He began to shrug and then seemed to stop himself, as if he realized that such an off-hand gesture didn't really fit the seriousness of the situation.

Even so, I gave him a startled glance. Yes, I'd thought the same thing myself, but I hadn't really expected Connor to agree with me. He'd always seemed fairly quick to defend Marie's behavior.

"I saw it," he said. "I didn't like it, and it wasn't really overt enough for me to call Marie on it. And then when we discovered who your father really was, it made total sense."

I nodded, then stared down at the photo once again. It was so odd—for most of my life my father had been a specter, a shadow, someone with no name, no identity. Now I knew his name was Andre Wilcox, and this was what he'd looked like, once upon a time. Better than nothing, but it still didn't help us get any closer to discovering why he'd gone to California all those years ago and what had happened to him, never mind whether finding any of those answers would get us any nearer to breaking the Wilcox curse.

"And she left this…why? As a clue?"

"Maybe. Or maybe she wanted to look at it one last time before she left."

"Left for where? I mean, where would Marie even *go?*"

"I have no idea," Connor said grimly. "So I'm going to call the only person who might."

Sitting in Marie's living room, Lucas appeared stunned as he glanced from me to Connor, his gaze finally coming to rest on the photo where it sat on the coffee table. Then he reached over and picked up the snapshot, eyes narrowing. "Andre Wilcox. Jesus Christ."

"So you knew him?" I asked.

"Well, he was my cousin—okay, we're *all* cousins, in one way or another—so yes, I knew him. Not well, since that branch of the family was a little standoffish, and he was about seven years older than I was. Enough that we weren't in the same subgroup of kids who hung out together at family parties, that sort of thing."

Lucas shifted on the couch, the photo still in his hand. Again I was struck by how he had to be about the least warlock-looking warlock I'd ever met, with his expensive jeans and golf shirt and polished loafers. He'd probably come straight from the country club when we called.

Now he scrubbed his free hand through his dark hair, disarranging the expensive haircut, and shook his head. "And this thing with Marie? I don't get it."

"So she never said anything to you?" Connor inquired.

"Well, she's said lots of things to me over the years, but she certainly never mentioned that she was planning to just up and disappear on us." His expression clouded as he leaned down to return the snapshot to the coffee table. "She might not be the world's friendliest person—"

No, that would be you, I thought with a mental grin.

"—But she's always been there when we needed her. We just sort of accepted that it was Marie's way and rolled with it."

"Do you have any idea where she might have gone?" I was mentally sifting through the few bits and pieces I did know about Marie Wilcox, trying to figure out the most logical destination for her. "Maybe to the reservation? That's where her mother is, right?"

"Was," Lucas corrected me, dark eyes troubled. "I heard she died a few years ago."

Well, damn. "But maybe Marie still could have gone there for some reason? Can't we, I don't know, try poking around to see if someone knows something?"

Both Connor and Lucas had the oddest expressions on their faces, as if they both wanted to call me on my ignorance but at the same time didn't want to seem rude. After an awkward pause, Connor said gently, "Angela, the Navajo lands are *huge*—bigger than some states. It would be worse than a needle in a haystack."

"Well, I refuse to believe that we've hit a complete dead end," I retorted. "What about my father's family? Are they still alive? Would they know anything?"

Connor looked blank, and I had a feeling he wasn't sure he could even remember who they were. Well, Lucas had said that part of the family wasn't exactly sociable.

"Maybe," Lucas said slowly. "That is, I know Andre's father—your grandfather—died awhile ago. I can't remember for sure. Your grandmother was a civilian, actually, and once her husband was gone, she pretty much had nothing to do with any of us. No one pushed it, since it was her choice. Our only concern was that she keep quiet about her husband being a warlock, and as far as we know, she never said anything to anyone, so there was no real reason to disturb her, since she obviously wanted to be left alone."

That was something, at least. "But do you know where she is? Can you set it up so we can talk to her? She may not even know that she has a grandchild."

Lucas' face was a study in mixed emotions: pity, worry…reluctance. "We haven't kept in touch, for obvious reasons. I hadn't heard if she even stayed here in Flagstaff after her husband died, but I'll do what I can. It might take a few days, though."

I chafed at any delay, but with Marie gone, we didn't have many alternatives. Maybe this would turn out to be nothing more than another wild-goose chase. Then again, even if Andre's mother could offer no insights, I felt as if I should at least get to meet her. She was the only living grandparent I had left.

"That's okay," I said, sounding heartier than I felt. "We have to go back to Jerome anyway, since the remodel on my house is starting tomorrow."

Lucas lifted an eyebrow; clearly he thought working on the house in Jerome was a wasted effort. "But you're still going to look at the property here on Thursday, right?"

"Yes, we already said we would," Connor replied. "We'll drive up Thursday morning and meet you there. In the meantime, I guess ask around and see if

Marie talked to anyone, mentioned anything about going out of town."

Being Lucas, he was too polite to point out that Marie really didn't take anyone into her confidence. Maybe she had, just a little, with Damon, but as he'd moved on to a higher plane of existence, that wasn't of much use to us.

"I'll do what I can," he said, in a tired-sounding voice that didn't sound much like the Lucas I knew. Then he got to his feet. "You two have a safe drive down to Jerome. Watch out for all those holiday drivers."

We both nodded and said we'd see him in a few days, and he let himself out. A minute later, we did the same, Connor making sure the door was securely locked and warded behind us. After all, even though we'd technically broken into her house, we didn't want anyone else to do the same.

Who knows…maybe one day she would return.

The contractors showed up at seven on the dot the next morning. I greeted them with as much enthusiasm as I could muster at that hour, although I knew seven was starting late for them. In Arizona it was common practice to start work as soon as the sun was up, noise pollution be damned. However, since I felt as if I were already on shaky ground with my neighbors, considering I was shacked up with a Wilcox, I'd told the contractors they couldn't begin to work until after seven, and to hold off on the power tools whenever possible until eight.

I supposed I'd see how long that lasted.

They were a professional crew, though, all recommended by the architect. Civilians, just because although the McAllister clan did have some talented carpenters and painters and such among its ranks, I thought it was safer to have a nonmagical group working on the house. Besides, my cousin Adam had been doing a lot of construction and contractor work around town and down in Cottonwood, and the very last thing I needed was him underfoot, shooting daggers with his eyes at Connor while attempting to braze a pipe or something. He'd made himself scarce the past few weeks, probably wanting to avoid seeing me with Connor. Although I still felt a twinge of guilt over the way things had shaken out between us, I couldn't help but be relieved that he apparently wasn't going to force a confrontation this time. Things were already complicated enough when it came to interactions with my family members.

Thank the Goddess that Connor had insisted on coming down with me to Jerome, even though I'd protested feebly that it would be fine and he didn't really need to subject himself to the noise. He'd only lifted his eyebrow at me—oh, I did love it when he did that—and said, "Of course I'm coming with you. Did you really think I'd let you suffer through all that on your own?"

And when he said "suffer," he wasn't kidding. The first hour or so was quiet enough; it looked like the workmen were taking final measurements, clearing out any last-minute stuff that I'd forgotten about. I'd already packed most of the kitchen, but there were always a few odds and ends that escaped capture. But after that?

Wham! Wham!

Connor and I had been sitting in the library upstairs, trying to keep out of the way, when the whole house shook. I would've said it was an earthquake, but we didn't get many of those in northern Arizona. No, it was just the capable wrecking crew from Yavapai Construction Associates.

After wincing and sharing a look of mutual commiseration, we tried to go back to our respective books…which lasted for a whole ten seconds.

"You want to get out of here?" Connor said, laying aside the paperback he was holding.

"Thought you'd never ask," I replied, and blanked the screen on my iPad before laying it aside. Okay, true, I'd come back to Jerome to be here in case the crew needed me, but after that last bit of clean-up and a final consult with the architect, it seemed I wasn't much needed.

So we fled to Sedona, where we caught an early movie, went out to lunch, wandered around a few galleries, saw another movie, and then finally ate dinner, coming home at dusk when we deemed it would be safe.

And it was, more or less; the crew was packing up as we pulled into the garage. Connor and I headed into the house, where there was a gaping hole in the side of the kitchen, now carefully covered with plastic sheeting. Good thing monsoon season wasn't due to start for another month and a half.

"Good first day," Brad, the foreman, told me. "We'll see you tomorrow morning at seven."

I think I managed a watery thanks, looking at the destruction around me. On paper, a remodel sounds great. Take an outdated, inconvenient space and turn it into something worthy of a magazine spread. The problem is, no one bothers to tell you how much of a godawful mess it's going to be during that all-important time between the "before" picture and the "after."

Wisely, Connor held his tongue, and only went with me into the family room, where we watched a little TV before going to bed. And as much as I enjoyed making love in the big king-size bed in my bedroom, I wasn't feeling it that night. Maybe it was hormones, maybe it was frustration over trying to figure out where Marie had gone, maybe it was worry about how the days were slowly ticking away, and eventually these babies—plural—would show up, and then my own clock would start winding down. It might not happen right away, or even within a few months, but eventually, something would happen to take me out of the picture. I definitely would not be around to fret over them getting into a good college.

Or maybe it was none of those things, and I was only worrying about what sort of mayhem the contracting crew would wreak the next day.

It also didn't help that the room felt horrendously warm to me. True, it had been warm verging on hot that day, but the house should have started to cool down by now. We always got a pleasant night breeze in Jerome.

After I adjusted my position for what felt like the tenth time, I heard Connor's voice in the darkness.

"What's the matter?"

"I'm hot," I said irritably.

"It is a little warm. I'm surprised you don't have air conditioning."

"It's on the list," I snapped. "I just thought the kitchen was more important. Anyway, the heat's never bothered me before."

"You've never been pregnant before."

Well, that was true. "I'm barely three months pregnant," I said. "I thought the heat issues didn't kick in until you were actually, you know, showing."

A soft little sound that might have been a chuckle, quickly repressed. "Okay, maybe, but different things affect people differently." I felt the bed rock slightly as he adjusted his position. Now, as my eyes were adjusting to the darkness, I could see he had turned on his side so he could face me. "Are you sure that's all it is?"

"Of course that's not all it is. It's just the most recent thing." I took a breath. "I think I may have taken on more than I can handle with this remodel." *And Marie's disappeared…and it turns out I'm half Wilcox…and every day I have a little less time to unravel this curse thing so I don't die before I'm twenty-five.*

I didn't say any of that, though. I had a feeling Connor already knew what I was thinking.

"Well, I doubt even your relatives will give you too much crap for not staying here while half the house is getting ripped apart. That's asking a bit much, don't you think?"

Under normal circumstances, maybe. But since I was *prima*, different rules applied to me. Even the short jaunts I'd been making to Flagstaff with Connor had upset them, I could tell. It just drove home that my consort was the last person they'd ever wanted or expected for me. Well, okay, second to last. I had a feeling that, if pressed, they would admit Connor was the lesser evil when compared to his brother.

"So you think we should go back to Flagstaff?"

"Well, considering no one's tearing up my apartment and it tends to be about ten degrees cooler there most of the time, I'd say yeah, that might be a better place to spend the summer." He grinned then, his teeth flashing in the near-darkness of the bedroom. "Of course, I'll admit that I might be a bit biased."

Maybe he was biased, but he was also making a lot of sense. Sure, there were places here in Jerome I could've crashed for the summer, such as my old bedroom back at Rachel's apartment. However, Connor would be excluded from such an arrangement, and I refused to be separated from him again. We'd already lost almost two months. I wouldn't give up any more.

"No, you're right," I said. "At least, I think you're right. It all makes so much sense when I'm alone with you, and then I get the elders giving me the hairy eyeball whenever I so much as mention your name, or Flagstaff, and I have to remind myself to stand my ground."

He didn't reply at first, only reached out and pulled me against him, held me close so I could hear the reassuring rhythm of his heartbeat. "Well, maybe you don't need to make any huge decisions right now. Just say the noise and the heat were getting to you, and that you needed to get away for a couple of days. Besides," he added, "we're looking at that house on Thursday. Maybe it'll be perfect, and that'll be the sign you need to tell you it's okay to spend part of your time in Flagstaff. I have a feeling they might not protest so much if their *prima* is shacked up in a million-dollar house rather than a walk-up over an art gallery."

"You might be surprised," I said. "The McAllisters aren't all that into external signs of wealth."

"That much is obvious. I've seen the cars most of you drive."

That remark left me no alternative but to give him a mock punch in the arm, to which he gave an equally false wince before pulling me even closer to him, his mouth hot on my neck, tracing a line of kisses down to my breast. In short order my tank top had been flung away to land somewhere on the floor in the darkness, and my fingers were pulling at the waistband of his boxer briefs, and soon after that we had joined once again in an embrace that erased all doubt and worry and clan politics.

...if only for a little while.

CHAPTER TEN

Habitat

"HOLY CRAP, LUCAS," I SAID. "IS THIS FOR REAL?"

"Of course it is," he said, pushing a button on the fob he carried. His bright red Porsche beeped once.

Connor stood in front of the FJ Cruiser we'd driven here, craning his neck to take in the property in its entirety. "And he's only asking nine-fifty?"

"You should've seen him salivating when I told him you could pay cash. Apparently the soon-to-be ex has him over a barrel, and he needs to liquidate as soon as he can. Avoiding a lengthy escrow is worth taking a mild hit on the price. The market is sort of stagnant right now anyhow, which doesn't help. No one else has come to look at it." Lucas shoved his car key in his pocket. "Anyway, let's go inside, and see what you think."

Inside? Well, if it was half as impressive as the outside, I was sold. Like Damon's former home, the house was built of a combination of stone and wood, with several chimneys rising above the steeply pitched roof. On the drive over, Connor had told me the property was just a hair over three acres. I had a hard time computing that; lots in Jerome, even for the larger houses, weren't very big. What I could see was that the rolling curves of the property were bounded in sturdy stone walls, and ponderosa pines and other evergreens dotted the landscape, clustering around the house, making it feel like something tucked away in an enchanted forest. And, in what seemed an utter extravagance to me, the four-car garage was detached and sat some distance away from the house, with a covered wooden walkway joining the two buildings.

Gawking at the place, I'd fallen a little behind the other two, so I hurried to catch up, even as Lucas was entering the code into the lockbox on the door. I wondered if he had the same talent with locks as Connor and I, and whether he was using the code to be polite.

But then I followed the two of them inside, and I stopped wondering about the locks.

"Holy crap."

"You said that already," Connor pointed out with a grin. "So good, so far?"

I could only nod dumbly. Now, Damon's house had been very impressive, and this place shared some of the same architectural features—huge windows that let in a view of the forest and impossibly blue skies, a stone fireplace that stretched all the way to the ceiling, shining wood floors. But when I'd been at Damon's, I couldn't allow myself to like it, because it had been his. Whereas this house....

This house could be mine, if I wanted it.

Granite kitchen counters. Thermidor appliances. A separate refrigerator for wine. A second fireplace in the family room, and yet another in the master bedroom. Spotting it, Connor sent me a significant glance, and I grinned back at him. Never mind that we were heading into the time of year where you really didn't need a fireplace—it was still something that was important to us.

And I couldn't find fault with the furniture, either. Nothing stuffy or overdone, or too kitschily Southwest, or anything like that. Big and solid, the dining room table with a top of what looked like solid copper, the couches and chairs covered in warm brown leather, contrasting with the reds and beiges and soft, dusty turquoise blues of the Navajo rugs on the floor.

In a daze, I trailed after Connor and Lucas as we returned to the kitchen. There were flyers from the realtor sitting on the granite-topped island. *Price reduced! Prime property in Forest Highlands!* I barely glanced at them, since the two men were watching me expectantly.

"Well?" Lucas said at last.

"It's—it's incredible," I replied, glad to see Connor nodding. We hadn't spoken much as we followed Lucas from room to room, preferring to remain silent so we could let the other person form their own judgments.

As I spoke, I noticed that Connor relaxed slightly, as if he'd been waiting to hear what I had to say. "Yeah, it is pretty amazing. And tons of room."

That was for sure. The place had five bedrooms and was more than four thousand square feet. Plenty of room for the twins, and whoever might come after that.

Assuming there would be any more after that, of course.

"I should've shown you the garage, too," Lucas said. "It was built with two stories, and although Dave is using the upper level for storage right now, it has lots of windows. It would make a great studio for you, Connor."

Who was silent, considering…although what he had to consider, I wasn't sure. The house couldn't have been much better, frankly. I felt a pang as I thought of the big Victorian back in Jerome, one wall knocked out, the counters and cabinets already demo'd. Buying this place felt like an abandonment, although I knew that wasn't true. Connor had already made a comment about splitting time between the two locations. Summer here and winter in Jerome? It wasn't quite living the bicoastal lifestyle, but it seemed like a reasonable compromise to me.

Finally he said, "Are you sure you want to do this, Angela? I don't want you to feel as if you're being rushed or pressured."

"I'm not," I said at once. "I mean, yes, this is happening sort of fast, but I've always thought if the right opportunity comes up, you should go for it. And this place…it feels right. Quiet and sheltered. The trees are amazing. And I love that the one bedroom already has bunk beds in it. It'll be perfect for the twins."

The word just sort of popped out. I hadn't really intended to say anything about it, as Connor and I were still keeping that piece of news under wraps.

Too late now.

Lucas' eyes widened. "You're having *twins?*"

Connor smiled and sort of ducked his head, as if not sure exactly how to handle this. Then his shoulders lifted slightly, and he said, "Yeah, that's what the doctor told us. It's too early to know much more than that."

"Well—congratulations, you two!" Lucas' expression of surprise might have been comical under other circumstances, but I knew now that part of it was him trying to figure out how twins fit in with the whole Wilcox heir conundrum. *There can be only one,* and all that.

"Thanks," Connor and I said, nearly in unison. We both laughed a little, more to break the tension than anything else.

Then I said, "So...what now?"

"Now I call Dave and tell him the good news, and we'll set up an appointment with the realtor. This will happen pretty quickly, since you won't have to deal with getting a loan approval or anything, but I'd still recommend a house inspection, and then there's a title search, deed transfer—" He broke off and peered over at me. I must have been looking a little green, because he went on, "Yeah, I know, it sounds like a lot. But buying a house is a big deal. Even with all that, we might have everything ready to go in as little as a week. I'll see what I can do to help...move things along."

And I had no doubt that he would. After all, Connor had told me that Lucas' particular gift was luck. All we needed was him to assist in overseeing the transaction, and I had no doubt everything would go as smooth as silk.

"Sounds perfect," I told him.

"It sure does," Connor chimed in. "And it means we'll have a lot to do."

"Not that much," I pointed out. "I mean, the house is already furnished. And most of the clothes I can fit into are at your place anyway, since I just bought them here in town."

"Okay, so it won't exactly be a typical move. But...." He seemed to stop himself, and gave a quick glance at Lucas before returning his attention to me. "I guess we can figure out the logistics later."

"That's for sure," Lucas said. "Let me get this call in to Dave so he can be in touch with his realtor, and then I'm taking you two out to lunch to celebrate."

His tone was so firm that I knew I couldn't really protest. I smiled, then went over to Connor and held hands with him as Lucas called his friend to let him know we wanted to buy the house. After that we had lunch at the country club nearby, and I was glad I'd put on a new pair of dark jeans and a pretty peasant top so I didn't look too out of place. As it was, I couldn't help shooting surreptitious glances at the other people dining in the restaurant during lunch. After all, these people would be our new neighbors. Compared to Jerome, they looked pretty buttoned up, and I couldn't help wondering what they'd think if they ever discovered that the young couple who'd just bought the house on Bear Allen Way were a couple of witches.

"Did you like it?" Lucas asked as we headed out to the parking lot afterward.

"Lunch was great."

"Good. I'm glad you enjoyed the food—once you've purchased the house, you'll be members here, so you can come any time you want."

Seriously? I looked over at Connor, whose mouth was twitching a bit. Probably trying to keep from bursting out laughing at the idea of Angela McAllister, *prima* of those bohemians from Jerome, being a member of a country club.

"Oh," I said faintly. A thought struck me. "So how are *you* a member here? Your house isn't in this neighborhood."

A devilish grin, one almost worthy of Damon Wilcox—except that I knew there was nothing more sinister than amusement behind Lucas' current expression. "I might have called in a few favors." His phone rang, and he pulled it out of his pocket, glanced at the display, and said, "Hey, Dave. Hmm… two o'clock at the realtor's?" He paused, raising his eyebrows at us as if for confirmation that this would be okay. We both nodded, and he continued, "Sounds perfect. Down on Riordan Road? We'll be there." After ending the call and slipping his phone back into his pocket, he asked, "Are you ready to do this?"

As one, Connor and I nodded. It was crazy, and it was scary, but it also felt right. If the worst happened, I wanted to make sure my children would be someplace safe with their father. Yes, I was a McAllister, too, and they'd need to know that side of the family, but they needed to be with Connor more.

So we drove to the realtor's office, and met the mythical Dave, who seemed to be a few years older than Lucas and far more high-strung—which, if he was going through a nasty divorce, made some sense. He did seem to relax visibly after Connor and I signed the offer paperwork, and even more so after Lydia, the realtor, said she was fast-tracking the whole process and could have a house inspector out to look at the property the next day, and the title search wrapped up by the end of the following week.

Feeling a bit punch-drunk, Connor and I made our goodbyes to Lucas a little after four, then drove back to his apartment, which did feel a little cramped and small after the splendor of the house in Forest Highlands. I couldn't drink champagne, obviously, but Connor broke out a bottle of San Pellegrino, and we ended up toasting with that.

But after the high faded a bit, he asked, "So what are you going to tell your family?"

Crap. "The truth, obviously." Much as I really didn't want to do that, I knew it was only fair. "They're going to have to come to terms with it eventually. You and I are together, and you can't relocate to Jerome permanently, and I can't live here in Flagstaff permanently. They're just going to have to…share…us."

"That sounds very reasonable," Connor said. "Which means they're probably going to bitch and moan."

"Not probably," I told him. "They will." I paused, thinking. The wheels had been set in motion, so unless the house inspector found termites or wood rot or lead paint—none of which was very likely in a newer-construction luxury home—that meant in less than two weeks Connor and I would own a home together. The McAllisters and the Wilcoxes would just have to learn to work together, and I figured there was no time like the present. "Maybe if we sat down with everyone and told them how it was going to be...."

"'Everyone' who? The McAllister elders?"

"Well, yes, them, but also the Wilcox elders."

"We're not really set up the same way," Connor pointed out. "I mean, Lucas and Marie served sort of the same function in some ways, but since she's disappeared off the face of the planet—"

"Yes, but we still have Lucas. Can you think of a better ambassador for the Wilcox clan than him?"

Connor didn't reply right away, only rubbed a hand over his chin, apparently deep in thought. Then he asked, "Margot's one of your elders, right?"

"Yes, so?"

"I can only imagine the scene if Lucas tries to buy her a drink."

I couldn't help grinning. "Well, if she has any brains, she'll take him up on it. Anyway, they're adults—I'll let them sort it out."

"I smell a disaster."

As much as I wanted to call him out for his negativity, I had a feeling that Connor had a point. But we all needed to move forward, to understand that we were treading new ground here, and getting the clans to cooperate was part of that bigger picture. Yes, we still had to work on that damn curse, but I also wanted to make sure I left behind a more stable relationship between the two clans, should the worst happen and I not be around to raise my children. Connor and the two extended families would all have to do it together.

Who knows…maybe that would turn out to be my legacy.

Since she seemed the most sympathetic to my situation of the three elders, I called Allegra Moss to say Connor and I would be coming back to Jerome over the weekend, and we had some important matters to discuss.

"Yes, I imagine you do," she said in her sweet voice, one that always sounded as if it had a hidden undercurrent of laughter in it.

"And—I want to bring Connor's cousin Lucas with us."

Silence for a second or two. Then she asked, "Whatever for?"

"Because what I have to say concerns both our families, and—well, Lucas is sort of the clan elder for the Wilcoxes. He's been an enormous help to Connor and me. So I want him there when we all sit down to talk."

"Margot and Bryce won't like it," she warned me.

"They don't have to like it," I said, my tone curt. "They just have to be there. Let's tentatively plan for meeting at my house at one-thirty on Saturday."

Whether it was because she heard a note of command in my voice, or whether she didn't want to argue with someone she thought might be experiencing some early-pregnancy mood swings, she replied quickly, "Of course, Angela. I'll let them know. You take care."

"You, too," I said, and hung up.

Although I'd gotten permission to bring Lucas with me to the house on Saturday, I thought it would be pushing things to have him stay anywhere in Jerome. Cottonwood was still technically McAllister territory, but having him put up for a night or two there wasn't quite the same thing as impinging on Jerome's hallowed ground, so I suggested he see if he could find a place down the hill where he could stay. If not, I'd have him crash in the guest bedroom, and we'd all just have to deal with the consequences.

But, being Lucas, of course he found a last-minute cancellation at a highly rated local B&B, and reserved two nights. "Just in case," he said cheerfully. "If nothing else, I'll hit a couple of the wine-tasting rooms down on Main Street before I head back to Flagstaff."

I had no doubt he would. If this meeting went anything like I feared it might, I'd ask him to have a couple of pours in my name as well, since I wouldn't be drinking any wine for a long time. If ever.

Those thoughts kept skittering through my mind, refusing to be still. Yes, I could tell myself that I wasn't due until December, and that gave us plenty of time to work on the curse, even with Marie taking a powder…but I was still worried, and scared…and trying desperately to conceal those emotions from Connor. It wasn't good for him, me, or the babies for me to be in a state of perpetual anxiety. I knew that intellectually, but my emotions weren't being good biddable things, unfortunately.

At least the wreckage in the kitchen wasn't visible from the dining room. I whispered a thank-you under my breath to the formal Victorian architecture, so unlike houses being built now, with their "great room" concepts and everything open to everything else. To be fair, the contractors were very good about cleaning up after themselves, and they'd made great progress over the past few days—the extension of the one side of the kitchen was already framed and wired, and they'd also extended the roofline and laid down tar paper in preparation for installing composite shingles. It could have been a lot worse.

We did have Lucas come up early, though, and took him out to lunch at Grapes, where he charmed Tina, our server, so much that she was blushing like a schoolgirl and giggling at almost everything he said.

"You really ought to behave yourself," Connor said, trying to sound stern, but I could tell he was more amused by Lucas' antics than anything else.

"I thought I was," Lucas replied.

Even I laughed at that remark, although I sobered up pretty quickly as we climbed the hill back to the house. Although I'd called this meeting, now I was sort of regretting setting it up in the first place. Well, there wasn't much I could about it at this point, although I couldn't help wishing that I'd inherited some of my Great-Aunt Ruby's commanding air along with her *prima* powers. It would've really helped to keep the clan elders in line.

Since the kitchen was so torn up, I couldn't offer much in the way of refreshments, although that was partly why I decided to have the meeting at one-thirty. If the elders hadn't eaten lunch by then, it really wasn't my problem. In the garage there was a Frigidaire even more ancient than the one I was replacing in the kitchen, and I sent Connor to fetch some bottled water I'd been storing out there, since the other refrigerator had already been hauled away—to the junkyard, or possibly a museum for antique appliances. Lucas helped me pull some glasses out of boxes, and I hurriedly cut some roses from the bushes in the backyard to set in a low vase in the center of the dining room table. By the time we were all done, the room looked downright respectable. You'd never know what chaos lurked on the other side of the door that led to the kitchen.

Not a moment too soon, though, since a knock came from the entryway just as I was shifting the vase of roses a fraction of an inch to the right. I straightened, as Connor and Lucas looked at me quizzically.

"I'll get it," I said. "It's probably better that way." I didn't add that I thought this meeting was going to be tense enough without my answering the door flanked by a couple of Wilcoxes.

Leaving the two of them behind, I went to the entry and opened the door. As expected, there stood Allegra and Bryce and Margot, none of them looking all that happy to be here.

"Come on in," I said, stepping aside so they could enter.

Bryce came in first, walking warily, as if he expected Connor and Lucas to be lurking somewhere in the foyer, ready to pounce, and he would be forced to protect the two women who accompanied him from bodily harm. I didn't quite heave a sigh, but there might have been some eye-rolling involved.

Margot and Allegra followed, Margot looking cool and summery in a pale coral dress, dark hair as always pulled back in a low ponytail on her neck. Allegra tended to subscribe to my Aunt Rachel's school of boho fashion, and wore a long embroidered black skirt and black T-shirt, her mousy graying hair piled haphazardly on her head in a bun.

Of all of them, she was the only one to smile at me, and even murmured, "How are you feeling?" as she entered the house. I nodded and sent her an answering smile, but didn't want to go into any detail then. They'd all find out soon enough.

"This way," I said, pointing toward the dining room, even though of course they'd been in there many times before and knew the way just as well as I did.

The briefest incline of her head from Margot and a furrowed brow from Bryce were all I got in reply. Great. If they were going to be this difficult now, when I'd barely said hello, how were they going to react to the rest of what I had to say?

Chin up, I led them to where Connor and Lucas were already waiting. They sat on the side of the table opposite the doorway, with Connor closest to where I would take my seat at the head of the table. As soon as the elders spied the two Wilcoxes, it was like watching the fur on a cat's back bristle. Bryce went ramrod straight, Allegra's eyes widened, and Margot's mouth tightened.

Speaking quickly, I said, "You've already met Connor, but this is his cousin, Lucas Wilcox. Lucas, this is Bryce McAllister, Allegra Moss, and Margot Emory."

As I said Margot's name, I could see Lucas' gaze linger on her, and I held my breath, praying he wouldn't do or say anything inappropriate. Flirting with the waitress was one thing, but Margot? She'd rip his head off.

However, he only smiled, the slow, lazy smile that most of the Wilcox men seemed to share, and said, "Very pleased to meet you."

For one long, horrible second, none of the elders replied. Then Allegra, bless her, said, "Very nice to meet you, Mr. Wilcox."

"Lucas, please."

"Lucas," she responded, a fluttery little smile playing around her lips.

Margot only tilted her head and then sat down, while Bryce said nothing at all, gruffly pulling out a chair with a brusque movement that surely would've scratched the wooden floor if it hadn't been protected by a rug.

"Well, then," I began, after everyone was watching me with expectant eyes. Well, except Connor; he knew most of what I wanted to discuss, and although he hadn't completely agreed with all of it, saying he thought the elders weren't going to react well to what I had to say, he'd told me he would support me in whatever I decided to do. Pulling in a breath, I continued, "There's been a lot going on lately, and since it affects both our families, I thought it was high time we sat down and talked about it like rational adults."

A sniff that might have come from Margot greeted this statement, but since she didn't actually say anything, I decided to just plow ahead.

"Our two families have been in—well, maybe not an all-out war, but definitely a cold war, for far too long. Maybe there was a reason for it once—"

"You damn well know there was a reason," Bryce cut in.

"—But now that Connor and I are together," I went on doggedly, "it's silly for us to keep acting like the Hatfields and McCoys or something. You all know that Connor and I are having a baby. Well, we recently found out that it's not just one baby. We're having twins."

Since Lucas already knew that, he didn't react, but only watched the other three. Both Allegra's and Bryce's eyes widened, while Margot's narrowed, as if she were trying to determine what such an unprecedented occurrence might actually mean.

None of them said anything, though, and I glanced over at Connor, unsure what to do. I hadn't exactly been expecting congratulations, not from this group, but I also hadn't expected to get quite so completely stonewalled.

Goddess help me, I could really use a drink right now. Since that was out of the question, I took a sip of ice water, then said, "Because these babies—these children—will belong to both clans, Connor and I think the best way to manage things is to have homes in both territories. We just made an offer on a house in Flagstaff yesterday."

That got their attention. Margot let out a shocked "what?" before she could stop herself, Allegra gasped, and Bryce spluttered, "You should have consulted with us before taking a step like that!"

"Why?" I said coolly, somehow relieved that they'd reacted in such a way. Now I could act like a calm and collected adult, rather than a transgressing child. "So you could have said no and given me a bunch of silly reasons why it would never work?"

"It's a very big step, Angela," Allegra began tentatively, only to have Margot override her, saying,

"I doubt any of our reasons would have been *silly*." She shifted in her chair, seeming to pin Lucas down with a sudden flash of her dark eyes. "Was this *your* idea?"

If it had been anyone else, I would've questioned how she could have possibly known that. Margot had said numerous times that she was not psychic, but I was beginning to have my doubts.

But, being Lucas, instead of appearing discomfited, he merely replied, "Well, I'd actually been telling Connor for some time that he needed to live someplace a little more suited to the Wilcox *primus*. And then when it came out that he and Angela were going to have a baby, it got more urgent. A house became available, they looked at it and loved it, and the rest, as they say, is history." He shrugged and reached for his own ice water, taking a sip before adding, "I really don't see anything that strange about any of it."

"You wouldn't," she said in cutting tones. "It's fairly obvious you Wilcoxes do things very differently from us McAllisters. But Angela should've consulted with us—"

"She's consulting with you now," Lucas responded breezily. "She could've just shown up here with her moving boxes and not told you anything. She is an adult, you know, and capable of making her own decisions."

For the first time in my life, I saw Margot Emory at a loss for words. Her mouth opened, then shut again, and I saw her knuckles whiten as she gripped the edge of the table. Whether this unprecedented response was due to what Lucas had said or the completely unconcerned way in which he'd said it, I wasn't sure, but in that moment I had to choke back the impulse to break into incongruous laughter. And that, I knew, would go over even worse than Lucas' reply to Margot.

Connor spoke for the first time, saying, "We're only trying to do what's fair—"

"Fair?" Bryce exclaimed. "How is any of this fair?"

"Is it fair to expect the *primus* of the Wilcoxes to live here full-time in Jerome?" I asked.

"No, we would prefer it if he stayed where he was supposed to be—in Flagstaff," Margot snapped.

"You know that wasn't going to happen," I replied. "Besides, if we were going to be completely *fair*"—I put an unnatural emphasis on the word, staring straight at Bryce as I said it—"then technically I should be spending three-quarters of my time with Connor in Flagstaff, considering I'm half Wilcox myself."

I might as well have thrown a live grenade into the center of the table. "*What?*" Bryce burst out, while Allegra shook her head, saying, "That's impossible!", and Margot stared at me as if she'd never seen me before.

"It's true," I said. "That's what we found out when we went to California. My mother was shacked up with a Wilcox out there. End result: me."

The words came out sharper-edged, more flippant than I had intended. Probably because the mystery of why my father had gone there at all, and had sought out Sonya McAllister, still hadn't been explained. It chafed at me, stirred up emotions I wasn't sure I wanted to analyze. All my life I'd wanted to know who my father was, but finding the truth had only caused more problems.

Finally, Margot spoke. "This—you must be mistaken."

"No mistake," Lucas said quietly, this time sounding quite sober, unlike his usual ebullient self. "Andre Wilcox left Flagstaff a little more than twenty-two years ago, and no one's seen him since. The timeline fits. Not that Angela's mother would have known. She thought his name was Andre Williams."

"So he lied to her. Typical," Bryce said.

"Enough," I told him, sending him what I hoped was my best *prima* stare. It seemed to work; he subsided and pushed up against the back of his chair, as if to create a little more distance between us. "Yes, it turns out I'm half Wilcox. Ironic, isn't it? Here you've been doing your damnedest to keep me here in Jerome, away from the Wilcox clans, and it turns out you both have an equal claim."

"Not entirely equal," Allegra said in her sweet voice.

Everyone turned toward her.

As if unsettled by being the center of attention, she reached up to smooth a wisp of flyaway hair from her forehead. "It may be true that you are half Wilcox, but you are also the prima of the McAllisters. That means our claim is the stronger one. You can't just…abandon us."

"Did I say anything about abandoning you?" I replied, irritated. "All I'm saying is that you have to accept that I'll be here part of the time and in Flagstaff part of the time. Even if there's some crisis, it's only a little more than an hour to get here. It's not like I'm buying a flat in Paris or something."

"And what happens afterward?" Bryce asked.

"Afterward?" I repeated.

"After you have the baby—I mean, the babies." His steely eyes seemed to bore into Connor, as if he held him directly responsible for my current condition. Never mind that I'd been a willing participant in those activities.

"You mean after the curse kills me?" I asked harshly. "No point in mincing words."

"Angela!" Connor and Bryce both burst out, even as Allegra recoiled and Margot watched all of us in silence, her expression grim. Lucas said nothing, only sat still in his chair, his dark eyes troubled.

"Why avoid talking about it? It's not that we aren't trying to do what we can about the curse, but seeing as we've hit sort of a dead end—"

"I'm working on that," Lucas cut in, his voice strained. "My own contacts didn't give me any leads on finding Andre's mother, so I hired a private investigator."

It was on the tip of my tongue to ask why there wasn't a magical solution to tracking down my missing grandmother, but maybe no one in his clan had that kind of talent. None of the McAllisters did, either; my cousin Becca was great at finding lost keys, earrings, and items like that, but people? Not so much.

"Well, then," I said. "We're doing what we can, but we always need to plan for contingencies, right? And if something happens to me"—pausing, I swallowed before pushing on—"then it's important that Connor and I have a proper home together in his own territory. You can fight about which clan has which rights, but in the end the children should be with their father. Now they'll have a good place to live, and if the curse decides to take me out, well, I won't be happy about it, but at least I know I won't have to worry about them being safe."

An uneasy silence fell. I supposed none of them really wanted to argue with what was, in effect, a spoken last will. Finally, Connor spoke.

"But we're not going to let that happen. We have months and months to figure this out, and we will. Angela—that is, *we*—just wanted to let you know where things stood with us. Her ob-gyn is in Flag, so as time goes on and her appointments come closer together, then we may be spending more time there than here. I hope you'll understand the reason why."

He said this last with a challenging note in his voice, as if daring one of them to protest. But although the three elders exchanged uneasy glances, none of them said anything for a few seconds. At last Allegra replied, "That does make sense, Connor. Thank you."

The tense line of his jaw relaxed slightly. I could tell he'd been expecting them to put up more of a fight on that point. Maybe they were just tired. I knew I was.

Since that seemed as good a point in the conversation as any to wrap things up, I told everyone, "The inspector went over the house yesterday and didn't find any issues, although we're waiting on the final report. That means we may be ready to move in as early as the end of next week, depending on how the title search goes. I'm going to talk to Rachel, of course, but I'd appreciate it if the rest of you could spread the word and let everyone else know that I plan to divide my time between here and Flagstaff."

Exactly how, I wasn't sure. Spending the summer up amongst the cool pines at seven thousand feet seemed infinitely preferable to the heat of the Verde Valley, but I knew I couldn't disappear for that long a stretch. Oh, well, we'd work it out somehow.

"We'll do that, *prima,*" Margot said formally.

They left after that, giving only a token goodbye to Connor and Lucas, whose gaze seemed to follow Margot as she went out to the foyer. I couldn't help giving a rueful shake of my head. Yes, he'd been on his best behavior, but that hadn't seemed to earn many points with her.

Not that I had time to worry about that now. I had enough problems of my own to deal with.

CHAPTER ELEVEN

Distant Relations

"ARE YOU *SERIOUS?*" SYDNEY SQUEALED INTO THE PHONE. "You bought a *house?*"

"Yes," I said, wincing a little and wishing that I'd turned down the speaker volume before I called her.

It was late Saturday afternoon, a few hours after the elders had departed. Connor and I had left Lucas to watch TV at the house for a while so we could go and talk to Rachel, tell her about the house and the twins... and Andre Wilcox. We'd brought up those subjects in basically that order, so by the time we got to Andre, my aunt was already looking a little glassy-eyed. "A Wilcox?" she kept repeating. "Your father is a *Wilcox?*" And I'd had to tell her that yes, we were almost positive, but that we were still trying to see if we could track him down somehow, just to confirm. Since she appeared so shell-shocked, I decided not to mention that we were also looking for him in case he knew something to help with breaking the curse. A long shot, but I couldn't forget Marie's words about going back to the beginning. He was my beginning…or at least the only part of my beginning still alive. Maybe. We really didn't have positive confirmation either way.

"I am so jealous," Sydney told me, and I had to drag my thoughts back to present. "And here I am, still living at my parents' house."

I didn't bother to point out that we were living very different lives. Trying to sound off-hand, I replied, "Well, Connor had the money from selling his brother's house, so it's really more that he's buying it and I'm just being listed on the deed. Anyway," I went on, before she could interject, "it's got a secondary master suite, so you and Anthony should come up and visit and hang for a while after Connor and I get settled."

"I am *so* there," she said, apparently abandoning the green-eyed monster for the moment. "When do you think you'll be settled? I need to know so I can ask for some time off from work."

Somehow I managed to avoid bursting into laughter. Patience had never been one of Syd's strong suits. "I don't know," I said carefully. "Maybe a couple of weeks?"

"So…mid-June?"

That might be doable, but it also felt like it might be putting some pressure on us. "I have a better idea. Why don't you guys come up for the Fourth of July weekend? I know it'll be a lot cooler here than in Cottonwood."

"That's for damn sure. I already feel like I'm dying of heat prostration, and it's barely *June*."

I knew the feeling. At least her parents' house had air conditioning. Lovely, lovely air conditioning. However, I figured I could put up with the heat for a while, since there was a light at the end of the tunnel. Or, more correctly, a big house with dual-zone A/C, in the unlikely event that you'd even need it in Flagstaff. "Well, check with Anthony and let me know. I haven't had time to research it much, but I'm sure they must be doing fireworks or something up in Flag."

"I will." She paused, then said, "I can't *believe* you and Connor bought a house."

Neither can the rest of my family, I thought, but only said, "I know, it's kind of crazy. But it was such a good deal that *we* would've been crazy to pass it up."

"So how long are you down here?"

"We're going back up on Monday, probably."

"Do you guys want to go out tonight, since you're in town? I feel like I haven't seen you in forever."

I hesitated. Normally I would've said yes, even though it wouldn't been a lot of fun to sit and drink mineral water while everyone else was having wine or cocktails. If nothing else, though, it might have helped to get out and socialize, and take my mind off my problems and my stiff-necked family.

But Lucas was here, and it would have been rude to dump him so Connor and I could go out with our friends. Not that Lucas probably couldn't find something to occupy himself, left to his own devices. Still, I hadn't been raised to treat guests that way, and I didn't think I should start now.

"I know," I said. "And we have so much more we need to talk about, but—"

"More?" she demanded. "There's more besides buying a house?"

You have no idea. "Um, yeah." Since everyone in town knew about the twins by now, I figured it was safe enough to mention it. "Well, I'm having twins."

"Twins!" she squealed, and again I had to hold the phone away from my ear. "Oh, my God, that is awesome! Do you know what they are yet?"

"No, it's way too early." Did I even want to know? Secretly, I was sort of hoping it would be one of each. Nice and neat.

"Oh," she said, sounding disappointed. "Well, it'll be fun no matter what they are. If they're the same, you can get them matching outfits and stuff."

Personally, I'd always hated it when I saw parents doing that to their twins, and so I vowed not to even if mine ended up being the same sex. But it wasn't worth arguing with Sydney over.

"Anyway," I said, not wanting to get too side-tracked, "I'd love to see you guys, but Connor's cousin Lucas is with us, and I don't really want to abandon him while we go out. Rain check?"

"Sure," she said. "We would've had to get a late start anyway, since Anthony doesn't get off work until eight."

I made a noncommittal comment, and after that we said our goodbyes and hung up. In the next few weeks I'd have to try to clear out some time to get together with her, even if it was just for lunch, but this weekend was already over-committed. I set down the phone, peered in the mirror, and realized I needed to do a little clean-up work to get ready for dinner. After meeting with the elders and then my aunt, I was looking just a little drained. Thank the Goddess for blush and lip gloss.

We took Lucas to Nic's in old town Cottonwood, since it seemed like the kind of place he'd enjoy. He did look right at home in the old-world atmosphere of the place, coaxing Connor into sharing a bottle of chianti after I swore it was okay for them to drink in front of me, then ordering grilled rib-eye and crab legs as if he did that sort of thing every day. Who knows—maybe he did.

Midway through dinner, though, his phone rang, and after shooting an apologetic glance at both of us, he pulled his cell out of his pocket, scanned the display briefly, and said, "I need to take this."

Connor and I both murmured, "Go ahead," and Lucas put the phone to his ear.

"Hey, Lester, you have something for me?" A pause. "Really? In Williams? And the address? Great, text it to me. Thanks for everything." He ended the call and returned to the phone to his pocket, dark eyes twinkling. "Well, I have some good news for you two. That was Lester, the private investigator I told you about. Turns out Angela's grandmother did move out of Flagstaff, but she didn't go very far. She's over in Williams."

I knew the name, but I'd never been there. Williams was in the Wilcox zone. Now, of course, I had nothing preventing me from going there. "That is great news, Lucas."

"Yeah, the reason I was having a hard time turning up anything about her was that apparently she changed her name after your grandfather passed away. She's going by her maiden name now. Jane Bryant. Lester's texting me her address, and I'll forward it to you."

"That was fast," Connor said. Something in his voice sounded tense, almost nervous, as if he wasn't as pleased as I'd thought he would be.

"Well, Lester's good." Lucas raised his glass of chianti toward me, and then Connor. "Here's to getting one step closer to your goal."

I had to toast with my water glass, but I found I didn't mind so much. Now the only trick would be figuring out the best time to go see Jane Bryant, the grandmother I had never met.

We saw Lucas off to his B&B, then drove back up to Jerome in silence. Since coming through the rear of the house was almost impossible right now because of the construction, I parked on the street—pregnancy had turned me into the designated driver—and we went in through the front entrance. After I shut the door, I said, "You're very quiet."

"Am I?"

"I thought you'd be happy that Lucas found my grandmother. You're sure not acting like it."

"I am. Really. It's just—" He hesitated, eyes downcast, as if he was studying the patterns of the rug beneath his feet to gain some sort of insight.

"Just what?" I asked impatiently.

"It's just—are you ready to hear what she has to say? What if she tells you things about your father that you really don't want to hear?"

"I'm touched that you want to protect me, Connor, but I can handle it. Even if she tells me he was a horrible person, that he made a bet that he could bang a McAllister and get away with it—or whatever—it's still better than not knowing *anything*. And maybe she'll know where he is, if he's still alive. I have to find out for sure. Can you understand that?"

"Of course I do," he replied, moving closer so he could take me in his arms and pull me close. "I forget what it must have been like for you, knowing nothing all those years. I had just the opposite problem—I often wished I could forget my father, forget what an asshole he was."

I snuggled into Connor's embrace, smelling the warm, familiar scent of his skin, feeling the strength of his arms around me. "I'm sorry you had to go through that."

"It's over. Luckily, in his eyes I was expendable, so he didn't pay a lot of attention to me. Damon was the one he focused all his energy on."

And see how well that turned out, I thought. "Well, joke's on him, considering you ended up as *primus* anyway."

Connor didn't reply, and I realized I'd stuck my foot in it with that response. "Sorry," I said quickly. "That came out wrong."

"It's okay. I've also been known develop foot-in-mouth disease on occasion." He let go of me, but gently, and not before planting a soft kiss on my forehead. "It's been a long day."

Had it ever. Hard to believe that it was only a little after eight. "So I say we veg out in front of the TV for a while and then go to bed. We can figure out what to do about visiting my grandmother tomorrow."

"Sounds like a plan."

And that's exactly what we did—headed to the family room, booted up Netflix, and watched *World War Z*. Strangely, it made me feel a little better. I might have a curse hanging over my head, but at least I wasn't trying to fight off a planet filled with zombies.

Since cooking breakfast was out of the question, the next morning we went down the hill and met Lucas for breakfast. I figured it couldn't hurt to ask for a little advice.

"So should I call, or just show up on her doorstep?" I asked after taking a sip of orange juice.

Both Connor and Lucas were drinking juice as well, since the smell of coffee still made me want to throw up. Once or twice as the waitress passed by our table with a pot in her hand, going to refill someone's cup, I felt a slight twinge of nausea, but it quickly passed. The problem was having it right in front of me, or filling the house with its scent as it was brewing.

"I wouldn't call," Lucas said, setting down his glass of grapefruit juice. "After all, she's taken some pains to disappear, to disconnect herself from the Wilcox clan. Calling and claiming to be her long-lost granddaughter might just make her take off again."

I hadn't thought of it that way. Neither had Connor, apparently; he nodded as he listened to Lucas' advice, but then remarked,

"And knocking on her door is better?"

"Well, at least then you have the element of surprise."

True. "Okay, so we drive out to Williams and hope she's there. What if she isn't?"

Connor shrugged. "Then we take a look around, grab something to eat. It's a cute little town."

I wasn't sure I could take such a setback quite that calmly, but he had a point. Sometimes you just gotta make lemonade.

"I'd say go ahead and give it a try today," Lucas told us. "I don't see how waiting is really going to help you."

Connor and I exchanged a glance. Yes, I'd known that we would be driving out to Williams, and soon, but…today? Was I mentally prepared for that?

"Well…." I hedged.

Perhaps misunderstanding my hesitation—or not; Lucas seemed to be a pretty shrewd judge of character behind that air of breezy cheerfulness—he said, "And don't worry about me. I did book a second night at the B&B, just in case, but I don't have to stay.

What you two need to do is far more important."

There didn't seem to be any way to argue with that. I shifted in the booth, turning toward Connor. "Are you okay with it?"

"Of course," he replied at once. "As Lucas said, this is important. Even if it turns out that your grandmother doesn't think she really knows anything, she could say something that makes sense to us, even if it doesn't make sense to her."

That seemed to clinch it. "Okay," I said. "We'll go this afternoon."

It was a longish drive, a little more than an hour and a half. We wound down the western slopes of Mingus Mountain, moving toward Prescott, and then turned due north to go through Chino Valley and hit I-40 in Ash Fork. Connor drove, since he knew I was tense enough without having to maneuver over unfamiliar roads. Well, some of it was unfamiliar; of course I'd been to Prescott and even Chino Valley, but no farther north than that, because then you'd start to run into Wilcox territory.

Funny how those arbitrary lines had now been more or less erased.

We pulled off I-40 into Williams, running along Route 66. Connor was right—the downtown area did look fun, full of restored buildings and shops and restaurants. In other words, not so different from the historic section of Flagstaff, although much smaller. From there we took a road that wound through a modest residential section, mostly of vintage homes that seemed to date from around the turn of the twentieth century, a little newer than most of Jerome, although not by much. The houses got bigger as we drove up the hill, and eventually Connor stopped his FJ Cruiser in front of a large farmhouse-style home painted white, with green shutters. The front lawn was brilliantly green, and bordered by carefully tended roses blooming in shades of red and yellow and pink.

All in all, it looked very respectable, the sort of place you might expect your grandmother to live.

Connor laid his hand on top of mine. "You ready for this?"

"Probably not," I admitted. "But we're here. If she slams the door in my face, we can turn around and go back downtown, and you can take me to that diner we passed and buy me a chocolate milkshake."

He smiled, heavy lashes almost concealing the green of his eyes. "Deal."

We got out and made our way to the front door. As we approached, I noticed that the dried-flower wreath on the front door had a simple wooden cross hanging in the middle of it. I glanced over at Connor, lifting my eyebrows, and he only shrugged.

Just do it, Angela, I told myself. So I reached out and pushed the doorbell.

I could hear the familiar Westminster chimes sequence from somewhere inside the house. A few minutes later the door opened, and an older woman with soft white hair pulled up into an elegant French twist opened the door. The afternoon sunlight hit the gold cross around her neck and made it gleam as if lit from within.

"Yes?" she said uncertainly, looking from me to Connor.

Since we'd put on "good" clothes to have breakfast with Lucas, we looked pretty respectable, Connor in jeans and a short-sleeved olive green shirt, me in a pair of my new jeans and a pretty sleeveless top with sequins and embroidery around the neckline. I could tell this woman was trying to puzzle out what we wanted, since we obviously didn't look like your usual solicitor.

The words seemed to stick in my throat, but somehow I forced them out. "Mrs. Bryant?"

"Yes?"

Okay, so we definitely had the right house. Not that I'd really doubted the information Lucas' P.I. had passed along. "My name is Angela—Angela McAllister. And this is my fiancé, Connor Wilcox."

At the name "Wilcox," she put a hand to her throat and took a step back. Then her gaze hardened as she seemed to really stop and study Connor's face, looking for the family resemblance. At last she said, her voice much colder than it had been, "Yes, you do look like one of them."

This was not going well, to say the least. I didn't know what kind of bad blood existed between this woman and the rest of the Wilcox clan, but I couldn't let it get in the way of our purpose for being here. "Mrs. Bryant," I said desperately. "I really need to talk to you. I'm—that is, I think I'm your granddaughter."

Dead silence. Her sharp blue eyes shifted, taking in my own countenance, seeming to study my features. For a second or two I thought I saw the thin lines of her mouth soften, but then she pulled herself up, saying, "Well, come in, I suppose. I certainly don't want to have this conversation on the front porch where the neighbors can hear."

An ungracious invitation, but one I'd accept nonetheless. I stepped inside, Connor hesitating before he followed me. I could tell he really wanted to be anyplace but here, and I couldn't blame him. At least he could comfort himself that he was only related to this woman by marriage, whereas she was the only grandparent I had left.

She led us into a formal living room, the kind of stiff, uncomfortable space, with its faux antique furniture, floral patterns, and ugly landscapes in oil on the walls, that I really couldn't stand. Just being there made me feel claustrophobic. But I made myself sit down on the couch, and Connor took a seat next to me, his hand reaching out to hold mine, to offer what reassurance he could.

I did notice that even with all the knickknacks sitting around, on the mantel and the side tables and in the curio cabinet in one corner, not one photograph was in sight, not one image of a husband, children…nothing. That disappointed me, because I'd been hoping for some visual evidence to corroborate Andre's identity.

No offer of a glass of water or anything like that. She sat down on a wingback chair covered in faded French blue velvet, then said, "How did you find me? Was it…*witchcraft?*" The word was uttered with such distaste you'd think she'd just mentioned child pornography or something.

"Actually, no," Connor said, his voice hard. "My cousin Lucas hired a private investigator to track you down."

She sniffed. "Lucas. Lucky Lucas. And how is *he?* Same as always, I would imagine."

"Very well. Thank you for asking." Polite words, but I could tell from the edge to his tone that he might as well have said "fuck you for asking."

"Mrs. Bryant"—there was no way I could call her "grandmother"—"was Andre Wilcox your son?"

"Was?" she repeated. "*Is,* as far as I know. At least, no one's contacted me to tell me otherwise."

A chill seemed to inch its way down my spine and then spread out, sending cold to every limb, even though it was quite a warm day, even here in Williams. "You mean…he's *alive?*"

"Why wouldn't he be?" she said irritably. "He's only forty-five years old, you know. To someone your age, I suppose that sounds like one foot in the grave, but I assure you it isn't."

"No, of course not," I agreed. Anything to keep her talking. "So…where is he? Because he never came back to Flagstaff after—that is, after…." I faltered, unsure as to how much she knew about her son's time in California.

"After he came back from California?" she asked. My eyes must have widened, because she went on, satisfaction at startling me clear in her voice, "Yes, he told me where he'd gone. At the time, I thought it was a good thing. At least it got him away from that Indian girl."

"'Indian girl'?" I echoed. "Do you mean Marie Wilcox?"

"Yes, her. Never could see what he saw in her, but he was just crazy about her, kept going on about how they were going to get married. I told him not to be silly, that he could do better than her, but he wouldn't listen. Always was hung up on all that

Navajo nonsense, just because his father's mother was an Indian."

Connor had already told me that he was fairly certain Andre's grandmother had been Navajo, so that wasn't much of a surprise. That my father identified with them so closely was, however. Then again, with a mother like this, I could see why he might have tried to cling to a part of the family that was more welcoming, for whatever reason.

I glanced over at Connor, but I could tell from his expression that he preferred to have me do the talking, that otherwise he might have a hard time remaining civil. Not that I could blame him. This Jane Bryant was no one I really wanted to claim as a relation. Unfortunately, it seemed we were connected by blood, whether I liked it or not.

"Did he say why he was going to California?"

"Not really. He went up to the reservation a good bit, visiting relations, I suppose. I don't know, because I never felt the need to meet that part of my husband's family. The Wilcoxes were bad enough."

Beside me, I could feel Connor stir, and I laid a calming hand on his knee. "So Andre went to the reservation…."

"Yes, he went this one last time, was gone for more than a week, then came back saying he had to go to California, that there was something he had to do."

I could feel my eyebrows shooting up. So this impulse to travel to California—possibly for no other reason than to seek out my mother—had come from the reservation? "Did he say anything else?"

"No, only that he didn't know how long he'd be gone. His father tried talking to him, told him the Santiagos would never allow a Wilcox in their territory, but Andre said that wouldn't be an issue. And so he went." She shrugged her thin shoulders. "At the time I wasn't too worried. I was just glad he was away from that Marie person. But then he didn't come back…and he didn't come back. And then his father got sick." Her blue eyes, in their frame of fine, wrinkled skin, narrowed. "Pancreatic cancer. Much good your witch healers were for *that!*" she added with venom, glaring at Connor.

"They're not infallible," he said quietly. "And cancer is the worst, especially something like pancreatic. I'm sure they did everything they could."

"Well, obviously they didn't, because he died, and left me alone, surrounded by *witches*." She transferred her scowl to me. "McAllister. So you're a witch, too, I suppose."

I nodded. Her lack of surprise at seeing a Wilcox engaged to a McAllister mystified me somewhat, but I certainly wasn't going to inquire about that. "So… if you never heard from him, how do you know your son really is still alive?"

"I didn't say I *never* heard from him," she retorted. "I said I didn't hear from him *then*. About a month after Gerard died, I got a note from Andre." A hesitation, as if she really didn't want to reveal what it had said. Her gaze raked over me again, lingering on my left hand. I'd introduced Connor as my fiancé, and I knew we regarded one another that way, but we really hadn't had much of a chance to make things formal with a ring and everything. "He said he was sorry he couldn't be there for me when his father passed, and that he wished he could come to be with me, but it was just impossible. And that was that."

Stranger and stranger. What in the world could have kept my father away from his mother at a time when she must have needed him? Then again, I had no real idea of what kind of a relationship they'd had. Maybe she hadn't been this prickly back then, had changed after she lost her husband…or maybe she'd always been like this, more or less.

I had to hope that she couldn't tell from looking at me what my opinion of her was, as I certainly didn't want to alienate her. So I said, "I'm sorry to hear that. But—"

"But what?" Her pinched expression told me she'd had just about enough of the questions.

"Do you remember where the note was mailed from? Maybe somewhere on Navajo land?"

"It was mailed from Flagstaff. I do remember that. It came as I was packing up the house and getting ready to leave. Another few weeks, and it would've had to be forwarded." She knotted her thin fingers, twisted with arthritis, on her knee. Her dress was blue linen, and she wore pearls in her ears. Not the usual sort of lazy Sunday outfit I was used to, but then I realized she'd probably gone to church earlier and hadn't changed out of her good clothes. "I don't know anything other than that. It's been more than twenty years, you know."

Yes, I did know. Twenty-two years of never knowing whether my father was alive or dead, or even what his name might be. I knew better than to say anything like that to this cold-voiced woman. Probably she had been very pretty in her youth; her hair was still thick, and her features were regular, her eyes bright blue, not faded from age at all. Then again, why should that surprise me? The Wilcox men did seem to have an eye for pretty women.

"And since I can't tell you anything else, I think you'd better go now."

Under different circumstances, I might have argued. But I could see the way she kept darting hostile, nervous glances at Connor, as if he were going to cast some dark spell at any moment, and I also realized that if she'd intended to display any sort of interest in me as her son's only child, the moment for that had long passed.

"Of course," I said, getting to my feet. "I'm very sorry to have intruded on your afternoon."

For the first time she looked vaguely discomfited, as if she'd realized that having your long-lost granddaughter apologize for intruding might mean she hadn't given the sort of reception one might expect in this type of situation. Not that she would apologize herself, though. She stood up, and Connor rose as well. He didn't say anything, only took my hand as I started to move toward the door.

"There's one thing," she added, just as I was reaching for the knob.

"There is?" I asked, stopping in surprise.

"I don't know if it'll help you or not, but I think my husband's Navajo relations' surname was Bedonie…Begonie? Something like that. Anyway, you might want to give it a try."

It was a small gesture, but one that meant a lot. Suddenly that haystack had gotten a good deal smaller. "Thank you," I said, hoping she could hear the gratitude in my voice.

She waved a hand, as if uncomfortable with even that small display of thankfulness. "It's nothing. Drive safe."

It was a clear dismissal, and I took it as such. Opening the door, I slipped out into the warm sunshine, glad of a chance to breathe fresh air after the stuffy confines of her house. By some tacit agreement, neither Connor nor I spoke until we were safely back in the FJ. He started up the SUV, pulled away from the curb, and began to head back toward downtown Williams. Only then did he say, "Jesus Christ."

I wasn't Christian by any stretch of the imagination, but I had to agree with his sentiment. "No kidding." For a few seconds I watched the slightly shabby-looking neighborhoods pass by. Then I said, "If she's that crazy, I'm not sure I even want to meet my father. Goddess knows what he's like."

Connor reached over and patted my knee. "Cheer up. Maybe he takes after the Wilcox side of the family."

"Oh, that's very reassuring."

Instead of being offended, he merely chuckled. Then his expression sobered, and he added, "She's definitely got issues, but I'm trying not to be too judgmental. Grief makes people do strange things. You can tell her husband's death hit her hard, especially with her son being gone. And expecting the healers to magically fix things, and then when they didn't…." He let the words die away, mouth tightening as he guided us back onto Route 66. "Well, I suppose I can see why she'd feel betrayed, by the Wilcoxes in particular and witchcraft in general. I'm not saying she didn't swing way too far in the other direction, but it does make some sense."

"Okay, maybe, but she's had twenty years to get over it," I said. Even I could hear the hurt in my voice. I hadn't wanted to admit it to myself, but somewhere deep inside I'd probably hoped that she would welcome me, tell me she was so happy to know that she had a grandchild. Instead, I'd only been given a little more courtesy than someone going from door to door and pushing religious tracts. Actually, she probably would have been friendlier to someone like that. At least she would have known they weren't a heathen.

He looked over and gave me a quick, sharp glance before returning his attention to the road. "You can't take it that way, Angela. The woman has issues. It has nothing to do with you personally."

In my heart, I knew he was right. But knowing something and believing it can be two very different things.

"We're passing that diner," he said, in a completely different tone of voice. "Do you want to stop for anything?"

I shook my head, staring out the window without really seeing. "No. Just take me home."

CHAPTER TWELVE

Ascension

By the time we got back to Jerome, I was feeling a little better—mostly because Connor had called Lucas from the road with the information on my great-grand-mother's possible family name. Lucas then promised to pass it on to the private detective right away. And since the man had done such a good job of locating my paternal grandmother, I had to hope he could do the same thing here.

On Monday we headed up to Flagstaff, partly to get out of the way of the remodeling crew, and partly so we could be on hand in case something happened with the house, or Lester the P.I. dug up something for us. But we didn't hear anything on either front, and I found myself getting discouraged all over again. In fact, I felt close to tears half the time, which was ridiculous. Was I going to be a complete mess for the next six months?

It's just hormones, I told myself. *Don't worry about acting crazy. Everyone's expecting it from you anyway.*

On Tuesday and Wednesday, Connor and I did do a little packing around his apartment, mostly of nonessential stuff that wouldn't be missed if the title search dragged out longer than planned. It was fun to look at old sketchbooks of his to see how his style had evolved over the years, and it was even more fun to dig out his high school yearbooks and giggle at his over-long emo-looking hair.

"Actually," I said, studying him closely as he shoved the yearbooks into a box and shook his head, "you're almost there now. Are you planning to cut it anytime in the near future?"

"I don't know," he replied, running a hand through the heavy black strands, which were now long enough to tuck behind his ears. "Do you want me to?"

"To be honest, I'm not sure. You're kind of hot with it long."

"I am?" he inquired, green eyes glinting.

I knew that look. "Yeah, you are."

He reached for me then, and we rolled over on the rug, kissing, fingers fumbling with buttons and zippers that were suddenly in the way. For some reason I'd thought being pregnant might kill my desire for him, or at least mute it a good deal, but that didn't seem to be the case here. I still wanted him just as badly as that first time we'd reached out to touch one another, on a spot only about a foot from where we lay now. His hands roamed over my bare flesh, caressing me, and I reached out to wrap my fingers around him, feeling the hard evidence that the slight rounding of my belly didn't bother him at all. And then we were joined, moving together, the soft whir of the ceiling fan overhead the only sound besides our ragged panting.

We were just pulling our clothes back on when Connor's phone rang. He shot me an apologetic look and went to pick up his cell from where he'd left it lying on the dining room table. I didn't mind, actually; we were waiting on too many important calls to ignore one now.

"Hey, Lucas," Connor said, and I pricked up my ears even as I finished buttoning my jeans. Man, I'd already bought them a week before, and they were already feeling tight. Dr. Ruiz had obviously been a little premature in her concern over my lack of a healthy weight gain.

Elastic waistbands, here I come.

Connor told Lucas, "No, nothing important. Just packing a few odds and ends."

"Is that what you're calling it these days?" I joked.

He shot me a grin before saying, "Oh, really? Okay. No, I understand. It's fine. I know he's doing the best he can. Thanks for the update."

That didn't sound good. "What is it?" I asked as he ended the call and stuffed the phone into his pocket.

"Just an update on the hunt for your father's Navajo relations. Apparently Bedonie and Begonie are both very common names, and since we don't know for sure which one it is, it's going to take Lester more time than he thought. He's working on it, but it's tough because of the name problem, and because the Navajo clearly aren't thrilled to have some P.I. poking around in their business."

"Well, it's not like he's trying to bring a criminal to justice or something," I protested. "All he's trying to do is find my relatives."

"Yeah, we know that, but to the Navajo, it probably just sounds like a cover story. So he's having to tread cautiously. That's all."

I had to admit to not being very knowledgeable about Navajo politics, so I decided to let it go for the moment. Clearly, Lester was doing a good job under difficult circumstances. I was impatient to find my father, if he really was on the reservation at all, but I told myself it was fine, that we still had six months to get everything resolved. All the time in the world.

So why did it feel like time was running out?

The next day we did get a piece of good news, though—the title search was completed, and now all we had to do was sign off on the paperwork and initiate the money transfer.

All. That was a joke.

I didn't recall there being a great deal to do when I inherited Great-Aunt Ruby's house, maybe because it was simply an inheritance, and her will had been very clear. Yes, I'd signed a few papers, just to make everything legal, but that was about it.

Now, though, I sat in the realtor's office and put my signature to what felt like an unending pile of papers with teeny type—"initial here…sign here"—until I felt like my eyes were about to start bleeding. "If it's like this when we're not even getting a mortgage, how many papers do you have to sign if you're actually taking out a loan?" I asked plaintively.

Connor looked like he was holding in a laugh, and the realtor gave me an indulgent smile. "Quite a few more, I'm afraid," she replied.

I held in a sigh and went back to signing.

Eventually, though, it was all done, the transfer of funds processed, every "i" dotted and "t" crossed.

After what felt like all afternoon but was probably closer to an hour an a half, the realtor pushed a set of keys and a couple of remote controls—for the garage, presumably—toward us.

"You're all set," she said. "Congratulations."

Feeling a little stunned at the speed with which everything had happened, we headed out toward the parking lot. Then Connor threw his arms around me, lifted me up, and spun me around. I let out a startled squeak and burst out laughing.

"Put me down, you nut," I told him.

Which he did, but not before he gave me a hearty kiss. "I guess I just can't believe that we actually have that house. I mean, we could drive down there right now, unlock the door, and walk in."

And so we did, wandering through the rooms, making notes here and there on the few pieces we didn't like or thought we should replace.

"We're definitely getting a new bed," I said, gazing around the master bedroom. "Sleeping on someone else's bed is just creepy, especially someone who's getting a divorce. Who knows how many fights they had while lying in that bed. It's bad juju."

"I agree. I'll put that on the list for tomorrow. There's a place in town that'll do same-day delivery. It's where I got my bed. Are you okay with another one just like it?"

Connor's bed was super-comfy. "Sure."

"Then that means we can probably be here—*really* be here, starting on Saturday."

I gazed around, taking in the stone fireplace, the gleaming wooden floors. Yes, I had the house in Jerome, but in the back of my head it was still "Great-Aunt Ruby's house," despite all the remodeling I'd done and was currently doing. This place—it was ours, Connor's and mine, and I vowed then that we'd be happy here for whatever time we had together.

But no, I shouldn't be thinking like that. Everything with the house had gone smoothly, and so I had to believe it would happen that way with the search for my father, even if it was taking a little longer than I would have liked.

We went back to the apartment and called Lucas with the good news, and then I phoned Sydney as well, and made dutiful calls to Margot Emory and my aunt.

Margot took the news with equanimity, only asking when I thought I'd be back in Jerome, but Rachel didn't handle it quite so well.

"I just can't believe that you really did it," she said. "Your place is here, Angela."

"And it will be, for half the year. And the other half I'll be here in Flagstaff, as is only fair. Everyone will learn to adapt over time.

She didn't reply right away, and I could tell she was thinking basically the same thing I'd been thinking only a short while earlier…that there might not be all that much time to work with.

But she didn't bring it up, thank the Goddess, and so after a few more reassurances, I hung up, glad that was over with.

"Hungry yet?" Connor asked, bringing me a glass of water.

"Silly question. I'm *always* hungry."

"Then let me go out and get some tapas. No point in trying to cook something, not when we need to start packing the kitchen tomorrow."

I nodded, and he went out, promising to be back in a few minutes. That was an optimistic estimate, since it was now verging on six-thirty, and even a Thursday night could be busy, especially on a mild summer evening like this one.

Not that waiting had to be bad. I settled down on the couch and began to reach for the remote, glad of a chance to rest and relax for a few minutes, only to see a pale flicker at the corner of my vision. Startled, I got to my feet, and realized the pale flicker was the ghost Mary Mullen in her white dress, standing in front of the window.

"Mary!" I exclaimed. "I haven't seen you for a while."

She didn't blink. "You're leaving, aren't you?"

"What?"

"Here." Her gaze seemed to wander over the living room, pause on the fireplace, and then move back toward me. "You and Connor. You're leaving."

"Well, yes," I said, feeling inexplicably guilty. "Because of the babies."

Her expression turned dreamy. "Oh, yes, the babies." Then the faraway look disappeared so quickly it might have been turned off with a switch. "Why can't you stay here with your babies? I had two children here. There was plenty of room."

I didn't really feel like getting in a discussion with her over the inadequacies of a two-bedroom walk-up when it came to raising twins. Times had changed a lot since she'd had to look after two small children. Fumbling for an excuse, I said, "Well, but it's much busier here than when you had your little girls. I'm afraid I don't think it would be safe for the babies. All that traffic."

She seemed to accept that explanation, nodding slightly as she moved soundlessly from where she stood in the living room to pause next to one of the dining room chairs. Running a hand over the back—or appearing to, anyway, as I was fairly certain she couldn't actually touch it—she let out a sigh and said, "I still miss them so very much."

"I know," I said in soothing tones. But as the words left my lips, I felt the oddest sensation deep within me. Not the babies moving; of course it was far too early for that. No, it was more like the stirring of the *prima* power, awakening from where it seemed to have slept for the past few days, somehow telling me I needed to do something to help Mary.

But what do I do? I asked of the power, as if it was a separate entity living inside me, rather than a gift I had inherited, one as much a part of me as the color of my eyes or the sound of my voice.

Tell her it is time to stop being alone.

That was all, but I thought I understood. I didn't want to leave her here with no one to talk to. The chances of someone else who possessed my same gift coming to live in the apartment were very slim. Yes, Connor had mentioned offering it as an affordable rental to any one of a number of Wilcox cousins currently attending Northern Pines, but our plans hadn't gotten much past the discussion stage. At any rate, no Wilcox I'd heard of was able to speak to ghosts, and so even if one of the cousins moved in, Mary would once again be relegated to watching only, unable to communicate with the living person who shared her home.

"Maybe," I ventured, trying to find the right words to tell her she didn't need to exist in this limbo any longer, "maybe it's time for you to be with them."

Her fine penciled brows lifted. "What do you mean?"

"I mean that they've been waiting for you—waiting such a long time. Your girls need their mother... and your husband needs his wife."

"But they left me," she protested, her tone almost petulant. "I waited and waited here—"

"I know, I know," I broke in. "But it's sort of like"—I racked my brains, trying to think of an analogy she'd understand—"it's like you made a plan to take the train, only you got off a stop ahead of them. So they've been waiting for you at their stop all this time, while you've been here, thinking that they must be horribly late. All you have to do is go meet them at their station."

Blue eyes widening, she nodded. "Of course. Ralph was so absentminded, he was always forgetting the timetables for the trains and such. I can see how he would have gone to the wrong place to wait for me."

The power pulsed within me again, and I asked, following its inner guidance, "What would Ralph be wearing to meet you at the station? And your girls?"

"Well, if it was Sunday, he'd have on his good black suit, and that fedora of his I loved so much, the one with the green feather. And the girls would be wearing the dresses their Nana smocked for them, and their patent-leather shoes, and—oh, my!"

I could understand why she'd let out that shocked exclamation, because the window that overlooked the street suddenly didn't seem to be a window any longer, but rather a portal through which a pure white light blazed. And out of that light stepped three figures, the tallest one in the middle, flanked by smaller shapes that resolved themselves into two small girls, probably four and six at the most, wearing, as Mary had described, darling smocked dresses in pink and blue, and the shiniest patent-leather Mary-Jane shoes I'd ever seen. The man with them wore a black suit, his fedora cocked at a jaunty angle.

His hazel eyes widened as he caught sight of Mary, and he cried out, "Mary! Oh, Mary—is that you?"

Tears streamed down her face. "It is, Ralph. Oh, my darling, I thought I would never see you again!"

She ran to him, and he took her in his arms, holding her close. In that moment they looked very solid—or perhaps it was more that they were solid to one another. The two little girls ran to them, reaching up with their arms to be hugged as well, and the whole family embraced in the middle of the living room, while the white light continued to pour in from the place where the window used to be.

At last I said softly, "Ralph, you'll be taking Mary with you now, won't you?"

He nodded. His face was pleasant, not handsome, but something in the way Mary was gazing up at him told me she thought he was the most beautiful thing she'd ever seen. "Yes, I will. I've been waiting a long time for her." He turned, searching her big tear-filled eyes. "Are you ready, my dear?"

"I am." She wrapped her arm around his waist and took the hand of the little girl wearing blue, while he clasped the small fingers of the younger child in pink. "I'm sorry I didn't come with you from the beginning."

"You're here now, and that's what matters."

He began to lead them toward the light, but at the last minute Mary paused and looked over her shoulder, her eyes meeting mine. "Thank you, Angela," she said, and they walked into the light, the radiance blazing brighter and brighter until I had to shield my eyes from that retina-scorching glare.

Then they were gone, the window just a window, the living room returned to its regular self, the abandoned remote sitting on the coffee table. I began to laugh, and then for some reason, the laughter turned to tears.

And that's how Connor found me when he returned, his hands full of takeout bags. Just me standing in the middle of the living room, crying for no apparent reason.

"So how did you know what to do?" he asked some time later, after he'd calmed me down enough for me to tell him what had happened.

"I—I don't know," I confessed. "It was sort of like…well, when we had to confront Damon. Somehow the power in me understood, even when I didn't. I guess I just felt so bad for her, thinking of her being here by herself after we moved out, and it woke up something in me. Sorry—I know that sounds kind of crazy."

"Not as crazy as you think." Quietly, he picked up the last bacon-wrapped date and set it on my plate. I flashed him a grateful smile. He reached over, touched my hand for a brief second, then went on, "Just like you said, you've had the power come to you when you needed it. For whatever reason, you understood it was time for Mary to move on. So… you helped her."

"But that's not my talent!" I protested. "Talking to ghosts, yes. Helping them cross over? That's what a medium does, isn't it? We McAllisters had one once, but she died when I was just a little girl. I even tried a few times, thinking I could coax a few of our ghosts into moving on, since it was so clear that they were clinging to what was familiar in Jerome rather than facing the next step in their existence. But I could never get them to listen to me. Not until now, I mean."

Connor seemed to ponder my comments for a moment, one index finger tracing idle swirls on the tabletop. "We don't have anyone like that, either. Nor anyone who can talk to ghosts like you do. Most of our powers seem to be concentrated pretty firmly in this world, for whatever reason. I know you think your talent is just talking to ghosts, but people grow and change. Why not their talents, too? Maybe yours are simply…evolving."

"I'd say yes, but I've never noticed that about any of the McAllisters. What they do is just…what they do. So my aunt never loses anything, can tell you down to the square inch where anything is in the apartment or the store, or even Tobias's place, come to think of it." I smiled, recalling the time he'd dropped a contact lens and she'd gone unerringly to the very spot where it had fallen. "And Margot can cast illusions so real you'd swear you could touch them—until your hand goes right through the wall she conjured, or whatever."

"So that's her talent," Connor murmured. "I was sort of wondering. Now we've got to get her and Lucas together. They'd clean up in Vegas."

"I'm serious, Connor."

"So am I."

There didn't seem to be anything for it except for me to smack him in the arm. He managed to wince and chuckle at the same time. "Anyway," I went on, trying to shoot him an evil glare, one that wasn't very effective because I could feel my lips start to twitch with answering laughter, "what I was trying to say is that I know what the people in my clan can do, but it's the same thing they've always done. It doesn't really change. Our powers start to show up when we're around ten or eleven, sometimes later, but after that, they are what they are. So I don't see how mine could suddenly morph into something new."

He lifted his glass of mineral water, polished it off, and then poured himself some more from the bottle sitting on the table. Afterward, he tilted it slightly toward me, offering me some. I shook my head. The fizzy bubbles were starting to get to my stomach. "Well, remember what Maya said?"

I shook my head, not understanding what he was getting at.

"She said nothing like this had happened before, that never had a *prima* and a *primus* been together the way we are, so we're basically in uncharted territory."

"But she was only talking about us being together," I pointed out. "She wasn't talking about our talents."

"Okay, maybe, but take it a step further. Maybe the mere fact of us being together, being joined like this, is doing something to our talents…having them, I don't know, evolve or something."

That sounded vaguely ominous. Not that I'd always enjoyed being able to talk to ghosts, but at least I was used to it by now. Although I was happy for Mary, glad that she had finally been able to reunite with the ones she loved, my role in her moving on made me uneasy. I'd already had enough changes in my life. I didn't really want to cope with the possibility that I myself might be changing, too.

"Well, if that's your hypothesis," I said, "then it should be easy enough to prove. Try taking on the appearance of someone who isn't your approximate size."

Now it was his turn to look uncomfortable. He didn't protest, though, only asked, "Like who?"

"How about Maya herself? She's at least a foot shorter than you are."

He expelled a breath, then nodded. "Okay. Let me think about that for a second." His lids dropped, as if he were trying to visualize her with his mind's eye and didn't want any interference from the outside world.

And there was Maya sitting at the table with me, her dark eyes glinting with mischief.

"Holy shit!" I exclaimed, and Connor winked back into existence, replacing the Maya illusion that had been there a second earlier.

"So I'm guessing it worked," he said.

"That's for sure." Pausing, I studied him for a few seconds, making sure he looked exactly like himself and nothing else. Which he did, from the sweep of the heavy black hair at his brow to the finely sculpted lips, those lips I loved to kiss. "Did it…feel…any different?"

His head tilted slightly as he considered the question. "Maybe. I was definitely seeing the world as she would see it—you know, from about a foot lower down. That did feel kind of strange."

I supposed it would, for someone used to seeing things from a commanding six-foot-three. "Anything else?"

"Not really. I mean, I visualized Maya in my mind, the same way I visualized Lucas when I took on his appearance. And it just…happened. But I'd never been able to do anything like that before."

So it seemed we were both changing…or at least our powers were. What that meant, I had no idea.

Although we really didn't have that much stuff to move, several Wilcox cousins I vaguely recognized from the Christmas party came over with their pickup trucks and SUVs to assist with transferring our things to the new house. I didn't know if they were just trying to be helpful, or whether what they really wanted was a peek at their *primus'* new digs. Whatever the reason, I was grateful for their help, because pretty much everything was taken care of by the time four o'clock rolled around. Connor shared a beer with them, then waved goodbye as they all took off, leaving us alone in the new house.

"Well," I said.

"Well, indeed." We were standing on the front walkway, watching as the last of the vehicles disappeared around a bend and into the trees. Connor reached out and brushed away a wisp of hair that had escaped my ponytail. His expression was hard to read—tired, yes, but there was a peace to it I hadn't seen for a long time. But then a corner of his mouth lifted, and he asked, "Do you want me to carry you over the threshold?"

"Connor, I've been in and out of the house all day," I replied. "Do you think it matters?"

"It matters to me."

I laughed. "Okay, then. Just be glad we're doing this now and not when I'm seven months pregnant."

"True." And he scooped me up in his arms, lifting me like I weighed nothing, then carried me through the open doorway. After pushing the door shut with one foot, he set me down in the entry. "Maybe I'm doing this backward," he said, "but I really do want to make it official."

Before I could do anything but stare down at him in stupefaction, he got on one knee and fished a small black box out of one pocket.

"Connor—"

"We've danced around this, Angela, and there's no reason to do that anymore. We're together. I can't imagine a life without you. So will you marry me?" And he opened the box, revealing a beautiful ring, obviously an antique, with a filigreed mounting of either white gold or platinum, and a square-cut diamond flanked on either side with emerald-cut sapphires.

I didn't even stop to think, my heart answering as the words rose to my lips. "Oh, yes, Connor, I'll marry you. Of course I will."

He slid the ring on my finger, and I reached out and took both his hands, pulled him back to his feet, brought him toward me so I could kiss him again and again and again. And then his arms were sliding around me, lifting me, and he carried me upstairs, through the welter of boxes in the master bedroom, to the bed that had been delivered that morning and which I had just finished making up.

That bed definitely got a proper christening.

Afterward, we lay there for a while, feeling the breeze blow in through the open windows, a breeze that smelled of pine and sun-warmed grass. I gazed down at the ring, thinking how perfect it was, how perfectly it fit me. "How did you pick it out?" I asked, turning my hand so the light from the window struck the diamond, scattering sparks all around the room.

"I guess it sort of picked me out. There's a shop around the corner from the tapas place that sells antiques but also has a selection of antique jewelry, and when I was out I stopped in to take a look. Can't even say why, really—it was just an impulse, I guess." We exchanged a smile at that comment; lately, our impulses seemed to be directed by a higher power. "I saw the ring, and just thought it looked like you. I couldn't really imagine you wearing some mass-market ring from a regular jewelry store."

How well he knew me. If he'd bought me something like that, I would've worn it, because it had come from him. But this ring was an individual, something I knew I'd never see coming and going.

"Also, I know you like blue, have all that turquoise jewelry, so I thought the sapphires were nice."

"It's perfect," I told him. "Just like you."

"You're going to give me a swelled head if you keep talking like that."

"I'd rather give you a swelled something else."

My hand moved lower, touching him, feeling him already growing hard as my fingers brushed against his shaft. He chuckled, shifting so I could reach him better, and I listened as his breathing quickened, felt my own body throbbing in response, the warm golden rush of heat going all through my veins. It seemed right to make love here, in this house that was ours, with the amber light of late afternoon slanting through the trees and making everything seem as if it were adrift in an enchanted forest, in a place of perfect peace, perfect harmony, perfect joy.

And then, content, we fell asleep in one another's arms.

The ringing of Connor's phone roused us both. I startled awake, blinking into the half-light of late dusk, a little disoriented. Then I remembered where we were. The new house. We were home.

Connor muttered a curse, then fumbled for the phone on the nightstand, nearly knocking over the lamp in the process. His reflexes were good enough that he was able to grab it before it crashed to the floor, though, and, still grumbling, he righted it before finally grabbing the phone.

"It's Lucas," he said after glancing briefly at the display.

"Then you'd better get it, I suppose."

He tapped the screen and then held the phone to his ear. "No offense, Lucas, but this had better be important. We just moved everything over, and—" Falling silent, he seemed to listen intently, at last saying, "Okay, we need to write that down. Angela…?"

I made a flailing motion with my hands. Right then I had no idea where anything I could write with might be, belatedly realizing that I'd dumped my purse on top of the dresser hours ago, and that I should at least have a pen in there, if not any actual writing paper. Grabbing my underwear, I sort of hopped into them as I crossed the floor and retrieved my purse. The pen had of course drifted to the bottom, but eventually I dug it out and gave it to Connor. No paper was to be had, but then he seemed to spy the discarded packing slip for the mattress on the floor, and leaned over to pick it up. Scribbling furiously, he said, "You're sure? I don't want to drive all the way out there and then…. No, okay, you're right. Well, I'll tell Angela. Thanks for everything, Lucas." He hung up and turned back toward me, as I'd slipped under the covers once I'd given him the pen.

"What is it?" I asked.

A pause, during which he reached out and cupped my cheek, ran those long, sensitive artist's fingers of his along my jaw. "He just heard back from the private investigator.

"He found your father."

CHAPTER THIRTEEN

On the Reservation

No big surprise that I had a hard time sleeping that night. The P.I. had done enough poking around that eventually he found someone who admitted that an Andre Bedonie was living a few miles outside Cameron. I'd asked Connor where Cameron was, and he said, "It's a wide spot in the road about fifty miles due north of Flagstaff. There's a trading post—kind of a tourist trap, but they have good food."

At the time I'd thought that was a good sign. Even if we drove out there and it was the wrong Andre Bedonie, or it turned out no one with that name lived there at all, we could at least get a decent meal to assuage our disappointment.

Now, though, I lay in the unfamiliar bed and stared at the unfamiliar ceiling, hearing the exotic night sounds of the forest outside. In fact, the only thing around me that *was* familiar was Connor, sleeping soundly, breaths too light to quite be called snores escaping from his open mouth. I wanted to reach out, snuggle into him, but he needed his rest, since he'd been slinging boxes with the rest of the cousins that afternoon.

I was tired but not sleepy, my mind roiling with the news of this latest development. My father, only fifty miles away. For how long? How many years had he lived there, tucked away on Navajo lands? Ever since he got back from California?

From what his mother had said—I still couldn't think of her as my grandmother—it sounded as if that was exactly what he'd done. Gone up there to hide. What else could you call it, when he'd discarded his father's last name and taken that of his maternal grandmother's family? Clearly he'd taken some pains to hide who he was, where he had come from.

I had no idea how he'd react when I came knocking at his door....

Although I'd had grand plans for getting up early and driving out to Cameron around nine, my body had different ideas. Between the moving stress and the sex and those tiny little people inside me who needed every spare ounce of energy I had, I crashed hard that night, and didn't even wake up until it was almost eight-thirty. And then there was hardly any food in the house, and of course here we couldn't just stroll out the back door and be in downtown Flagstaff, with plenty of places to get something to eat. We ended up showering and getting dressed, and then finally making it to breakfast at the country club around ten-thirty. Thank goodness it was a Sunday, a day when people liked to brunch, so we didn't need to worry about it being too late to get some actual breakfast food.

How they knew we were members, I really didn't know—some seamless behind-the-scenes magic of their own, I supposed. But no one challenged us as we gave our names, and after a short wait we were shown to a table next to the window, where we could look down at a putting green and the calm blue of a manmade lake.

"So are you going to take up golf?" I inquired with a grin, after watching Connor gaze out the window at a group taking their turns on the green.

"God, no," he said with such vehemence that I knew he didn't find my question amusing in the slightest. "That's Lucas' thing, not mine. Can you really imagine me in khakis and a polo shirt?"

"Um, no," I replied. Since we were coming here to eat, he'd actually tucked his shirt in, but Connor wasn't exactly what you'd call buttoned-down when it came to his clothes. Jeans all the time, long-sleeved henleys in the winter, short-sleeved ones in the summer. In fact, the only time I'd ever seen him wear actual trousers was at Damon's funeral.

A waiter came up and asked what we'd like, and I ordered a glass of cranberry juice and Connor some mineral water, since he knew better than to drink any coffee around me. Afterward he said, "So, from here it'll take us about an hour to get out to Cameron. It might be kind of busy, since it's the weekend and that's one route you can take to get to the Grand Canyon."

"Have you been there a lot? To Cameron, I mean."

"Couple of times when I was driving someplace else. It's not exactly what you'd call a destination." He hesitated, fingers playing nervously with the edge of the napkin in his lap. "It's Navajo territory, so we need to be respectful and understand that they're allowing us to be on their land."

"I get it," I said, although I wasn't sure I did, not completely. The Navajo nation truly was another country embedded within our own.

Connor went on, "I looked the address up on Google maps, and it's a little bit outside Cameron itself, up in a canyon. You can only get there by a dirt road. From what I could tell, it looks like a little compound…there are several buildings, and what looked like a small solar array. Makes sense, because otherwise it's hard to get power out to a place like that." Another one of those pauses, and then he looked me directly in the eye and said, "You'll need to prepare yourself."

"I know," I told him. "He may not be there at all, or he may slam the door in my face. I get it."

"That's not what I meant. There's a lot of poverty on the reservation. No one's living out there in a McMansion, you know? It can be kind of a shock, if you aren't used to it."

My first impulse was to say I didn't care about any of that. I just wanted to see my father. But I realized that I'd never really witnessed that kind of need before. Oh, sure, I knew a lot of people who were far from rich. But there was poor, and then there was *poor*.

"It's okay," I said at length. "I mean, you know more about it than I do, but I promise not to gawk like a tourist or flip out because my father isn't living in a split-level ranch house or something."

"Do they even have split-level ranch houses in Jerome?" he asked with a grin.

"No, but they do in Cottonwood, and that's where most of the people I went to high school with live."

Connor nodded, and then the waiter came by with our drinks and took our food orders. We both got omelettes, his the sort of thing Sydney would call "heart attack on a plate"—two kinds of cheese, bacon, sausage—while I decided to be conservative and have tomatoes and black olives and feta cheese. After the waiter left, I added, "I appreciate you trying to prepare me, Connor, and honestly, I'm not sure what to expect. I mean, just because the private investigator found someone who sounds like he's the right person—right name, right age—it doesn't mean he'll really turn out to be who we're looking for. Did Lucas say that the P.I. had actually even seen my father?"

"No. He asked around, and finally got it from one of the women who works at the trading post. Traded a couple of six-packs for the information."

At that revelation, I raised my eyebrows, and he added, "They don't sell alcohol on the reservation. From Cameron, you have to drive down to Flagstaff to buy booze, and it's actually illegal to bring it onto Navajo land. I guess the P.I. thought it was worth the risk, since they really don't have enough reservation cops to enforce the law. So the woman who told him about your father wasn't quite as much of a cheap date as you might be thinking…and Lester was taking a risk, too, although I think the worst that would have happened is that the beer would have been confiscated."

This was all news to me, but up until a few months ago, I'd never thought I'd have a chance to explore Wilcox territory, which overlapped with the land the Navajo nation called their own. Well, at least if we did end up eating at the trading post, I wouldn't have to worry about watching people chug beer and wine around me while I was stuck with water or herbal tea.

Our food came soon after that, and I focused on eating. It had been a long time since the cheese and crackers we'd eaten around eight the night before, since there wasn't much else available. Yes, we'd brought over the food from Connor's apartment and stocked the enormous Sub-Zero refrigerator in the new kitchen, but most of what we had were the components to make meals, not any ready-made dinners, and I was really not up to cooking by the time we finally stopped organizing and putting away things. Maybe it was time to revisit the policy I'd adopted from my Aunt Rachel of not having any processed food in the house. It might not have been the healthiest thing ever, but it sure was convenient.

At any rate, I shoveled in that omelette at a rate that probably wasn't very ladylike, but at least it silenced the raging monster in my stomach. Connor seemed to understand, not eating quite as quickly—and also not protesting when I snagged one of his pieces of toast, since I finished so much sooner than he did.

"Eating for three!" I chirped as he gave me the side-eye.

At that he could only shake his head. Maybe he understood that I was trying to act normal, to pretend there was nothing unusual about this pregnancy, so I wouldn't drive myself crazy wondering how this was all going to play out, whether I'd make it to the twins' first birthday, or whether I'd fall down the stairs the day after we brought them home from the hospital, or one of seemingly a hundred gruesome scenarios my mind had begun to conjure up. None of that was helping, of course, so instead I tried to think about the drive to Cameron, and the person we were going out there to see. I didn't see any way how Andre Wilcox…or Bedonie, I supposed…could be any more dreadful than his mother, but…*could* he?

"Can we stop by the house before we hit the road?" I asked Connor as the waiter came by with the check. Without even looking at it, Connor handed over his credit card, then replied,

"Sure. Want to primp?"

"I want to brush my teeth. I don't want to go meet my father with feta cheese breath."

"Understandable."

I did brush my teeth when we went back to the house…and applied some eyeshadow and eyeliner, which I hardly ever did, and then decided to change my top and slip the concho belt Connor had bought me around my hips. Before I got pregnant, I'd been wearing it on the last hole before the conchos started, but today I had to slip the buckle a few notches over. At this rate, I'd be lucky to get another month or so of wear out of it before I had to pack it away with all my non-pregnancy jeans and everything else I couldn't fit into.

Well, at least it still fits now, I told myself, and regarded my reflection solemnly. Would my father see some of himself in me—the green eyes, the cheekbones, the oval face—or would he only see my mother's straight nose and wide mouth, her arched brows, and claim that he wasn't my father at all?

"You look beautiful," Connor said from behind me, and I jumped.

"You shouldn't sneak up on a person like that."

"I wasn't sneaking. You're just not used to how this house is set up. Anyway, you're beautiful, and your father is going to be proud of you." He dropped a kiss on the top of my head—lightly, so he wouldn't mess up my hair. "Now let's get going."

I knew I couldn't delay our departure any longer, so I nodded and followed him downstairs, then out that amazing covered walkway to the garage. What would it be like in the winter, to have this sheltered path shielding us from the snow? If the property looked like fairyland now, I could only imagine what it must be like in December or January, the ground a smooth blanket of white, the trees looking as if they'd been swirled with pale frosting.

If, of course, I made it that long.

No, that was silly. Of course I'd make it to December—I was due on the 11th, although the doctor had warned me that the date wasn't set in stone, especially for a first pregnancy, and even more so for twins. But it seemed pretty clear that I'd still be around in December. January? That was an entirely different story.

Well, I'd just have to make sure the curse was broken by then.

Oh, yeah. Easy peasy.

I got in the passenger side of Connor's FJ. We could've taken my car, which also had four-wheel drive, but the Cruiser was bigger and sturdier, and Connor knew it better. If we ended up having to take rough roads, it made more sense to be in the vehicle he was most familiar with.

It was a beautiful early June day, the sun bright, not a cloud in the sky. Here in Flagstaff it was just comfortably warm, enough that you could wear sandals and a short-sleeved shirt and be just fine. Of course it was a good deal warmer back in Jerome, although I hadn't a clue about where we were headed. Maybe I should've thrown my jean jacket in the back, just to be safe, since I knew it could get pretty cold at night here, even in June.

June…why was that tickling at my brain?

Then I got it. I shifted in my seat and shot Connor an accusing glare. "I just realized it's June, and you told me once that your birthday was in June. If you let me miss it, I'll never forgive you."

He shot me a startled look, then relaxed slightly and smiled. "No worries on that front. It's the twenty-first."

Wait…*what?* "You mean your birthday is on the solstice, too?"

"Yeah."

"And you don't find that just a little bit of a coincidence?"

"Angela, pretty much *everything* to do with us is a weird coincidence. I'm kind of just rolling with it at this point."

I couldn't really argue with that. Still, it had to mean something, didn't it? That we should have been born on the two most significant dates in the sun's calendar? Something in Connor's expression told me I shouldn't push it too much, so I only said, "Well, I'm glad it's still a few weeks off yet. That gives me some time to shop."

He gave me a mock-worried glance. "Don't go overboard. Please. I really don't need anything."

"Really?" I inquired. "Nothing? Not even me wrapped in a red silk teddy?"

"Oh, okay," he said, relenting. "That might be one birthday present I'd be all right with."

There wasn't much I could do except chuckle and shake my head. Yes, I'd definitely spring the lingerie on him, but maybe some new paintbrushes, too, and his wallet was so beat-up it looked like he'd backed the FJ over it a few times. For all I knew, maybe he had.

And so I distracted myself as we jogged east on the I-40 for a few miles, then got off at Highway 89, which led all the way to Page and the Grand Canyon. Not that we intended to go that far, as Cameron was a lot closer. We passed the mall and headed north, climbing through residential neighborhoods before beginning to drop down into the dry, dusty valley where Cameron was located.

It was hotter there, too; I watched the outside temperature reading on the dashboard rise from the comfortable eighty-two it had been in Flagstaff up into the low nineties, then rise even more. By the time we were nearing the trading post, it was almost a hundred degrees outside. I really wasn't looking forward to getting out of the FJ's powerful air conditioning.

We didn't stop, though, but turned west on Highway 64, going slowly because, although the crews weren't working on Sunday, the road was carved up by what looked like a massive construction project. Out here there wasn't a lot of vegetation, except some trees clustered around the trading post and what Connor pointed out as the Little Colorado River. Off the road I saw small settlements, a few houses clustered together, all small and consisting of a single story, some of them mobile homes, a lot of them surrounded by collections of broken-down-looking vehicles.

As Connor had warned me, none of this appeared very promising. I sat quietly in the passenger seat as we drove a few miles down Highway 64. Then Connor slowed and pulled off on a dirt road that wasn't even marked.

"Good thing you looked this up on Google maps, huh?" I said.

He gave me a quick, tight smile but didn't take his eyes off the road. "I also programmed it into my GPS, just in case. But it looks like I found the turn-off okay."

On this side of the highway there was a series of steep hills with shadowy canyons in between. It looked like we were headed toward one of those, and I peered through the dust swirling up from the FJ's tires to see that we were approaching another one of those meager little compounds, this one with two one-story houses, both painted a light sand color, an outbuilding that looked as if it might have been made of adobe, the pale cylindrical shape of a propane tank, and, incongruously, an array of shiny solar panels. Up toward the canyon there seemed to be one more building, but I couldn't quite make out what it was. A stable, maybe?

There were two vehicles parked under the shade of a large oak tree, one a battered white pickup truck, the other a Jeep even older than my Aunt Rachel's, maybe twenty years or more.

My heart seemed to stutter and then resume a normal rhythm. Had that Jeep once been new and shiny, carrying my father to his assignation with my mother in California?

Only one way to find out.

Connor pulled up on the far side of the pickup and then put the FJ in park. Although we must have made a good deal of noise coming up here—and brought a conspicuous dust cloud with us—no one had emerged from either of the houses to see who was trespassing on their property. Maybe they were out, but then why were both vehicles here?

"You ready?" Connor asked, reaching up to turn off the engine.

Not really, but of course I couldn't tell him that, not after making him drive all the way out here. I swallowed. "Sure. Let's do this."

He pulled the key from the ignition, and I reached over to open the door. A blast of dry desert heat hit me, and I had to fight the urge to cough, feeling as if I'd just swallowed half the dust particles we'd stirred up as we entered the property. I did wave a hand in front of my face to ward off a few flies that descended almost as soon as I moved two feet away from the SUV.

Both of the houses looked roughly the same, paint peeling in places, a chaotic assortment of potted succulents clustering around their front doors. Off past them I caught a glimpse of what appeared to be a small garden, carefully covered with shade cloth. They'd certainly need it out here.

Since I really didn't know where I was going, I angled toward the house that was slightly closer to us. Connor followed a pace or two behind me, the sound of his hiking boots on the gravelly dirt a welcome sound. Once again I had to thank the Goddess for bringing him to me. I knew I could never have done this without him.

When we were a few yards away from the nearer house, the door to the other one opened, and a tall man stepped out onto the uncovered front stoop, lifting his hand to shield his eyes from the pitiless sun. He wore a loose white linen shirt with an old-fashioned band collar, the sleeves rolled up to his elbows, revealing sun-browned forearms. His hair was long and dark, pulled back into a ponytail, but when I got closer, I saw that his eyes weren't dark to match, but hazel, their green-gold unexpected against the warm brown of his skin.

My breath caught, and it wasn't just because of the dust and the oppressive heat. The man stood there watching me for a second or two, and then he smiled, teeth flashing.

"Come in. We've been expecting you."

The house was cramped, but cooler than I had expected, thanks to a swamp cooler going at full blast. As Connor and I entered, I saw an old, old Navajo man sitting in a worn leather chair tucked into a corner. The furniture was minimal—that chair, a cracked leather sofa, a plain wooden chair with a woven rush seat and the remnants of red paint on its surface.

I found my voice. "You were expecting us?"

Another smile, and this time I was looking for the Wilcox resemblance and saw it immediately, in the sculpted bones of his face and the strong, elegant nose. He could have probably passed for Connor's uncle…if Connor had one, of course.

"Yes. The time is here. Please sit down."

Since I didn't know what else to do, I took a seat on the leather couch, Connor following suit a second or two later, after giving the place a quick surveying glance. I could tell he was uncomfortable, and

I didn't feel much better. During all this the Navajo man sitting in the corner remained silent, watching us with bright dark eyes almost buried in wrinkles.

"So you're…." I began, and the man who'd let us in nodded and said,

"Yes, Angela, I'm Andre Bedonie—Andre Wilcox, once. And your father."

It was all so surreal, I couldn't quite decide how to respond. Maybe if he'd said, "Angela, I am your father," in a sepulchral Darth Vader voice, I could have handled it a bit better. But after all the years of not even knowing who my father was, and then not knowing whether he was alive or dead…well, I suppose I can be forgiven for staring at him blankly, then finally bursting out, "If you knew who I was—knew you had a daughter—then why did you abandon me all these years? Why didn't you come and tell me who you were?"

Instead of being taken aback by my outburst, he gave me a long, sad look, finally shaking his head. "I couldn't do that because I had to wait until you were ready."

"Ready for what?" I demanded, voice sharper than I'd intended. Dealing with all this was tough enough without factoring raging pregnancy hormones into the equation. Connor took my hand in his, not really squeezing it, but just surrounding my fingers with his, letting me know he was there.

The Navajo man spoke for the first time. His voice was deep and strong, belying his feeble appearance. "Ready to right an ancient wrong."

"What?" I asked, although I had a feeling I knew what he meant, a chill beginning somewhere low on my spine and spreading throughout my body.

"This is what we all have been waiting for," my father replied. "It's time for you to break the curse, Angela."

CHAPTER FOURTEEN

The Waiting

CONNOR'S FINGERS TIGHTENED AROUND MINE. FOR A FEW seconds I didn't reply—*couldn't* reply. At last I took in a breath, then asked, "And how do you know it's the right time…or even that I'm the person to do it?"

A short silence as my father folded his hands on the knee of his well-worn cargo pants. Clearly, he was waiting for the older man to speak. And how strange that I'd already started thinking of Andre Wilcox as my father, when I still couldn't make myself admit to any kind of real relation to my grandmother.

The old man did reply eventually, bright black eyes fixed on my face. "Many years we've waited. It is no easy thing, to wait and watch, knowing the time will come eventually but also knowing we can do nothing to hasten its coming."

"What time?" Connor asked. "What were you waiting for?" His gaze shifted to my father, then hardened. "Was it worth leaving Angela with no father all these years?"

I could see my father's mouth compress slightly, deepening the laugh lines that bracketed it, but his voice was calm as he replied, "And do you truly think the McAllisters would have accepted a Wilcox as the father of their future *prima?*"

Good question, one whose answer was most likely *hell, no*. I honestly didn't know quite what my family would've done if Andre Wilcox—or Bedonie, I supposed, since I got the impression he'd been using that name for a while—had shown up out of the blue and tried to claim me back when I was still a minor. They were less than thrilled now, but at least that particular truth hadn't come out until I had already inherited the *prima* gifts. Would they have tried to find an alternate for me after they realized I was tainted with Wilcox blood? Was that even possible? I'd never heard of the *prima*-in-waiting being passed over for another candidate once she'd been identified, but it had to have happened once or twice over the years because of sickness or an accident or some other twist of fate.

"Probably not," I admitted to my father, after a hesitation I was pretty sure everyone noticed.

"Many times I've had to counsel patience," the old man said in his slow, deep voice. "Andre knew what was at stake, and yet he chafed at the waiting, wishing he could go to you."

"With all due respect," Connor cut in, "maybe you could explain that a bit better. You expect Angela to break the curse? Why her?"

"Because it was this purpose for which she was born."

I looked from the old man—whose name I still didn't know—to my father, who was regarding me with a deep sadness in his eyes. At first I couldn't quite figure out where that sadness had come from, but then the realization seemed to bubble up from somewhere deep inside me, perhaps the well of knowledge that seemed to be joined to my growing powers.

"That's why you went to California, isn't it?" I whispered.

He nodded, the sadness now tinged with pride. "Yes. Lawrence, my great-uncle"—he nodded toward the old man, and I realized how old Lawrence must be if he truly was my great-great-uncle—"told me of what he had seen in the movements of the stars, what he'd heard in the wind. The time was coming when at last the curse could be broken, but only if I could turn away from the woman of my heart and go to the one who was destined to bear the curse-breaker.

That child needed to be born of a witch with the strength to be *prima*, even though your mother had denied what was supposed to be her own destiny."

The woman of his heart. That would be Marie Wilcox, I supposed. "So, what…you just dumped Marie and shacked up with my mother to fulfill a *prophecy?*"

A wince, but he didn't look away from me, didn't try to deny it. "I had to think of the greater good. And your mother was a lovely woman, full of her own strength and fire. I couldn't love her the way I loved Marie, but I did care for her."

Pretty words. I wasn't sure I believed them, though. How *could* I believe them?

Actually, in that moment I wasn't sure what I did believe.

"Well, this all sounds very noble," Connor said, and I could hear the edge of disbelief in his voice as well. "But…*why?* I mean, we Wilcoxes didn't do so well by the Navajo back in the day. So why should you care whether the curse continues or not?"

Lawrence's piercing dark gaze rested on Connor for a moment, and then he smiled for the first time, showing teeth so straight and white I guessed they had to be false. "The sort of question a Wilcox would ask, I suppose. So little trust among you, even now, when you are the masters of your own kingdom down there in Flagstaff." Beside me, Connor stiffened, but the old man appeared not to notice. "You ask why. I will tell you it is because the order, the balance of things, has been upset, and must be righted. Whatever happened all those years ago, it was between Nizhoni and Jeremiah Wilcox, and should have stayed between them. What she did brought dishonor upon all of us, using her gifts in such a way."

"Nizhoni?" I repeated. "That was her name—the Navajo woman Jeremiah married, I mean?"

"Yes, Nizhoni was of the Diné, although she came to live with the Wilcoxes."

"Deen-eh?" I questioned, sounding it out.

"The true name of the Navajo," my father said quietly.

My head was spinning. Maybe in time I'd be able to absorb all this, but right now I was starting to feel more than a little overloaded. "Okay," I said. "So you think I'm the one to break the curse. How exactly am I supposed to do that? I mean, Damon Wilcox failed miserably at it, and he was a hell of a lot smarter than I can ever hope to be."

"He was intelligent, but he was not wise," Lawrence replied calmly. "He thought to use power for his own ends, and showed no respect for the ways of others. He was warned, but he did not listen. I do not think you are as foolish."

Connor shifted, the leather couch creaking under his weight. Although he didn't say anything, I could tell that Lawrence's words had upset him; he released my hand and crossed his arms, a scowl pulling at his brow despite his best efforts to erase it.

"You may try to defend your brother, if you wish," the old man said, apparently missing none of this. "But you know in your heart of hearts that what I say is true." Incongruously, his eyes twinkled. "And it is also true that you will make a far better *primus* than he."

"Leaving that aside for now," I broke in, since I could tell that my great-great-uncle's remark had done nothing to mollify Connor…rather, the reverse, "could you share a little of your wisdom with me and help me understand how this curse-breaking is supposed to work?"

"You already know, even though you think you don't," the old man told me. "But the power is waking in you. Did you ever wonder why it was that you could speak with ghosts? Nizhoni is not a ghost, precisely—not in the way you might think, not like the earthbound spirits who have been your companions since you were a child. But her soul is a restless one, trapped on this plane, the strength of her ill will ensuring that the curse continues, generation after generation. You must convince her that it is time to move on. When her soul ascends, the curse will be broken, since she will no longer exist on this plane."

Convince her that it is time to move on. His words shook me, because that was exactly what I'd done with Mary Mullen. However, it was one thing to convince sweet Mary, already missing her husband and children, that it was time for her to finally go and join them, and quite another to do the same thing with this Nizhoni, whose hurt and anger and sorrow had fueled a curse that had lasted for many generations. Also, Mary had always come to me; I'd never been forced to seek her out.

"Okay," I said at length. "I suppose that makes some sense. Any idea where this Nizhoni might be hanging out so we can have a chat?"

At my question, my father shook his head, and Lawrence let out a rusty chuckle. "Angela, you know it is not that easy. She is not haunting any one place, but rather is all around us."

"Well, unless you can tell me how to pin her down somehow, I'm not sure how I'm supposed to make this work. I'm used to dealing with regular garden-variety ghosts. They all have their particular haunts, so to speak."

Apparently unperturbed, the old man responded, "Soon the time will come when the veil between the worlds will thin, and you will use the power of the longest day to give you the strength to approach her on her own ground."

By "longest day," I had to assume he meant the solstice, now less than two weeks away. I opened my mouth to confirm this, but he had already moved on, saying,

"Not only is it the solstice, but it is also a new moon. Many years will pass before such a combination comes again. In the time of the dark moon, you will meet with Nizhoni, and use your powers to convince her to move on to the next world. This is what I have seen, and what I know will come to pass."

It must be nice to have that kind of confidence. Personally, I wasn't feeling it, but I couldn't deny the potent combination of the summer solstice, with its power of the light, joining with a new moon and its shadowy strength. Would it be enough to propel me into the dark world of the spirits, to the place where Nizhoni's tormented soul had wandered all these years?

Instinctively, my hand moved to my belly, as if to protect the two tiny souls that lived within me and who depended on me for everything. What would happen to them if I failed, if somehow I remained imprisoned in the same limbo that had trapped Nizhoni for more than a century?

"Yes, you risk much," Lawrence said, apparently catching my gesture. "But the reward will be all the greater—that you will be here to see these two grow up, and the ones to come after them. No longer will the Wilcox clan experience grief at imminent death mingled with the joy of knowing a new *primus* has been born to them. It is a time for healing. You have already begun it, with this mingling of McAllister and Wilcox. Yes, the blood of those two clans was joined in you as well, but this is different. This is no secret, but an open bond between the *prima* of the McAllisters and the *primus* of the Wilcox. To you, progress may still feel slow, but sometimes it is the tiniest of breaches that bring a great dam tumbling down."

I didn't bother to ask how he knew the struggles I'd been facing, trying to convince my clan that things would be very different from now on. True, the McAllisters didn't have a seer, but I'd seen Marie's powers in this area, and Lawrence's seemed to be even greater than hers. Clearly he knew what had been happening in my own world. For all I knew, he'd been watching over me for years, relaying that information to my father so at least he'd know I was well, and thriving.

"Yeah, it's easy for you to ask her to risk her life and that of her unborn children," Connor snapped. His green eyes were narrowed, and I could tell by the way his fingers were clutching the edge of the worn leather sofa that he was doing so to keep himself from launching right off that couch and getting in the old man's face. "You get to sit on the sidelines and wait to see what happens. But you're asking too much of her."

"Of course your instinct is to protect her. This is good. But would you really prevent her from making the attempt when you know it is the only thing that will guarantee you two can grow old together? Don't let fear rule you, Connor Wilcox, as that same fear can only lead to you stopping Angela from doing this…which means you will be looking for a new mother for your children in a year or two."

"Son of a bitch—" Connor began, and actually began to rise from the sofa. I reached up to grasp his wrist, even as my father looked at me and said quietly,

"Angela, this is your choice. We can't make you do it. On the other hand, Connor can't stop you if you decide to take the risk. Just—" He paused and reached up to grasp the turquoise amulet he wore on a brown leather thong around his throat. "Just remember how much suffering this curse has already caused. Think of what we've all done to get to this point."

How could I forget, when I knew I'd be another one of those Wilcox wives gone too soon into the dark if something didn't change? Connor subsided but watched me with anguished eyes. Possibly he was in the worst situation of all, knowing that I would surely die if I didn't break the curse, but also understanding that I risked not only myself but the twins if my attempt failed. If that happened, he would lose everything.

Oh, Goddess, I moaned to myself, not knowing what I should do. I was only one person, but if I should lose the twins....

It was as if she had spoken within me. *The worst thing to do is to do nothing at all.*

But was it, truly? Even if I died, the twins would live.

But they are still only two. What of all the others to come after you, generation after generation, if this curse is not ended now?

Harsh logic, the kind I wished I could ignore. I couldn't, though. Not and live with myself. If all the signs and portents had pointed to me, pointed to this one particular day, then I had better do them proud and give Nizhoni the talking-to she so clearly deserved.

"Okay," I said. "I'll do whatever I can. But I hope you're up to giving me some coaching, because I really have no idea what I'm supposed to do."

Connor slumped beside me, face blank. I could read the defeat and worry in every line of his body, and I reached out and took his hand in mine.

"They're right," I said softly. "This has to end. We're scared. It's okay to be scared. But we can't let it stop us. Do you really want our children and our children's children to go through this all over again, generation after generation, with no end in sight?"

Raising his head, he stared at me for a long moment. We could've been the only two people in the room, although I was dimly aware of Lawrence and my father sitting still and quiet, waiting for us to work this through on our own.

"No," Connor said at last. "I don't. I want this to end."

"Do you trust me?" I asked him, an echo of a question he'd asked me so many months ago.

His fingers, strong and warm, squeezed mine in return. "Yes, I trust you."

After that the atmosphere became a little more relaxed, my father getting up from his chair to fetch us some long-overdue water, Connor leaning against the back of the couch, looking as drained as if he'd just run a marathon. But I knew he wouldn't fight me on this any longer, had realized we couldn't let this singular opportunity slip by.

As my father came back with two tall glasses incongruously decorated with strawberries—probably a thrift store or yard sale purchase—Lawrence said, "You asked for my instruction. I can assist you with this part at least, help train you in the sort of meditation that will help you when it comes time to walk the paths of the otherworld."

"Today?" I asked faintly. Even though we'd probably been here no more than half an hour, I was already feeling drained, brain and body exhausted by the revelations Lawrence and my father had just shared.

Lawrence smiled in understanding. "No, you are tired. You can come back in a day or two. We have a little time, and I can tell that your mind needs its rest."

After taking another sip of his ice water, Connor murmured to me, "So do you want to go?"

I shook my head. "Not quite yet," I replied in the same undertone. The water glass was sweating under my fingers, the humidity in here higher than it would be in a house with regular air conditioning rather than this swamp cooler. I drank as well, glad of the cold fluid coursing down my throat. Raising my voice a little, I said, "I'd really like to talk to my father in private."

It turned out that the house where we'd been talking was Lawrence's, and the other one belonged to my father. I wasn't sure if he actually owned it or not, or whether they were both technically Lawrence's and my father just lived there. Their setup probably wasn't all that formal.

After Connor gave me a quick encouraging squeeze of my hand, letting me know it was okay for me to leave him for a few minutes, my father and I emerged into the blistering heat and then went into the house that was his.

Here, too, the swamp cooler was blasting away, but the windows only had thin paper shades, so it felt much brighter than the other house. The furniture looked newer, too, although still plain—a couch and chair covered in plain brown canvas, Navajo rugs on the floor.

Actually, it reminded me of Marie's house, although much smaller, of course. Maybe those two really had been meant to be together.

Thinking of that just made me uncomfortable, though, because it reminded me of how artificial my father's relationship with my mother actually had been. He'd said he'd come to care for her, but how much of that feeling was good old-fashioned guilt?

I paused, standing in the middle of the living room.

"Some more water?" my father asked.

"No, thanks." Now that we were alone together, I began to wonder if this had been such a good idea. The tension between us seemed thick enough that it lay as heavy as the heat outside on my skin. I pulled in a breath, then said, "What did you fight about?"

"Excuse me?"

Since I'd asked the question out of nowhere, I supposed his look of bewilderment was understandable. "We talked with Linda Sanderson, the woman who lived next door to you in Newport Beach back when you were…with my mother. She said you two had a huge fight a few days before I was born, and that you drove off and didn't come back. So what was the fight about?"

He pushed up his sleeves, a nervous gesture, since they weren't in any danger of sliding back down past his elbows. "Linda. I hadn't thought about her in years. She's still in the same house?"

"Yes. I got the address of the place you and my mother were renting from my birth certificate. Connor and I drove out there, looking for answers."

Like me, my father was sort of hovering in the middle of the room, ignoring the couches and chair as if they weren't even there. At last he said, "We fought because your mother found out about Marie."

"So my mother didn't know anything? Who did she think you were?" *What lies did you tell her?* was my unspoken question, and from the twist of my father's mouth, I got the impression he'd picked up on the unvoiced query loud and clear.

"She thought I was one of the Santiagos."

"Because that's what you told her."

"Yes."

"And none of the real Santiagos figured out that there was a Wilcox living in their midst?"

The hazel eyes, so similar in shape to my own, were full of anguish. "Things are bad now in California, but they were bad then, too. So many witches and warlocks coming there without permission, and the Santiagos trying to police them all—well, let's just say I slipped in under the radar. Of course I knew better than to use my powers, do anything to attract attention. Lawrence had seen your mother going to Newport Beach, and that's where I found her. She was standing on the sand, watching the sunset. Most of the other girls on the beach were wearing bikinis or tank tops and shorts, but Sonya, she had on a pale blue sundress and her hair was blowing in the breeze." He paused then, obviously attempting to choose the right words. "I guess I hadn't expected her to be that pretty."

So she had been, at least from the few photos I'd seen of her. Had he looked at her, that day on the beach so long ago, and thought perhaps the duty he'd been tasked with carrying out wouldn't be quite as bad as he feared?

"So you…hooked up."

A frown touched his mouth. "Well, that's not what people called it back then, but…yes. Not that she needed much persuading. It was as if she'd gone there determined to lose her virginity at the earliest opportunity."

As much as I really didn't want to think that about my mother, I knew it was only the truth. The best way to avoid bonding with her consort and becoming *prima* was to throw away that virginity as soon as she could. No one in Jerome or Cottonwood or Clarkdale would have touched her, knowing what was at stake, but a handsome stranger she met on a beach in California was a completely different story.

"And so...."

"And so...we were together. She was staying in a little motel down on the peninsula. We spent a few weeks there, and then we thought we'd try renting a house together."

"Her idea or yours?" I asked, knowing the question had come out more sharply than I'd intended.

He didn't blink. "Mine. To be honest, I don't think she had a real plan. She'd gotten away, gotten out, and made damn sure she wouldn't be the McAllisters' newest *prima*. Maybe in her head she'd thought she would just go back to Jerome after that. But she was having fun in Newport and decided she might as well stay for a while. And then...." The words died away, but I knew what he'd been about to say.

"Then she got pregnant."

"Yes. And we were together, and I didn't see that changing anytime soon. Lawrence hadn't been all that clear on exactly how everything was supposed to pan out, whether I was supposed to stay with Sonya, be with her to raise our child or what, so I had to wait and see how things developed. We were doing pretty well, until the argument."

"Yeah, that." I hooked my thumbs in my belt and shifted my weight to one leg, considering him. My father's expression was still troubled, although that could have simply been from dredging up memories he would rather have forgotten. "How did she find out? I mean, obviously you kept things secret for a good chunk of time, considering you had that blow-out only a few days before I was born."

"I got sloppy." He didn't exactly sigh, but his lips parted slightly, the slightest gust of breath escaping them. "It was right before Yule, of course, right before the holidays. I did care about your mother, but I'd loved Marie since I was barely fifteen years old. I'd brought a picture of her with me, one I kept hidden in my wallet. Your mother wasn't the nosy type, so it wasn't as if she was snooping or anything like that. But I'd pulled out the picture to look at it, wondering what Marie would be doing back in Flagstaff, with the two of us so far apart for the holidays, and your mother walked into the bedroom and saw me holding it. Naturally she wanted to know who it was. I tried to shrug it off, say it was a cousin—which wasn't even a lie, of course—but she could tell I wasn't telling the whole truth. Funny how she saw through that one, when I'd managed to convince her I was a Santiago for all those months."

"So she never knew you were a Wilcox?"

"No. She thought I'd been cheating on her. I tried to explain that I hadn't seen Marie for almost a year, but she didn't believe me, said if that were really true, then I wouldn't be carrying around another woman's picture. And the more I tried to talk to her, the more upset she got. She didn't want to listen. It almost felt as if she wanted an excuse to get rid of me."

"Why would she feel that way?" I asked, sending him an accusing glance. Not that I really suspected him of doing anything worse than lying to her about who he was, but I had a hard time imagining a woman nine months pregnant who'd want to be left alone to have her baby by herself. Then again, my relationship with Connor was very different from whatever it was that my mother and Andre Wilcox had shared. Their entire history together was built on lies. Maybe Connor's and my relationship had started out that way, but things had changed dramatically for us. I knew he would never lie to me again. I trusted him implicitly.

After a heavy pause, my father said, "I don't know what she was thinking. Maybe she was tired of being out in California and wanted to go home to her family, and the only way she could think of to do that was without me. I think maybe she was scared about raising a child so far away from the support structure she knew. She did talk about her sister Rachel from time to time, almost as if she wished her sister was around so she could help with the baby and Sonya could get back to what she was best at—partying and having fun." He stopped himself there, as if he were about to say more but didn't want to be seen as maligning my mother to my face.

It wasn't anything I hadn't heard before, though. "Don't worry," I told him. "My Aunt Rachel has made it pretty clear what she thought of her my mother's character flaws. And it's not as if I'm going to nominate for sainthood someone who went out drinking only a few months after her baby was born and managed to get herself killed because she was riding on the back of a Harley with no helmet."

"I am very sorry about that," my father said quietly. "When Lawrence told me what happened, I wanted to go to Jerome, go fetch you and bring you back here, but he said that wasn't right, that you would be the next *prima*, and as much as it hurt, I had to leave you to be raised by your McAllister relatives."

He might have lied to my mother, but I could tell he wasn't lying now. "And so…you just stayed out here, and took your grandmother's family name? You never went back to Flagstaff?"

"Never. What I had done needed to be hidden from both the McAllister and Wilcox clans. I did send one note to my mother, so she would know I wasn't dead…too." The last word was tacked on, and I could tell how much it still bothered him that he hadn't been there when his father had passed away, and had to stand by and do nothing while his mother turned her back on that part of her past, repudiating the witch clan her husband had come from.

"So…what have you been doing all this time?" *Besides waiting, that is….*

He gestured for me to follow him, and we left the living room and went down a short hallway. Through one open door I spied what must have been his bedroom, with a full-size bed and one dresser, and not much else. But our destination was the other bedroom, now turned into a workshop. I recognized the assortment of pliers on the large table, and the boxes of polished stones—mostly turquoise, with some coral and sugilite and lapis mixed in, and the long bands of silver and copper used for bezels in cabochon settings. There were also chunks of raw stones, which meant he probably did his own gem-cutting as well. His jewelry-making equipment was more elaborate than mine, though, since I could see he also had a kiln for lost-wax casting, something I'd never attempted. On the shelf were various carvings he'd done for ring and pendant settings; a few half-finished pieces still sat in the middle of the worktable, along with a ring that looked ready to be sold.

"You make jewelry?" I asked, trying not to sound too flabbergasted. After all, what were the odds that both my father and I would end up with the same vocation? "That's amazing. I mean, I make jewelry, too."

"I know," he said.

Of course he did. He knew a good deal about me, whereas I knew hardly anything about him. But I was learning, and however I might fault him for staying away, no matter what any prophecy might say, I had to admit that he'd been very honest with me today, even when he knew some of the things he'd be telling me would put him in a bad light.

"Anyway, this was the trade I took up. I have some pieces down at the trading post, and the rest goes to the co-ops that run the roadside stands. It hasn't made us rich, but the tourists like Navajo jewelry. They don't need to know that I'm only a quarter Navajo."

"It's very beautiful," I said. I took a few steps over to the table and then picked up the ring that sat there, a piece of beautiful pure blue Sleeping Beauty turquoise with a fine rope bezel and detailed flowers and leaves encircling the entire piece.

"It's yours," he said, coming to me and closing my fingers around the ring.

"Oh, no, I couldn't—"

"Angela," he said quietly, and something in his tone made me stop and look up at him. His gaze was earnest, pleading. "I've done so little for you. Please, let me do this."

My protests died on my lips. I nodded, and he let go of my hand, watching as I slipped the ring onto my middle finger. "Thank you."

He smiled then, just a little, a smile that slipped away as he said, "I suppose we should go back so your fiancé doesn't think you've completely abandoned him."

"You're probably right."

So we headed back to Lawrence's house, where Connor looked very relieved to see us. He shot a questioning look in my direction and I nodded slightly, indicating that I'd gotten some answers, if not all.

"Come back the day after tomorrow, and we'll begin our work then," Lawrence told me.

Although I knew it was important to be as prepared for the confrontation with Nizhoni as I possibly could, I wasn't really looking forward to coming back out here, partly because I wasn't sure what this "work" would really entail, and partly because I had a new house full of boxes that weren't going to unpack themselves.

Now, there would be another handy magical skill to have.

But I promised I would be back on Tuesday afternoon, and after that Connor and I said our goodbyes and went back to the car. It wasn't until we'd gone back through Cameron and were heading south on 89 toward Flagstaff that he asked,

"So, what do you think?"

I think my head's beginning to hurt. But I said, "I think they're telling us the truth. And my father was pretty honest about what really happened with my mother. I'm not saying I like it—finding out your father never loved your mother and was only with her to fulfill some sort of prophecy isn't exactly fun. But my not liking it isn't the same thing as not believing them. Because I do."

Connor was silent for a bit, eyes fixed on the road. Late afternoon sunlight slanted through the car, bringing out unexpected glints of copper and mahogany in his dark hair. Finally he spoke. "I get that feeling, too. And I kind of have to respect someone who's patient enough to wait twenty-plus years for his plans to pan out. But still…." He lifted his right hand from the steering wheel and rested it lightly on my thigh, as if to reassure himself that I really was sitting there next to him. "I'd be lying if I said I wasn't scared about what's coming next."

"I know," I told him. "I don't even want to think about it. But somehow, knowing how patient they've been about waiting for the correct time to arrive, for me to grow up and be ready…well, in an odd way it actually helps. I'm not going to let them down…or us, either."

His fingers tightened on my thigh, squeezing slightly. Then we went over a jarring bump, and he returned his hand to the steering wheel.

As I watched him, something struck me. "But you want to know what's really strange?"

"Beyond what's already happened?" he asked, mouth curling a bit.

"Yeah, beyond all that." I mentally ran through the conversations with my father, both the one he and I shared in private, and what we'd discussed at Lawrence's house. "In that whole time, my father didn't ask one question about Marie. Not about where she was, or what she was doing. Doesn't that seem a bit odd?"

Connor shrugged. "Maybe he wasn't sure how you would react to that kind of question, so he decided to leave it alone for now."

Possibly, but I couldn't shake the feeling that there was more to it than that.

CHAPTER FIFTEEN

The Waiting

I REALIZED WHEN WE WERE HALFWAY HOME THAT NEITHER my father nor Lawrence had asked for our phone numbers, or offered theirs. Maybe they didn't have phones. Crazy as that sounded to me, I'd noticed that I had basically zero cell reception out at the house, and it didn't seem to me as if they were doing well enough financially to afford a satellite phone. I asked Connor about it, and he told me quite a few people on the reservation used CB radios to keep in touch, since they were cheap and reliable.

So, even if I'd wanted to change my mind about going back out there on Tuesday, there wasn't any way to back out politely. And actually, there wasn't as much work to be done at the new house as my brain had manufactured. By the time Monday evening rolled around, we were fairly settled. I almost wished we weren't, because at least unpacking the kitchen and the bedroom stuff meant I was occupied with figuring out where things should go, and therefore not brooding over what this training with Lawrence might entail.

I was relieved to see that by Tuesday it had cooled down a bit, which meant the temperature might not be past the century mark out at the compound where my father lived. We headed out after lunch, Connor bringing the iPad with him, since he'd gotten the distinct impression he was going to be doing a lot of sitting around while Lawrence worked with me. Of course there was no Internet out there, but you didn't need connectivity to read a book or play a game locally.

I was wearing the ring my father had given me, proudly displacing the much plainer turquoise piece I'd bought back in high school. On my other hand glittered Connor's diamond. Looking at them, I thought of how they represented both my past and my future.

And I was going to make damn sure that future extended farther than just another year.

Both Lawrence and my father came out to greet us this time, the two of them looking about the same as when we'd first met them, although today my father's shirt was a sand color that almost matched the house, the front streaked with rusty stains that

I guessed were from the jeweler's rouge he used to polish his sterling silver pieces. They guided us back to Lawrence's house, where we all sat down once more.

"It is simpler than you might think," he told me after my father had once again brought us water. "All of us have a stillness at our center, but most have forgotten how to find it. Once you locate it, always remember what it feels like, since that calm, that quiet, is what grounds you to who you are, where you have come from. It is easy to get lost in the otherworld if you don't remember to hold on to yourself."

"Are we—are we traveling to the otherworld today?" I asked, wishing my voice didn't sound so tight, so frightened.

Chuckling, he shook his head. "No, I will not ask that of you on your first day. Now it is only about meditation. You are afraid, but there is nothing to fear. You, Angela, know more than most people that this world is one of many, and passing from it is nothing more than walking from one room to another. For now, think on these words:

"May it be beautiful
before me.
May it be beautiful
behind me.
May it be beautiful

All around me.
In beauty
It is finished;
In beauty
It is finished."

He fell silent, watching me. Then he asked, "Do you understand?"

I wasn't sure I did, not really. But then I thought of the green line of the cottonwoods along the line of the Verde River, and the way the pale golden grass waved in the summertime. I thought of the cool dark shapes of the pines surrounding Flagstaff, and the glint of snow on the San Francisco Peaks, and the way the lightning would flash against bruise-colored clouds in monsoon season. The warmth in Connor's eyes, and the bright gilded fall of Sydney's hair. Everything around me was beautiful, if I just stopped to truly look at it. That beauty was complete and perfect, and the thing that would anchor me here, in this life.

"I think so," I said at last, and he gave me an approving nod.

"This is good. Then close your eyes, and let yourself merely be, here, on this couch. Think of who you are, and where you are. Think of the world surrounding you, and be one with it."

Feeling more than a little self-conscious, I closed my eyes and folded my hands in my lap. At first I was acutely aware of Connor sitting on the couch a scant foot away from me, the hum of the evaporative cooler, the faint aromatic tinge to the air, something familiar. Sage, probably, as if they regularly smudged the house to keep it clear of unfriendly influences. A little farther off I sensed the presences of Lawrence and my father, both of them sitting quietly, their breathing calm, controlled. Maybe they were meditating along with me.

Something in me wanted to push beyond them, beyond the four walls of the cramped little house. It was as if I felt myself rising, seeing spread below me the small stucco structures the two men called home, the dilapidated garage, the equally shabby stable and small corral where a bored-looking pinto horse grazed. Even beyond that, and my eyes took in the sere golden undulations of the landscape, the dark gash a few miles off where the Little Colorado River gorge began, the cluster of deep green trees and buildings at the trading post.

Within me I felt a push to rise even higher, but somehow I knew now was not the time. It was enough that I'd been able to do this, to leave my physical self behind and take in the world through an eagle's eyes. Now I needed to return to myself, and so I thought of me, of Angela, sitting there on the shabby couch in her new jeans that were already starting to feel too tight, in the sleeveless embroidered blouse, dark hair pulled back in a ponytail because of the heat, pink polish on her toes starting to chip. All that and so much more was myself, and so I slipped into my body the way I might slip into my oldest and softest beat-up sweatshirt on a cold winter's night.

I opened my eyes, and saw Connor staring at me in wonder, and Lawrence and my father watching me with quiet approval on their faces. Oddly, I felt stiff and sore, as if I'd been sitting in one position for far longer than the five or so minutes I'd just spent in meditation.

"Very good," said Lawrence, even as Connor shook his head and asked,

"Where did you go?"

"Go?" I repeated, putting one finger to my temple, where I felt a slight twinge. "Up—and out, I guess. It was weird. Definitely an out-of-body sort of thing. But I'll have to work on staying in it longer next time."

"Longer?" he demanded. "You were out of it for almost forty-five minutes!"

And then I noticed the iPad lying next to him, screen still showing the Kindle app. I had no recollection of him pulling out the device. Unbelieving, I stared at Connor for a few seconds, then transferred my gaze to Lawrence, who inclined his head slightly.

"This is true," he said, not sounding surprised at all. "I was not sure that you would be able to make such a journey on your first try, but it seems you have a natural talent for this sort of travel. It is good. It will be easier for you when the time comes."

"And you didn't have any trouble getting back?" my father asked.

"No," I said, recalling how I had seen myself clearly, down to the chipped polish on my toes. "It was easy, like slipping into an old comfy sweater or something."

"That is kind of amazing," he said. "When I first tried this sort of thing, I couldn't manage that until I'd been doing it for several weeks. Good thing Lawrence was patient."

"There was no rush. I knew you would work it out eventually." Lawrence gestured toward my neglected glass of water. "But drink, because this sort of travel can be taxing on the body, even if you don't feel it immediately."

"There won't any bad side effects, though, will there?" Connor asked, worry clear in his voice.

My father gave him an understanding smile. "Just a bit of dehydration. That's all."

I hadn't noticed anything up until they mentioned it, but now I did feel extremely thirsty. Reaching over, I plucked the glass from where it sat on the scarred wooden tabletop and drained the contents in one long swallow. "I'm fine, Connor," I said once I was finished. "Just thirsty. No big deal."

"You say it was no big deal, but you were in basically a trance for almost an hour—"

"Not a trance," Lawrence cut in. "A deep meditation. It is important for Angela to learn how to follow where her spirit walks, to let it lead her back to herself. She seems to have a talent for it, which can only help her when she goes to seek Nizhoni."

Connor still looked troubled, but he didn't offer any further arguments.

"So what now?" I asked. "Should I try again?"

"No, once is enough for now. It isn't good for you to over-tire yourself. You can come back on Thursday and try again, after giving yourself some time to rest."

I knew that wasn't going to work. Things had been hectic and crazy the past few days, but not so crazy that I'd forgotten my next appointment at the ob-gyn was on Thursday afternoon. I explained, and Lawrence said, "Then come on Friday. I would not ask you to miss such an important appointment."

Relieved that he wasn't going to push on that point, I said, "Is there anything else I should do between now and then?"

"You can meditate, as you have done here, but make sure to do it with Connor near you. That way, he can wake you from the meditation if for some reason you don't find it as easy to return as you did today."

"No worries," Connor said. "I'll be standing by, ready to stick a pin into her if necessary."

I shot him a pained glance, but to my surprise, Lawrence chuckled slightly, not offended at all. "A pin would work," he said, eyes twinkling, though his tone was serious. "But let's hope it will not come to that."

We got up from the couch then. I stumbled, feeling oddly lightheaded, and at once Connor reached out and took my hand to steady me. "You okay?" he murmured.

"I'm fine," I told him. "Just sitting in one place for too long."

"The dizziness will pass," my father said. "But let Connor help you out to the car to be safe."

That remark made Connor frown a little, although he didn't say anything. I thanked Lawrence for helping me with the meditation, and gave my father a quick, awkward hug before Connor and I went out to the car and headed for home. All in all, I thought it had gone very well, strange dizziness or no, but I could tell Connor wasn't feeling quite so optimistic.

"I'm not sure if I like it," he told me, almost as soon as I shut the car door.

"I'm fine," I said. "I was sitting motionless in one place for almost an hour. I don't think it's so strange that I felt a little lightheaded. It's gone now."

"You're sure?"

"I'm positive." And it was no more than truth. I did feel fine…now. Of course, I also knew that even if I didn't feel fine, I'd still keep practicing the meditation. I needed to be prepared.

After all, I really didn't have a choice.

The doctor's appointment went just fine, though, with Dr. Ruiz saying that everything was moving along right on schedule. The babies' hearts were beating nice and strong, and I'd put on seven pounds, which relieved her somewhat. "Make sure you keep that up," she told me. "Not that I want you to sit down and eat a pint of ice cream at a time, but don't worry about having too many carbs or whatever."

I could tell she thought I must have been someone who watched her weight pretty carefully, considering how slender I'd been when I got pregnant. Maybe my comment about having a fast metabolism hadn't really sunk in. Anyway, I was relieved that at least I had begun to gain some weight, and everything else seemed fine, so that relieved some of my worry. Some.

They made my next appointment for June 30th, and Connor and I exchanged a significant glance. Either everything would be settled by then…or it wouldn't. Hard to believe that the solstice was now only ten days away.

We didn't go back to the house immediately, but rather headed over to the apartment. Connor's cousin Mason was interested in taking it over, as the lease on her own loft downtown was about to end. She'd just been accepted into a master's program at Northern Pines and preferred to stay in the downtown area if she could swing it, and Connor and I both thought she'd be a great tenant.

"At least you wouldn't have to worry about her having blow-out frat parties here the way you might with some of your guy cousins," I'd remarked upon hearing she was interested in the place, and Connor agreed.

"Yeah, some of my cousins would have a great time trashing this place…or at least they would if they weren't worried about pissing off the *primus*," he said. "But I'm going to be a big old sexist and say that I'd much rather have a woman renting the apartment, so if Mason thinks it'll work for her, then it's hers."

Judging by the expression on her face as she looked the apartment over, I got the feeling she thought it would definitely "work for her."

"And the timing is perfect, because my current lease will be up on July 1st, and I haven't had any luck finding a place I like."

"Great," Connor said. "We've already gotten most of our stuff out of here, but we'll make sure it's cleared out, and I'll have my cleaning crew come in to really get into the corners."

"It's perfect," she replied, dark eyes shining as she looked around again. "So much nicer than where I am now."

"And the rent's okay?" he asked. He'd told me he felt funny charging anything at all, but I'd said he should ask for some kind of rent, even if doing so went against his familial instincts. Paying for something tended to make people take better care of it.

Mason laughed. "Are you kidding? You should be charging double what you're asking, and you know it. Not that I'm going to argue," she added hastily.

"No worries." He glanced over at me, then said, "Since we're here, I'm going to run next door and grab a few more supplies. Just give me a couple of minutes."

"Sure," I replied. Although he'd cleared out a lot of his stuff from the studio next door, there were always odds and ends left over. Since we were here anyway, it made sense for him to get what he could.

He went out, and Mason wandered into the kitchen, obviously eyeing the cupboard space. Then she let out a contented little sigh. "I cannot believe I'm lucky enough to get this place."

"I'm glad it could all work out," I said sincerely.

"Same for you two," she said. "I was a little worried for a while there, but it looks like you're all okay now." She ended the comment on the slightest of questioning notes, as if she wanted to make sure.

"Definitely okay," I told her with a smile, then lifted my left hand and flashed the diamond at her. "Actually, more than okay."

"Oh, wow!" she exclaimed, and emerged from the kitchen so she could give me a hug. "Why haven't you two announced it?"

"Well, things have been busy with the house and...everything," I finished, waving one hand vaguely in the air. No one knew about our meetings with Lawrence and Andre, and I wanted to keep it that way. If I succeeded and the curse was broken, well, then we'd tell everyone what we'd been up to. But I didn't see the point in getting everyone's hopes up beforehand.

"I'm really happy for you," Mason said, but then her smile wavered a bit, compelling me to ask,

"What is it?"

"Oh, nothing," she replied. Then she bit her lip, glanced away from me, and added, "I've just been getting some flak from my parents. They don't see the point in me getting my master's degree when all I'm going to do is end up staying here in Flag and getting married eventually."

She sounded so unimpressed by the prospect that I had to inquire, "You don't want to get married someday?" To be honest, she hadn't talked much about guys, but then again, when she and Carla and I had gotten together for coffee or whatever, the conversation hadn't really veered in that direction. But maybe she was into girls.

"Oh, someday," she said. "But Carla just got engaged—"

"Did she? I didn't hear about that."

"Well, you and Connor have had other things going on, so that's probably why Carla hasn't said anything. And it's not that I'm against the idea in principle, it's just…." She sighed, shaking her head. "It's one thing if you're fated for one another or something interesting like that. But in my case it's marrying some cousin I've known my whole life, which isn't all that romantic, you know? Or finding a civilian I think'll be open-minded enough to deal with marrying into a witch clan, which isn't as easy as it sounds. So I figured if I stayed in school and got my master's, it would put off the evil day for a few more years."

"There's no law that says you have to get married," I said gently. "I mean, it's not as if the Wilcox clan is going to die out if you decide to stay single."

She let out a reluctant laugh. "True that. No, I don't really like the idea of spending my life alone, but I also want to *do* something with it. That's partly why I'm getting my master's in education—I'd really like to go on the reservation and make a difference, assist in setting up new programs and things to help improve the situation there."

"Wow," I said, impressed. This was a side of Mason I hadn't seen before. Then again, we'd never really had a chance to talk alone like this. Before, it had always been Carla and Mason and me, and when Carla was around, the conversation tended to be a lot more gossipy. "I think that sounds incredible."

"I'm glad someone thinks so," she responded, voice glum. Then she seemed to shake it off, adding, "At least my parents haven't said I can't get my master's, or take this apartment. Yeah, I'm an adult, but you know how it is in a clan."

Did I ever. I was still battling the weight of unmet expectations from the McAllisters. Some days it seemed as if I could feel their disapproval radiating all the way from Jerome. But I hadn't really chosen this path, it had chosen me, and now all I could do was attempt to walk it as best I could.

"Well, if anyone tries to give you crap, just tell them the *primus* supports you fully in what you're doing," I said, just as Connor walked back in, carrying two overloaded Sprouts canvas shopping bags.

"What am I supporting?" he asked.

"Your cousin in going to school and getting her master's and not marrying some random Wilcox cousin just because her parents expect it of her."

"Oh," he said, nodding in understanding, "I fully support that. If they give you any crap, tell 'em to come talk to me."

She grinned, the shadows gone from her face. "I definitely will. Thanks for everything."

We both murmured words to the effect that it was nothing, but I could tell Mason didn't think it was nothing. She ducked out after that, telling Connor to be in touch when he was ready to hand over the keys. After she was gone, he said, eyes glinting,

"It's good to be the king."

"'King'?" I inquired, lifting an eyebrow. "Getting a little full of yourself, aren't you, Mr. *Primus*?"

"Nah. I didn't want to be *primus*, and, despite what Lawrence might say, I don't really know how good I am at it, but if putting my stamp of approval on Mason's college plans will get her parents to back off, I'm okay with swinging my dick around a little bit."

"Hmm," I said, and pursed my lips. "I say we go home so you can show me how this whole dick-swinging thing works."

"Deal," he replied immediately. "Let's get out of here."

"Oh, so now we're in a hurry?"

"Damn straight. Too bad teleportation isn't in my *primus* bag of tricks."

"Nor mine," I said with some regret. "So I guess we'll just have to do this the old-fashioned way and drive."

"Good thing the house is only fifteen minutes away."

Laughing, we went out, Connor locking the door behind us. As he did so, I couldn't help feeling a tiny bit sad. Yes, we had a new home to share, and I loved it already. But the apartment had felt like home for a while, too, and now we were handing it over to someone else.

I'd just have to hope she would be as happy there as Connor and I had been.

The days slipped by, seeming to move more quickly of their own accord, although I would have been more than happy to have them slow down, give me more time. I practiced my meditations at home, Connor at my side. He would hold my hand, and for some reason his touch would make it easier for me to use that strange power to lift myself out and away from my body.

I experienced the thrill of rising above myself, looking down at the dark pine trees from high above, seeing the smooth, narrow roads that twisted through the development, the sparkle of the man-made lakes at the country club. Each time it got a little easier, and I felt a little less drained as I returned to my body. Just three days before the solstice, we drove back out to the shabby little compound in Navajo territory, this time so Lawrence could show me the next step—how to cast my consciousness, now free from my body, into the world of the spirits.

"You know there is nothing to fear," he told me, every line and hollow in his face etched by the flickering candles inside the house. This time we'd come at night, as he'd instructed, telling us that this sort of work was easier in the quiet, cool hours of the evening.

Well, "cool" being a relative term. Yes, the sun had gone down and the temperature dropped a bit, but it still had to be hovering around ninety outside.

"You have spoken with spirits, and know they mean no harm, even the ones who linger here out of fear or anger or resentment," he went on. "So you may walk amongst them without doubt or worry. But it is easy to get lost there, and so you must always remember your body, waiting here for you. Remember as well that those who love you also wait for you here, and so do not linger."

So much for not worrying. But since I certainly couldn't turn back now, I only nodded, Connor's hand lying on top of mine, just a gentle pressure to show that he was there. His presence wasn't enough to distract me, but it was a solid reminder that I was not a being of spirit and shadow, but a young woman who needed to return to her body before too much time had elapsed.

When Lawrence spoke again, his voice was barely above a whisper. "It is time."

I breathed in deeply—not a gasp, but a full, rich breath that seemed to fill my lungs all the way down to the very bottom of my ribcage. Again I was lifting away, leaving the house and its occupants behind, but this time I had a destination. I floated over the dark landscape, the only points of light the highway and the trading post, coming ever closer. Lawrence had suggested that I go there, as it was more than a hundred years old and had its own attendant spirits.

Moving silently as a ghost myself, I drifted toward the cluster of buildings. The parking lot was empty, save for a few cars belonging to people staying at the motel there; it was now a little after ten o'clock, and everything else was closed up for the night. Not that it mattered. I hadn't come here in pursuit of the living.

There was a garden behind one of the buildings, a little oasis shadowed under the half-light of a waning crescent moon. I knew in a few days there would be no moon at all, and although I had no real body, still I shivered.

Dark shapes moved in the garden, then paused on one of the paths, staring up at me. Again a chill went through me, but I forced myself to keep going, to meet them. This felt very different from chatting up Maisie, with her blonde curls and big blue eyes.

But as I drew closer, I could see the shapes were those of a man and woman. Probably a mother and son, as she was much older than he. They watched me with hostile dark eyes as I drifted along the pathway to meet them.

"You are not supposed to be here," the woman said, her English halting but clear enough. "Your world is that of the living."

"True," I said, glad I could agree with her on that point. "But it's necessary that I come here to the world of the spirits. I'm looking for a woman named Nizhoni."

At that remark, the man and woman looked at one another, and I thought I heard the man chuckle. However, his face was sober enough as he replied, "That is a common name among the Diné. But I know of no one with that name who lingers here with us."

Damn. I should've known it wouldn't be that easy. Anyway, Lawrence had said Nizhoni was not an ordinary spirit, tied to one place. Her energy was more powerful, and yet more diffuse, than that. Anyway, if I recalled my history correctly, this place had been built about forty years after she laid down her curse and died. I'd never found out where she was buried, but I assumed it was somewhere in Flagstaff.

"She would not be here," I said slowly. "Her people might have come from around here, but I know she passed from this world down in Flagstaff. I'd just hoped that maybe you would have heard of her. She was taken away from here, married to a man named Jeremiah Wilcox."

The man and woman exchanged an unreadable look, although something in their stance seemed to indicate fear, mixed with disgust. "Ah," the woman said at last. "Her people did come from farther up the river, beyond the trading post. But she is not here, and we would not want her."

Can't say as I blame you, I thought. "But if she is not here, do you know where she might be?"

The woman didn't reply, but the man lifted his head, looking southward. "Sometimes an ill will blows with the south wind," he said, somewhat cryptically.

"So she's down toward Flagstaff?"

Again they shared an inscrutable glance. "You should not be here. This is not your place," the woman said, and although she made no movement, it was as if I felt an invisible hand shoving against my chest, pushing me backward.

I gasped, not stumbling exactly, but somehow I was now yards away from them, moving faster and faster, the trading post dropping away beneath me. I felt the pull of my body like the weight of a dead star, sucking me downward, and the next thing I knew, I was blinking my eyes open, clutching at Connor's hand.

"What's the matter?" he said at once. "Are you okay?"

After pulling in a ragged breath, I made myself nod. "Yes, I'm fine. I guess I just didn't expect to meet resistance like that."

"Resistance?" he asked, his tone sharp. "What kind of resistance?"

I glanced across the room to where Lawrence sat, watching me carefully. Next to him, my father looked on, his expression tense even in the dim flickering light of the candles, but he didn't say anything.

"You met the two at the trading post," Lawrence commented finally. It wasn't a question.

"I did. They weren't exactly what you'd call friendly."

"Why should they be? You cannot go into the world of the spirits and expect them all to welcome you, or help you. Did they do anything to hurt you?" His voice was mild, almost uninterested.

"No, they didn't hurt me," I replied. "But they made it pretty clear they didn't like my question."

"And what was that?"

"Where to find Nizhoni."

He laughed a little, perhaps at my naïveté. "Ah, that is something I doubt they would tell you, even if they knew the answer. But they died many years after she did, when her name had become only an echo of malice."

"Well, they did tell me one thing," I said, a little rankled by his amusement. "They made it pretty clear that she wasn't to be found anywhere around here."

"Indeed? Because I've already said she's not to be found anywhere at all."

"Maybe. But the man did tell me that an ill wind sometimes blows from the south, by which I assume he must mean Flagstaff. When…when the time comes, it seems logical to try there first."

"It is possible. Perhaps we should start from there, then, rather than here."

My father looked alarmed. "You mean…go to Flagstaff?"

"You must face your past sometime," Lawrence told him. "The time for hiding will soon be over."

I could tell my father didn't like the sound of that at all, but he only nodded, face tight and still. What he was expecting from returning to his hometown, I wasn't sure. After all, the person who had the most reason to tell him off was gone. Lucas had just texted

Connor the day before to say he'd gone by to water her garden, and still no sign of Marie.

Connor, on the other hand, appeared distinctly relieved that my perilous journey would at least have its starting point on his home turf. "From the house?" he asked.

Lawrence shook his head. "No. It is too new. We'll go to your apartment."

How he knew about the apartment, I didn't know. However, it was clear enough that Lawrence knew a good deal he probably shouldn't. At the moment, I was just glad that we hadn't yet handed the keys over to Mason.

And, like Connor, I was relieved I wouldn't have to drive all the way out here on the solstice. It would happen at a little past ten o'clock at night three days from now, and blundering around in the darkness of the spirit world seemed infinitely preferable if that journey could be initiated on familiar territory.

"Okay, it's a plan," I said, trying to sound casual and probably not doing a very good job of it. "So we'll all meet there on Saturday night, say, around nine?"

Lawrence's expression told me he wasn't fooled by my tone. Luckily, all he did was incline his head ever so slightly, then reply, "We will be there."

And that, it seemed, was that.

CHAPTER SIXTEEN

Solstice

ALTHOUGH IN THE INTERVENING DAYS I ATTEMPTED TO DO my out-of-body meditations starting from the apartment, I never got any hint that this Nizhoni was anywhere around Flagstaff. I tried to not let myself be discouraged, but it seemed I should have been able to feel something...*anything*.

But I didn't, although I did make the acquaintance of two rather amusing bootleggers who'd shot each other in the middle of Leroux Street back in 1925. They didn't seem to hold a grudge, though. Maybe spending eternity in one another's company had mellowed them somewhat.

"You're sure you've never seen a young Navajo woman around these parts?" I asked them desperately on Friday night, knowing I was running out of options.

"Nope," said the taller of the two spirits, whose name was Isaac Ford. He scratched his thinning hair. "No Injuns."

I winced and tried to remind myself that racial sensitivity probably wasn't too much of a thing in 1920s Flagstaff.

"Me, neither," said the short, round one, who called himself Clay Wilkins. "I'd remember." He not-quite leered at me. "We don't get enough pretty girls that we won't remember the ones we do see."

Of that I had little doubt. He seemed like just the sort of ghost to pull the covers off attractive tourists as they slept in one of the nearby hotels. The problem was that, in the spirit world, I didn't have a lot of choices when it came to finding someone willing to talk to me. I couldn't force them—either they'd come to me naturally, or they wouldn't. At least I hadn't yet come up with a way to compel them to make contact.

Since these two didn't seem as if they were going to be of much assistance, I thought maybe I should try the second part of my plan on them, of convincing them it was time to move on. After all, I'd done a pretty good job of it with Mary Mullen.

"Have you two ever thought that maybe you've stayed around here long enough?" I inquired. "There's a whole new existence waiting for you in the next world. Staying stuck here can't be that much fun."

"Will there be pretty girls in the next world?" Clay responded.

Good question. "Um…probably," I hedged.

Isaac Ford shot a stream of brown tobacco juice out of one side of his mouth—luckily, the side farthest away from me. Don't ask me how a spirit can spit tobacco. Just one of the afterlife's little mysteries, I supposed. "But you don't know for sure."

"Well, no."

"Then I'm stayin' here," Clay said, and Isaac nodded.

"Yup. Why mess with a sure thing? I know there are pretty girls here."

"But—"

My protest died on my lips, because at that point they both tipped their hats to me and faded away—off to look for half-drunk pretty girls roaming the streets of downtown Flagstaff. It was a mild Friday night in June, so that probably wouldn't be too difficult.

I came out of that "spirit walk" frowning, and Connor peered at me, concerned. "You okay?"

"Fine," I said curtly, then relented. "I don't know. I'm not feeling very optimistic. I mean, if I can't get a couple of horny bootleggers to move on to the next world, how can I possibly handle this Nizhoni person?"

"Horny?" Connor repeated, looking bemused. "How can spirits be horny?"

"You don't want to know," I told him, and after taking a closer look at my face, he must have decided it wasn't worth pressing the issue, because he took me home shortly afterward.

On Saturday we returned to the apartment around seven-thirty in the evening, since we'd decided to fortify ourselves with some tapas before Lawrence and my father showed up. I didn't want to call it my last meal, because I thought that would be jinxing things before we even got started, but I couldn't help feeling as if our little feast might be that very thing. Instead, I called it Connor's birthday dinner, promising him that we'd do something more festive after...well, afterward. In fact, I made something of a show of getting us reservations the following evening at the Cottage, his favorite restaurant in town. All perfectly normal.

Whether he saw through my pretense, I wasn't sure, but he didn't comment, only said that sounded great and it was only a birthday, nothing to get that fussed about.

It had been sort of tricky, getting the chance to be here in the apartment, since both the Wilcox and the McAllister clans had solstice observances that they wanted us to attend, and Lucas had made some noises about a birthday celebration for Connor afterward.

That wouldn't work at all, of course, as we couldn't possibly be anywhere except here. Pregnancy, however, allows you all sorts of built-in excuses for getting out of social events. Connor simply put it out there on the respective family grapevines that I was having stomach issues just short of projectile vomiting, and that closed down the matter pretty quickly. Never mind that, except for my adverse reactions to the smell of coffee, I was probably having the most nausea-free pregnancy on record. Luckily, we hadn't really been spending that much time around most of our family members, except Lucas, and so no one found anything particularly odd about the excuse.

So we ate mostly in silence, each of us brooding about what lay ahead. I did make Connor let me have half a glass of wine. That little surely couldn't do any irreparable harm, and if I wasn't coming back from this journey into the otherworld, then I wanted a few last sips of malbec to accompany me to the afterlife. I know, I really shouldn't have been thinking that way, but it was how I felt.

We'd had to eat off paper plates, since of course all of the dishes were at the new house. There wasn't much clean-up to be done. After the last bit of trash had been shoved into the garbage can under the sink, Connor turned around and regarded me gravely.

"It's not too late—" he began, and I went to him and laid two fingers against his lips, hushing him.

"I'm not backing out now," I said, raising my hand from his mouth. Oh, that mouth. As anxious as I was, the touch of his lips against my skin still sent warm little thrills all through me. How I wished it were just another night here, and that we could go upstairs and make slow, languorous love in the king-size bed. But this wasn't our home anymore, not really, and besides, Lawrence and my father would be here soon.

"I know," Connor said, resigned. "You get this lift to your chin when you have your mind set on something, and you definitely have it now. It's just...." He let the words die away, and I wrapped my arms around him, pressing my face into his chest, breathing in the warm masculine smell of him, soap and the slightest tinge of clean sweat, and something beneath that, something comforting that had to be the scent of his skin.

"It'll be fine," I told him, knowing I was trying to convince myself just as much as I was attempting to convince him.

"I'm trying to make myself believe that."

Just as I opened my mouth to reply, I heard a knock at the door, and knew it was my father and Lawrence. I disentangled myself from Connor's arms, saying, "Showtime."

His mouth compressed, but he only nodded and went to the door. The two men stood outside, both wearing their usual loose-fitting light-colored shirts, my father in the inevitable cargo pants, Lawrence in Wranglers so faded I had to wonder if they were older than I was. My father held a small linen bag in one hand.

"Come in," Connor told them, his voice tight.

I smiled at them as they entered and asked, "Do you want something to drink? We have bottled water, and there's some cold tea—"

"Water later," Lawrence said. "But first we need to prepare the space."

"Um…prepare the space?"

In reply, my father drew a sage smudge stick out of the bag. "We weren't sure if Connor had cleansed the place lately."

Try ever, I thought. Smudging was something we McAllisters did a lot, but one thing I'd noticed about the Wilcox clan was that they didn't seem to follow too many of the old ways, except for observing the solstice celebrations.

"No, I haven't," Connor said, looking embarrassed, although I wasn't sure if his embarrassment was due to the fact that he'd never done such a thing, or because he couldn't believe the other two men had suggested doing it in the first place.

But they were deadly serious, and so we spent the next twenty minutes or so following them from room to room as Lawrence chanted quietly in

Navajo, touching the smudge stick to the four points of each chamber, tracing symbols I didn't recognize above each window and doorway. By the time they were done, it was only a few minutes before ten. I could feel my pulse begin to race when I realized what time it was. Not good. I needed to be calm, in control.

"It is time," Lawrence said at last. "Where in this place do you feel most comfortable?"

I was inclined to tell them it was upstairs in bed with Connor, but I had a feeling that wouldn't go over very well. "In the living room," I replied. That wasn't even a lie. We'd spent lots of good moments in the living room, including a few memorable ones on the rug in front of the fireplace.

Probably not a good idea to bring that up, either.

Lawrence directed me to sit on the couch, with Connor beside me. That was good; I didn't think Lawrence would separate us, not after we'd spent so much time with me practicing the meditations in Connor's company, but my anxiety kept ratcheting up and up, and right then I really didn't know what to expect.

My father sat down in the matching armchair, but Lawrence remained standing, his back to the cold hearth. I wondered if he was going to maintain that position the entire time I was off in my trance… meditation…whatever. But he probably had a much better idea of what he was doing than I did, so I didn't ask.

The clock ticked away, and I cast a worried glance up at it. Four minutes after ten. Almost there....

"Breathe," Lawrence said. "Reach out, and sense the powers at work this night."

As simple as that, and I knew it was time to begin. I gave a brief nod, then reached out and laid my hand on top of Connor's just before I shut my eyes and drew in a deep breath.

I could feel it, almost as soon as I shut out the physical world around me. This longest of days was coming to an end and would begin to tilt back toward the dark, even as the earth blocked out even the slightest trace of the moon's light. Their energies, wildly opposed and yet somehow working in concert, seemed to crackle on every side.

This time I drifted out the big windows overlooking the street as if they weren't there. The sidewalks below me were crowded with people; after all, to them this was just another Saturday night, another excuse to get out and party. I thought I caught dual shimmers of energy that were Clay and Isaac, moving through the throngs, but of course they were not my goal tonight.

Here in downtown I could feel nothing, no whisper of an alien presence that might be Nizhoni's. I wanted to curse, but I knew that would only break my focus. *No need to be impatient,* I told myself. *Time doesn't work the same way in the world of the spirits.*

No, it didn't. It could speed up, or slow down. During some meditations it would feel as if I'd only been gone for five minutes, when in reality nearly an hour had passed. Other times I'd think I'd been away for hours and hours, and would return only a minute or two after I shut my eyes. So I couldn't allow myself to worry about how much time this was all taking. It would take what it took, and not a second more or less.

I'd spent a little time the past few days doing research on early Flagstaff, and so I knew the downtown area, though old, had still been built decades after Nizhoni had been taken to be Jeremiah Wilcox's reluctant bride. The original settlement was to the north and west of here; when the railroad came through, that was when most people picked up and moved to what would be downtown's current location.

So although this was a good starting point, I knew I'd have to range farther out, to the approximate place where the first Wilcox clan members had settled in the area. Leaving aside the cheerful crowds and busy restaurants and bars of downtown, I drifted over dark residential neighborhoods, past the observatory on Mars Hill, heading in roughly the same direction where Damon Wilcox's house was located, although not nearly as far.

As I moved, I began to feel…something. At first I thought maybe it was my own nerves playing tricks on me, raising my anxiety level even more, but this was different. It felt wrong, like an instrument played out of tune, almost masked by the sound of the rest of the orchestra…but not quite.

Beneath me was a dry creek that cut between housing developments. As I watched, though, I saw the stony stream bed disappear, hidden by dark water flowing over it. On either side the houses faded away, becoming insubstantial as mist before they evaporated altogether. In their place were stands of ponderosa pines, interspersed with mountain meadows.

Icy sweat trickled down my back, but I ignored it. The perspiration wasn't real, was only a manifestation of my worry. And what I saw around me wasn't real.

Or was it?

I saw her then, standing by the side of the creek, long hair blowing like raven silk in an unseen wind. Her back was to me, but I could see she wore a dress of dark calico with a modest bustle, probably quite fashionable for 1870s Flagstaff. I wasn't sure why I hadn't been expecting that; in my mind's eye I'd always thought of her wearing some kind of native dress, although if I'd stopped to think about it, I should have realized Jeremiah Wilcox probably wouldn't have allowed his wife to go around wearing deerskin.

She turned around, and I had to catch my breath. Probably because of the way her curse had echoed down the generations, bringing such evil with it, I hadn't stopped to think that she might have been beautiful.

But she was, with that long black hair and tip-tilted dark eyes, those high cheekbones and full mouth. No wonder Jeremiah Wilcox had wanted her.

"Angela," she said, startling me so much that I dropped to the ground with an ungraceful thud.

Was someone traveling in the otherworld supposed to make a thud like that? I didn't know. It felt too real, just as the soft grass beneath my feet did, the cool mountain air against my skin. It didn't feel like high summer in this place, wherever it was; the wind had a bite to it, but I couldn't tell for sure if it was supposed to be early fall or late spring.

The sky was spangled with stars, but here, as it had been back in my own world, in my own time, no moon shone overhead. Not that it appeared to matter, because everything around me seemed to have a faint glow, the waters in the creek glittering so brightly that they might as well have been reflecting the sun.

"You have come a long way for nothing, Angela Wilcox," Nizhoni said. Her English was good, although spoken slowly, as if she had to consider each word before she pronounced it.

"My last name is McAllister, not Wilcox," I told her, a little surprised at my own boldness.

Her shoulders lifted. "Is the Wilcox *primus* not your intended husband? Is your own father not a Wilcox?"

"Well, yes, but—"

"Then you are a Wilcox, no matter what you may call yourself, and so I have nothing to say to you." Turning, she began to walk away from me, up the stream toward a stand of cottonwoods that clustered around the water.

"Wait!" I called, feeling like an idiot, and ran after her. I was dressed here exactly the same as I had been when I went into this meditation, and so I had on a pair of flip-flops. Not the best footwear for tearing along a rocky creek bank, and once or twice I slipped and nearly lost my balance. What would happen if I did a face plant here? Would I wake up back in my physical body sporting a new black eye?

But I didn't slip, and because I was running while she was only walking, albeit with a purposeful stride, I did manage to catch up with her a minute later. She looked at me with scornful eyes and said, "I have nothing to say to you. Go back to your world, and learn to accept your fate."

"I don't think so," I snapped. "I'm not going to accept this stupid curse of yours, because that's what it is...stupid. Pointless. Hateful."

At that last word, I thought I saw her mouth tighten slightly, but she didn't reply, only stared at me, stony-faced.

"Whatever happened between you and Jeremiah Wilcox, it was between the two of you. I'm not saying it was right, and I'm sorry you had to go through that, but it doesn't give you the right to curse a bunch of innocent women, just so you can indirectly hurt the Wilcox *primus*."

"If a woman is with the *primus*, then she is no innocent," Nizhoni retorted.

"Oh, really? So what does that make you?"

Her eyes narrowed, turning to slits hidden by her thick lashes. "You have no idea what you are talking about."

"Then enlighten me," I said, crossing my arms. "Because I don't see why I should have to drop dead at twenty-two or twenty-three just because Jeremiah Wilcox was an asshole."

The profanity startled her, I could tell—her eyebrows lifted, and she pulled in a breath. I supposed anyone who counted herself a lady back in the day wouldn't have talked like that. But I was certainly beyond caring what she thought of me.

"Look," I said, attempting to soften my tone, "you can't right past wrongs by creating new ones. It doesn't work that way. You've stayed here, hanging on to your hatred, for far too long. What good is it doing you? Has it brought you peace? Acceptance? There's no dishonor in realizing enough is enough and moving on. Whatever Jeremiah did to you, you're only giving him more power by not letting it go. Can't you see that?"

The silence stretched out so long I was beginning to think she wouldn't answer me. Finally, she said, the words spoken so softly that I could barely hear them, "You don't understand. Not any of it."

"Then tell me," I begged her. "Please. I want to know. Help me to understand."

Silence again, and then her face darkened with fury. The wind picked up, causing her long hair to snap like whips, blowing loose twigs and branches and leaves toward me. I raised my hands to protect my eyes. Was she doing this? It seemed so.

"Stop it!" I cried. "This isn't helping!"

"Good!" she flung at me. "Leave me alone!"

"No!" True, she'd been a witch so powerful Jeremiah had wanted her for his own, and she'd had all these years to brood and let her malice build, feeding her strength, but I wasn't exactly helpless myself.

Reaching for my own power, I let it radiate out from within, golden light surrounding me, forming a barrier against which the branches and twigs and a few stray pinecones bounced off and fell harmlessly away.

Her eyes glittered when she saw the shield I had raised, but that didn't stop her. If anything, the hail of debris against me only increased, dirt flying now as well, so that I could barely see her through the whirlwind of forest detritus swirling around me. Biting my lip, I let my own energy surge forth, pushing against the spell-summoned tornado. At last the strain was too much, and the branches and leaves and pinecones exploded away from me, scattering in every direction.

Nizhoni, however, seemed untouched. Frowning, she said, "You are strong."

"Yeah," I agreed, trying not to pant, since that would sort of ruin the impression I was trying to give. "Care to go for round two?"

Her eyebrows pulled down at that. Clearly, she didn't get the reference.

"Okay," I went on, taking her silence as a tacit invitation for me to keep talking, "we can stand here and have magical battles like two characters out of a Harry Potter book, or we can talk like rational adults. Which is it going to be?"

"I do not know this 'Harry Potter' of which you speak."

"Never mind." I reached up and pulled a twig out of my hair. My cheek twinged, and I realized at least one piece of debris had gotten through, because when I touched my finger to my cheek, it came away smeared with blood. Ignoring the pain as best I could, I said, "Look, Nizhoni, I'm not here to hurt you or upset you. I just want you to move on to a place where you can be at peace. Don't you realize that the people you loved are waiting for you?"

"Not all," she said, in an undertone, looking away from me, and in that instant I thought I understood.

All that rage, all that hatred—it hadn't come from being taken to be Jeremiah Wilcox's wife. It had come because she must have loved him on some level, and hated herself for it. And that hatred had twisted in on itself, made her curse all Wilcox wives to come, because she thought herself cursed by a love she hadn't wanted.

"Oh, Nizhoni," I murmured then. "It's no weakness to love."

That made her whirl around, black eyes blazing. "I did not love him!"

And the skies cracked open, storm clouds rushing in from nowhere, lightning lancing down and hitting the ground only a few yards away from us. The sharp scent of ozone stung my nostrils and I blinked, seeing dancing reddish echoes of the lightning bolt etched into my eyelids.

This was not good.

I summoned the energy, praying it would be enough, and scared shitless that it wouldn't be. The forest flared with light again, the bolt this time hitting the tree directly behind me, splitting it with a *cra-ack!* so loud my ears began to ring. Even with the golden light enveloping me, I cowered, my hands up to protect my face against any further hurt. How in the world was I supposed to fight this? She was so strong. This wasn't like going up against Damon. He'd been driven nearly mad, but even using some of the darkest magic known to any witch, he was still just a man.

Nizhoni had once been a woman, but she wasn't that any longer. Now she was a vengeful, angry spirit, and clearly nothing I could say or do would convince her to change, to understand that she had no reason to stay here anymore.

Connor, I thought in despair, reaching out to where he was waiting for me in the mortal world, and sensing nothing of him. That frightened me more than anything, because I'd always been able to sense him during my previous journeys to the otherworld. But still I flung the thoughts outward, hoping against hope that he'd somehow be able to hear me.

I love you so much. I was wrong. I can't do this. I don't know how.

Forgive me.

And the clouds rumbled overhead, and the lightning surged once more, and I gathered every bit of strength I had, pushing it out to surround me, to fight her hostile power with my shielding energies. Even so, I didn't think it would be enough.

Actually, I knew it wouldn't.

CHAPTER SEVENTEEN

A Silver Stream

LIGHT SEARED THROUGH ME AND I SCREAMED, PAIN shrilling along every vein, every nerve ending. Was I going to die being burned from within?

Then I heard a man's voice, commanding and deep. "Nizhoni."

It was as if I had been on fire, and someone had thrown a bucket of water over me. I blinked, then looked down, expecting to see burns from Nizhoni's lightning running down my bare arms. But the skin was smooth and untouched, lightly brown with the faint beginnings of my summer tan.

And then I glanced up to see who had spoken, and saw a tall man walking toward us through the trees. His hair was as black as Nizhoni's, though cut short and slicked away from his face. In his features I could see an echo of the Wilcox men I knew today, the fine strong nose and chin, the well-cut mouth. Unlike most of the men of his time, he was clean-shaven, but otherwise he looked a lot like the historical re-enactors I knew who did Wild West demonstrations: long black frock coat, band-collared shirt, dark vest, dusty boots.

He stopped a few feet away from us. His gaze flickered toward me. "Are you all right, Angela?"

I guessed we were all on a first-name basis here in the otherworld. "I'm fine…Jeremiah."

Instead of being put off by the familiarity, he grinned, showing teeth better than I would've expected from someone not blessed with the gifts of modern dentistry. "Not for a lack of Nizhoni's trying, I'm sure."

I shook my head and glanced over at her. She was standing so still she might have been a statue. The wind she had summoned was gone, and now her hair didn't move at all, only hung straight as a skein of black silk down her back. And she was staring at Jeremiah as if she couldn't believe the evidence of her own eyes.

"Why?" she said at last, the word barely a breath.

"Why?" Jeremiah repeated.

"Why now, after all these years?"

"Because you've finally admitted it."

"I have admitted nothing," she replied, chin up, dark eyes flashing.

"You should listen to this girl," he said. "What did she say? 'It's no weakness to love'? She has the right of it, Nizhoni."

She didn't respond, only stood there, her chest moving as she heaved an angry breath.

"Look, Nizhoni," I began. It still frightened me a little to have her looking at me with those furious dark eyes, but Jeremiah had deflected her energy away from me, and I had to believe he would do so again if necessary. Why exactly he'd defended me, I wasn't sure—family loyalty?—but I wasn't going to worry about that now. I took a breath and continued, "It can't have been easy to find that you had feelings for him after he went and stole you from your people, but—"

"I did what?" he demanded, staring at me in disbelief. "Where did you hear that?"

"Well, uh…from someone in my clan," I faltered. Jeremiah looked equal parts angry and shocked, but I didn't think that anger was directed at me. Not exactly, anyway. "Um…that's not what happened?"

"I suppose it's not that great a surprise, that the McAllisters might twist the tale." He reached up to push away a lock of hair that had fallen over his brow, and the gesture was so like one of the gestures I loved about Connor that I pulled in a startled little breath. The Wilcox blood really did breed true.

"Do you want to tell her the truth of it, Nizhoni, or should I?"

She glanced away from him then, not meeting his eyes, and remained silent.

"Ah, then, I'll do it." His gaze lingered on her for a second or two more, and at last he returned his attention to me. "I don't know what you were told, but we came here in 1876, the year of the great centennial. There had been some trouble back in Connecticut—"

"You were practicing dark magic," I cut in.

"More McAllister lies."

"We don't lie."

His raised eyebrow indicated his disbelief, but he only said, "Very well. Let us say 'misinterpretation of history' and leave it at that. It was more that we were experimenting with magic, and the *primas* of the surrounding clans took exception to our work. So we left and headed west, where we thought we'd be allowed more freedom. All that open land, and no one looking over your shoulder."

Yeah, I thought, *that sounds like heaven to a Wilcox.*

"There had been some thought of pushing on to California, but we came here and saw the snow on the mountaintops and the pine forests, and knew we didn't want to go any farther." He glanced over at Nizhoni, but she was still standing there without moving, without speaking, although I could tell she was listening intently. Fine by me. If she'd decided to hang on Jeremiah's every word, it meant she most likely wouldn't be flinging any stray logs at my head. "We built a small settlement here, my brothers and my sister and their families, and started over. And after we'd been living here for a few months, we began to hear rumors of a powerful young witch who lived in the desert lands north of here, among her people.

"You have to understand that for the Diné"—he pronounced it correctly—"the word 'witch' does not mean the same thing that it does to us. Shamans and healers and medicine men and women, those they had, but they were not called witches. 'Witch' is a bad word to them, meaning one who practices evil magic."

"It was not evil," Nizhoni said proudly, speaking for the first time. "I tried to tell them this, but they did not understand."

"No, they didn't," Jeremiah agreed, before directing his attention back to me. "You must understand, Angela, that there were not so many of us Wilcoxes back then. A little more than twenty, when you numbered all the children of my brothers and sister, but my wife had died on the journey here, and I had no children of my own. I thought that I would like to meet this young woman, because if she was as powerful as the rumors claimed, then she would do better to be here with us, with people who understood her powers."

"And because you just happened to need a wife," I said dryly.

He did not appear offended by my comment, replying, "I will not lie and say the thought did not cross my mind. So my brother Samuel and I rode for three days, journeying to Navajo lands, and we met with Sicheii, Nizhoni's father, who had very good English, as did his daughter. He was suspicious at first, but soon realized I could be of some assistance to him."

I raised an eyebrow, and Jeremiah went on, "In my ignorance, I didn't realize the Diné did not have the custom of the bride price the way some other tribes practiced it, and Sicheii saw no reason to correct my mistake—not when he could be rid of the daughter who had been causing trouble in his tribe and be three horses and five bars of silver richer at the same time."

To me that didn't sound like all that much to exchange for a human being, but apparently Nizhoni's father had thought differently. "So…you didn't steal her."

"No." Another of those quick looks in his wife's direction. She was still standing in the same place, but now her arms hung relaxed at her side, and her head was tilted slightly, as if she had been listening intently. "And she did not seem unwilling to come back to the settlement with me."

"I was not," she said. "It was in me to know more of this white man's magic, and I knew I could run away later if I wanted to."

"But you didn't," I guessed.

Her chin went up at that, and I tensed, wondering if she was going to launch another one of those attacks. Then she seemed to deflate, head drooping as her hair fell forward to conceal her face. "No, I did not."

Jeremiah paused, his gaze moving from me to her and then back to me again. "In time she became my wife in more than just name. She learned from me, just as I learned from her. A little more than a year after she came to live with us, she gave me a son."

"Jacob," I supplied, recalling the name from the one and only time Connor had ever spoken of his long-ago forebears.

"Yes, and then you had all you needed from me, didn't you?" Nizhoni spat.

For a few seconds he didn't reply, only watched her from hooded dark eyes. "That is not true."

She shook back her head. "You may speak untruths to this girl, and she may believe them, but I was there. I know."

"You know what you have told yourself, but that doesn't mean it's the truth," Jeremiah told her. Surprisingly, his voice was calm and even a bit sad. "The world was a different place then, and men did not speak of their feelings as freely as they do now. That does not mean those feelings did not exist. I will be honest and say I did not love my first wife. She was a cousin my father urged me on his deathbed to marry, and I was a good son and followed his wishes. But she had suffered from ill health for some time, and in the end she succumbed to a fever as we were traveling down out of Colorado. I buried her there, and mourned for a life cut short, but I did not feel any great loss."

Kind of tough for her, I thought, but I didn't say anything. I had no experience of living in that kind of world with those sorts of expectations, so I thought it better not to comment.

"But Nizhoni," he began, then shook his head. His eyes met hers, and it was almost as if a spark jumped between them. Oh, yes, something still lay there smoldering, even after all these years, even after all the resentment and misunderstandings. "There was much made over Jacob, I know, because finally the *primus* had an heir, and so perhaps Nizhoni felt overlooked."

Glancing over at her, I could see that her expression had grown blank and cool again. Never a good sign.

I wasn't sure if Jeremiah hadn't seen the look on her face or was ignoring it, because he continued, "And then when Jacob was only four months old, typhoid fever struck our settlement and many others in the area. We fared better than most, as my sister Emma was a healer. But then the fever took Nizhoni, and it seemed that Emma could do nothing for her. You have perhaps seen this even now, with your science. If someone doesn't have the will to live...."

Something else Margot had gotten wrong. At the very least, she'd been given the wrong information, but I realized I shouldn't be that surprised by how the story might have gotten twisted over the generations. When you came right down to the point, I supposed it was a fine line between killing yourself outright and not wanting to live anymore.

"Why should I have continued to live?" Nizhoni demanded. "When you saw me only as a vessel to bear you powerful children?"

His mouth tightened, but his tone was even as he went on, "At the end, she was not herself, raving in a fever. It was very dangerous, that someone with her power should be in so little control of herself, and my brother Edmund was forced to put a spell of binding on her, so that she could not hurt anyone in the family. She cursed me then, cursed me with her last breath, saying I should have no joy of any of my wives, nor would any child of my line. At the time I thought little of it, for, as I said, the fever had quite put her out of her mind."

During this speech Nizhoni wore an odd expression on her face, a strange half grimace, as if she were recalling those hours of pain and delirium. "Do I look mad to you?" she said at last.

"Now, no, but then was a different matter. You were so wild, screaming in both English and Diné, that half the time we didn't know what you were saying…not until later, anyway." His gaze shifted toward me, although I could tell it was difficult for him to look away from his wife. "She died just before dawn, and was buried in a little stand of cottonwoods down near the stream."

Cold flooded through me as I realized that was where we stood now. Somewhere beneath my feet were Nizhoni's bones. No wonder she had lingered here, haunting this quiet spot, for almost a hundred and forty years.

"We all did mourn her, but life goes on. I had a son to raise, and I did not wish him to be without a mother his entire life. A little more than a year later, I married a woman from one of the neighboring settlements. That…did not go well."

"She died?" I ventured.

"Yes, four months gone with our child." His jaw tightened. "I tried to tell myself that these things sometimes occurred, but…."

"But you married again, and the same thing happened."

"Not precisely the same thing, but yes, she did not survive six months of marriage to me." During all this he had seemed remarkably calm, but for the first time I saw a flash of anger in his dark eyes as he looked at Nizhoni, cold and calm, listening but saying nothing. "I understood then that Nizhoni's dying curse had contained all her power within it, and there was no escape from it." He drew in a breath then, spreading his hands wide. "And that, Angela McAllister, is the truth of what happened."

"Your truth," Nizhoni said, and I shook my head wearily.

"Everyone's truth is a little different," I told her. "Are you going to fight for another hundred and forty years over whose truth is better?"

She didn't answer, but looked away, her gaze apparently fixed on the unnaturally sparkling stream a few yards away.

"It seems to me," I went on, thinking I really hadn't signed up to be some sort of afterlife marriage counselor, but knowing I had to do something, "that you two were always misunderstanding one another. I suppose it's not that strange, since you came from very different worlds."

Not that it really excused either of their behavior. As much as I wanted to shake both of them for their stubbornness, for their refusal to reach out to one another and tell the other person the true nature of their feelings, I knew that really wasn't going to help. What was done was done, as Aunt Rachel liked to say. All I could do was try to make sure the future didn't carry with it these dark echoes from the past. And, whatever I might think of the way they'd been so horribly at cross-purposes, I hadn't been there. I couldn't begin to imagine what it must have been like to live back in that place and time, when societal pressures on men and women were so very different from what they were today.

But love was love, whether it was experienced now or in 1876. Maybe getting them to admit that would be enough. I pulled in a breath, then spoke. "Jeremiah, I just want to ask you one simple question."

He inclined his head slightly but remained silent, waiting to hear what I was going to say.

"Did you love Nizhoni? *Do* you love her?"

"Yes," he said simply. "I did, and I do. It was wrong of me to say nothing, and ever since I lost her, I have berated myself for my silence, but—"

"That'll work for now," I broke in. "And Nizhoni, did you love Jeremiah?"

Silence. The air was so still that I thought I could hear the thudding of the blood in my ears, the faint creak of Jeremiah's boots as he shifted his weight.

What if she wouldn't admit it? I didn't have much left in my bag of tricks.

Something in the proud set of her shoulders seemed to slump, and she whispered, "Yes. I did. I was weak. I should not have allowed myself to care for him. I—"

Her next words were smothered, however, as Jeremiah strode forward, took her in his arms, and kissed her so thoroughly that I found myself staring, embarrassed, at the ground, although I could still catch a glimpse of what they were doing out of the corner of my eye. After a brief, muffled sound, she made no protest, her arms tightening around him, drawing him close.

As they kissed, the stream grew brighter and brighter, looking like a ribbon of molten silver in the dark landscape. At last they broke apart, but I noticed their fingers were still intertwined, as if, after spending so many years apart, they could not bear to be separated again.

"Will you come with me now, beloved?" Jeremiah asked softly.

"Yes, my husband." She raised his hand to her lips and kissed it softly. Pale metal glinted on his finger as she did so, and I realized he was still wearing a wedding ring. The briefest glance over her shoulder at me, and she said, "Be happy, Angela. For you will be alive to see your children grow to adulthood."

Then they were moving away from me, somehow stepping onto the gleaming surface of the water, walking along it as if it were simply a pathway, until the light surrounded them. It seemed to flow over their limbs, embracing them, and then they were gone, the stream now looking like just an ordinary stream, all trace of that extraordinary silver light disappearing as if it had never been.

I stood there in the dark starlit night, pulling in one deep, heaving breath after another. Nizhoni was gone, and she had taken her curse with her. The Wilcoxes were free.

I was free.

Stepping out of the little stand of cottonwoods, I expected to see the empty fields and hillsides around me gradually fill in with the shapes of the houses and roads and walls that should be standing here…but they didn't. Nothing changed, and I felt a stirring of fear inside me.

So Jeremiah and Nizhoni had gotten their happy ending…but did they have to leave me here in the otherworld she'd created with no way out?

Okay, Angela, I told myself. *Breathe. You just accomplished the impossible, so getting out of here can't be too hard compared to that.*

I thought of where I was. Northwest of downtown, with high hills on either side. That was clear enough in my head from looking at Google maps.

Now I just had to visualize how everything had appeared before Nizhoni's reality took over—the dry creek bed with the bridge over it, the big houses to either side, sitting on their half- and third-acre plots.

So I closed my eyes and brought those pictures up in mind, recalling every last detail I could, right down to the fancy wooden playhouse / slide / swing-set combo I'd spotted in someone's backyard. There. That should do it.

But when I looked around me, nothing had changed. Same cottonwoods, same stream moving briskly within its banks. Same vast, vast emptiness, with nothing around me except miles and miles of ponderosa pines.

My heart began to hammer in my chest. *Just walk,* I told myself. *It's better than standing here and doing nothing.*

Seeming to move of their own accord, my feet took me away from the little grove where Nizhoni's bones rested, down the creek, down in the general direction of the town center. What would happen if I made it all the way there, I wasn't sure. Would I find an older version of Flagstaff, or nothing at all?

No, that wasn't right. If I had somehow gotten stuck back in 1876, there wouldn't even be a Flagstaff in the place I was looking.

A little sob caught in the back of my throat, but I kept going. I wouldn't stop now, no matter what, not even if I walked over this stony ground until my flip-flops broke apart. If I made myself keep on, maybe I could still get back to Connor somehow. I tried to make myself feel the shape of his hand beneath mine, the way it had been resting when I went into the otherworld, but I couldn't. My fingers were cold in the chilly night breeze, unwarmed by his flesh.

I don't know how long I walked. The darkness never changed, and neither did the landscape. That is, maybe there were slight variations in the shapes of the hills and the locations of the trees, but I never saw a single sign of life. No buildings, no roads, no people.

Until....

Her back was to me, her long black hair lifting in a faint breeze that seemed to have sprung up out of nowhere. I froze, wondering if this was Nizhoni, returned from wherever she'd gone with Jeremiah. Had she come back to help me?

My pace quickened, gravel crunching under my feet, and the woman turned. No, this was not Nizhoni. Only the silky dark hair was the same, hanging almost to her waist. But this woman was older, her face more oval.

And then I realized who it was.

"Marie?" I said, voice incredulous, cracking a little on the second syllable. "What—what are you doing here?"

"I've come to take you home," she replied calmly, as if running into each other in this place was the most natural thing in the world. "I felt—I could tell you were having some trouble."

"Were you watching me? How did you know I was here?" My voice sharpened. "Did you see what happened with Nizhoni and Jeremiah?"

"I had a vision of you here, and knew I must come." Head tilting to one side, she asked, "What is this about Nizhoni and Jeremiah?"

"The curse is broken," I said simply.

Her eyes shut, and she whispered something under her breath. "So it did come to pass. I wasn't sure—"

"Yeah, it might have been good to know you weren't feeling totally certain, but since you bailed on us and only left a note—"

"I am sorry about that. It was just"—she made an impatient gesture with one hand, as if trying to wave away something that had irritated her —"it became too difficult for me, because I knew you would learn about your father, and then all those memories I had tried to push away for so many years would come flooding back. I went back to the reservation, to surround myself with stillness, to keep myself from knowing the truth. It was weak of me, and I apologize, but I did not want to know what had become of him, how he had moved on with his life. "

"But he hasn't," I said, my tone softer than I would have expected it to be. Maybe it was simply that I'd just seen how much damage love thwarted could do. "He's hidden himself all these years, waiting for tonight to come, but I don't think there's ever been anyone else. He never stopped loving you."

Her eyes widened, and it seemed as if she was struggling within herself, struggling to believe what I had just told her. Then she stood up a little taller, her shoulders straightening, and she said simply, "Then I think it's time for both of us to go home."

CHAPTER EIGHTEEN

Promised Land

Marie took my hand firmly in hers, and we walked along the creek bed, heading south and east. This time, though, the empty fields and thickly growing pines began to fade away, replaced with the familiar sprawl of suburbia. And as the real world fell in around us, we began to move faster and faster, not flying as I had in some of my meditations, but still doing a credible imitation of The Flash as we covered the miles to downtown in only a few seconds.

At the last minute she let go of my hand, and I felt my consciousness fall into my body with an almost physical thud. My eyes shot open, and I saw Lawrence and my father watching me in concern, even as Connor's fingers clasped mine and he said,

"Angela? What happened?"

It all seemed to hit me at once—Nizhoni, and Jeremiah, and how they had walked away from me up that shining creek, going into the light. "It's over," I whispered. For some reason, my throat felt as dry as if I'd walked a hundred miles of desert road.

"What do you mean, 'it's over'?" Connor asked.

"The curse. It's broken. They made up, and he kissed her, and they went into the light together."

None of that was probably very coherent, but he seemed to get the gist of it, because his eyes lit up and he pulled me against him, kissing my mouth and my cheeks and my forehead while somehow laughing at the same time. I didn't mind, even when he missed and kissed my eyelid. After all, it was Connor, and just to feel him and hear him was enough for me.

When he pulled away, though, he frowned, reaching out to touch my cheek. "You're hurt."

"Just a scrape," I said, so giddy with everything that had happened that I'd honestly forgotten about the cut on my face. "I'll clean it up later."

He didn't protest, although he did reach over and pick up a napkin from the coffee table and hand it to me. I pressed it against my skin, finally feeling the sting of the wound, although it didn't hurt nearly as much as it had when I first got it.

"You have done very well," Lawrence said, and my father nodded.

"We'll want to hear the whole story soon, but for now, let me get you a glass of water."

That sounded like a great idea. I watched him rise from his chair and head to the kitchen, and my gaze strayed to the clock on the wall in the dining room. Ten past ten. So I'd been gone for only a few minutes.

Or an eternity, depending on how you looked at it.

I heard the clink of ice in the glass, and then the soft gush of water from the dispenser in the refrigerator door. As my father was leaving the kitchen, there came a soft knock at the front door. He stopped in the hallway, looking back toward us where we sat in the living room. "Should I get that?"

"I don't know who it could be, but yeah, might as well," Connor said. "I doubt they'd be dropping by at this hour if it wasn't important."

My father nodded and went over to the door, opening it with his free hand. Since he was blocking the doorway, I couldn't see who was there—but when the glass of ice water fell from his hand and shattered on the wooden floor, scattering ice cubes everywhere, I thought I had a pretty good idea.

"Hello, Andre," Marie said.

It was, as they say, an evening of surprises. Once my father got over his shock, he brought Marie into the living room, then apologized about the mess and fetched me another glass of water. Then it was time to tell the story as they all listened intently, exclaiming at certain points—how Jeremiah had never kidnapped his bride, how he and Nizhoni had reconciled at the end—until at last we all sat there quietly, exhausted and overwhelmed. So much had changed, and yet —

Connor was sitting close enough that we were thigh to thigh, his warmth as always reassuring, solid, real. And so some things, the important things, were still the same. We had each other.

And now…now we had a future.

He did try teasing Marie about her disappearing act, but she'd only said, "There are some times when a person needs to be alone. This was one of those times." Her expression had been calm enough, but there was a certain sharpness to her dark eyes that told me she wasn't going to tolerate any more questions on the subject.

Luckily, he backed off. I got the feeling that he didn't want to push her, not when my father was sitting there and watching her with an expression of pure wonder on his face. It was clear that he didn't care that she wasn't the laughing, pretty young woman she'd once been. She was his Marie, and that was all that mattered.

They left together, taking Lawrence with them. It was a long drive back to Cameron, but I had a feeling they wouldn't mind too much. After all, they had a lot of catching up to do.

Connor shut the door after they were gone and raked a hand through his shaggy hair. "I don't—" He broke off, shaking his head. "I don't even know where to begin."

"I do," I said, going to him and putting his hand on the slight curve of my belly. "We can begin right here."

He let his fingers rest there for a minute, then smiled, as if it had finally hit him that there wouldn't be any more doubt or worry, no fears that I wouldn't be around to be a mother to these children. I would see them take their first steps…say their first words. And, since witch blood almost always bred true, cast their first spells.

Connor and I would be there for all of it. Together.

"Okay," I told Sydney, since she hadn't said one word, only stood there staring at me. "You can be honest. Do I look like a complete heifer?"

She blinked, then shook her head vigorously. "No. Oh, God, Angela, you're *perfect*. Look."

Then she turned me around so I could take a look at myself in the full-length mirror. She'd spent all day doing my hair and my makeup and my nails, helping me get dressed, but she hadn't let me see what she was doing, saying she wanted me to see it all when she was done so I could get the full effect.

Well, I was definitely getting the full effect now.

The gown had a high A-line waist to accommodate my baby bump, but even though I was almost six months pregnant, the crisp raw silk seemed to fall away from my stomach rather than accentuate it. The wide straps and the bodice were sewn with tiny crystals, the only ornamentation on the dress, and they sparkled as I turned to look at myself from different angles. Sydney had also curled my hair and put it up, a simple veil falling partway down my back. The antique diamond earrings Aunt Rachel had loaned me glittered as well. And the makeup was perfect, my eyes looking enormous, my mouth touched with color but not so much that it competed with the way Syd had done up my eyes. Eleanor, the Wilcox healer, had made sure that the cut on my cheek healed without a scar, so there was nothing to mar the perfection Sydney had just created.

"Wow," I said at last.

"I know, right?" She stepped away, surveying me with a critical eye in case she'd missed anything. Apparently she hadn't, because she gave a nod and pronounced, "It really is perfect. And you're looking perfectly boobalicious in that dress. Connor's going to pass out."

"Sydney!"

"Well, it's true. Pregnancy's done great things for your chesticular region. Makes me want to get knocked up myself."

"I'm pretty sure there are easier ways to make your boobs look bigger," I told her, then turned away from the mirror so I could step into my shoes. The heels were pretty high, so I had been putting off wearing them until the last minute. "Anyway, you know how big a pain it was to find a dress that worked for me, so I doubt you'd really want to go through that when your own wedding is only six months off."

Syd and Anthony had gotten engaged over Labor Day weekend. She was already plotting her nuptials with a vengeance, probably making Anthony very glad that he was currently embroiled in negotiations for purchasing a vineyard down in Page Springs… with a little funding assistance from Connor.

"You're right, of course." She went over to the mirror and cast a critical eye over her own makeup, which of course was flawless, as was the fit of the sky blue gown she wore, the beading on the bodice echoing that of my own.

I could hear laughter just outside the room, and Mason and Carla came in, also wearing long bridesmaids' gowns that coordinated with Sydney's, only in a soft coral-pink shade. "You've definitely got a packed house, Angela. Or I guess I should say 'packed garden,'" Carla added with a grin.

Well, when you combined the Wilcox and McAllister clans, you ended up with a pretty big gathering. To maintain the fragile peace between the two families, Connor and I had decided to have the wedding in Sedona. It would have been easier in a lot of ways to use the country club near our house, but asking all the McAllisters to go blithely trooping into what a good number of them still considered to be enemy territory felt like a bit much. So we compromised.

Not that having the wedding in a garden overlooking West Sedona with red rock views on every side could really be called a "compromise."

"Everything's ready," Mason added. "Your aunt sent us in here to see how you're doing."

"Just fine," I told her. "I was just climbing into these torture devices that Sydney insisted I had to have."

"Hey, they're totally hot," she protested. "It's okay to suffer a little for fashion."

"I'll remember to tell you that when you're six months pregnant and your feet are starting to swell up." Since I'd been practicing walking in the strappy sandals, at least I didn't wobble as I took a few experimental steps, then turned. "Everything looking okay?"

"You're beautiful," Mason said sincerely. "Connor's eyes are going to pop out of his head."

"Well, I hope they stay where they are, but thanks."

She grinned, and Carla added, "So can I tell them we're go for launch?"

"Yes," I told her. "I'm ready."

At least, I thought I was. Oh, I wanted to be married to Connor, no question about that. But part of me had thought it might have been easier for us to simply go to the courthouse and make things official in a much more subdued way. He wouldn't hear of that, though, saying that weddings were a big deal in his family and that people would feel cheated if they couldn't see us get married. Whatever lingering suspicions some of the Wilcoxes might have harbored concerning Connor's and my connection pretty much evaporated once word got out that I had broken the curse. And the discovery that my father was the long-lost Andre Wilcox probably didn't hurt, either.

It was a little tougher on the McAllister side, but people were gradually accepting the situation. That was all I could really ask for; the prejudices of generations couldn't be put aside in a day. I had, however, informed Margot Emory of the truth of the situation, and, true to form, she hadn't really apologized for the misinformation she'd given me, but only tilted her head to one side, gave me a tight-lipped smile, and said, "Oh, so that's what really happened? How...*romantic.*" And the way she said "romantic" made it sound just the opposite.

Well, she hadn't been there, and I wasn't going to bother trying to change how she viewed the matter. The important thing was that she'd spoken with the other elders, and they'd agreed—if somewhat grudgingly—that they would take down the wards that had been protecting Jerome from any Wilcox incursions. A small step, but one I appreciated. The last thing I'd wanted was Mason and Carla to get zapped when they were coming over to look at bridesmaids' dresses.

Now Syd went over to the door of the suite I was using for a dressing room and cracked it an inch. "Looks like everyone's seated, pretty much. I'll go give Rachel the signal." She slipped out and disappeared around a corner, while Mason went over to the suite's mini-fridge and extracted a bottle of water. "Do you want one, Angela?"

"Better not. Sydney will kill me if I mess up this lipstick."

She smiled and cracked the lid on the bottle, sipping at the water before sealing it again. I could understand her wanting to stay hydrated; now that it was mid-September, temperatures were starting to drop somewhat, but it was still fairly warm outside.

The door opened, and Sydney stuck her head inside. "Okay, we're really ready. So everyone get their game face on!"

They didn't exactly plaster on beauty-queen smiles, but both Carla and Mason perked up a bit, then went to retrieve their bouquets from where they'd been sitting on top of the dresser. Sydney came into the room and got hers, then handed me mine.

I grasped the bundle of snow white and pale pink peonies, fingers tightening around the tightly bound stems. This was really it.

"You're going to be fine," she murmured. "You look amazing, and you couldn't have ordered a more perfect day. Or did Adam have something to do with that?"

As a matter of fact, he had, but I thought it better to let that go for now. I just gave her what I hoped was an enigmatic smile and said, "No comment."

"That's what I thought. Okay, Cinderella, time to go."

I had to laugh at that, and followed her and the other two girls out of the room. They all went on ahead of me, but I paused at the tall hedge that separated the garden area where the ceremony was being held from the rooms at the hilltop hotel.

"Angela."

I turned at my father's voice, and had to pull in a deep breath at the sight of him standing there in a gray suit, his hair pulled back into a neat ponytail. He looked so handsome…and happy. Then again, he had every reason to be. He'd been reunited with Marie, and had moved in with her. They hadn't talked much about marriage, maybe not wanting to overshadow Connor's and my nuptials. Or maybe they knew that, after their long separation, they didn't need a piece of paper to tell them that they'd never leave one another's side again. And I won't say that Connor didn't tease me from time to time about having Marie as the equivalent of a stepmother, but I found I didn't mind so much. Like a lot of other people, she'd mellowed a good deal over the past few months.

"I'm so proud of you," my father said, and I felt tears prick at my eyes.

"Don't make me cry," I warned him. "Sydney spent an hour on my makeup, and if this mascara runs, I'm toast."

He smiled. "Well, we can't have that. But—I just wanted you to know how happy I am that you're allowing me to walk you down the aisle."

"Of course you're walking me down the aisle," I said, going to him and looping my arm through his. "You're my father, aren't you?"

"That I am," he agreed. "And I'll be here for you from now on. That's a promise."

"Good," I said with a grin. "Because I have a feeling Connor and I are going to need a whole bunch of babysitters in the near future."

He responded to that with a laugh. But then I heard the harpist beginning to play Pachelbel's "Canon," and knew the ritual walk down the aisle had begun. My heart sped up, and he patted my hand.

"Ready?"

"Ready," I replied.

We began the slow processional, moving out into the bright sunshine, a fresh breeze playing with my veil. To either side were crowds of people, many of whom I barely recognized—the Wilcox contingent, I supposed—but of course there were many familiar faces, including Sydney's parents, and then my Aunt Rachel and Tobias and the McAllister elders sitting in the front row on one side, and Lucas and Marie on the other, an empty seat next to her, waiting for my father when he was done walking me down the aisle.

Then I really didn't have eyes for any of them, only saw Connor waiting for me, Anthony standing next to him, along with Connor's friend Darren and a Wilcox cousin whose name totally escaped me at the moment. We were still a few yards apart, but Connor's gaze caught mine and held. I could see the way his eyes lit up when he saw me, and I almost gasped when I saw how handsome he was in his charcoal gray suit and deep teal tie. He'd kept growing his hair, and now it was long enough that he had it back in a ponytail. I actually loved that, because it was a lot of fun to pull off the elastic at night and let my fingers drift through the heavy raven tresses. And don't even get me started on the way that hair felt brushing against my inner thighs....

The woman officiating was someone we'd found at one of Sedona's funky New Age churches; she'd been more than happy to perform a sort of free-form ceremony for us, as I'd discovered that the Wilcoxes tended to have traditional sorts of weddings, more for appearance than anything else, and I knew the Goddess didn't care much how this marriage happened, as long as it did. For Connor and I were meant to be together—I knew that more than anything else—and everything else was just window dressing.

My father bent and kissed me on the cheek before going to take his seat next to Marie, and Connor stepped forward to take my hand in his. For a second I fumbled with the bouquet, totally forgetting I was supposed to hand it off to Sydney. Then I heard her laugh and come over to take it from me.

After that, things went smoothly, although I have to confess I wasn't paying much attention to the words of the ceremony, was only staring up at Connor, wondering how I could be so lucky to have found him, how I truly did have the man of my dreams. And at the end he kissed me, warm fire spreading through my veins, and I realized he was now my husband, and I was his wife, and the mingling of the two clans had truly begun.

Whatever their differences, everyone did stand up and cheer and clap as we made our way back down the aisle, hand in hand. After this I knew there would be a frenzy and a bustle for a while as the hotel staff broke down all the lines of chairs and set up tables in their stead, but Connor and I got to miss most of that as we had our pictures taken while the sun began to dip toward the horizon, and the rocks blazed redder and redder behind us.

And when we returned, the outdoor space had been turned into fairyland, with lights swagged from the trees and gleaming from the middle of the tables, and everyone looking a little more relaxed after using the downtime to hit the open bar.

A week before the wedding, I'd had another appointment with Dr. Ruiz, and she said I could have a small glass of champagne at the reception, as long as it was only the one. "I won't tell a bride that she can't have a little champagne at her own wedding," she said with a smile.

That hadn't been the only piece of good news she shared with us, though. She performed another ultrasound, and this time she was able to be fairly definite on the sex of the twins. "Looks like a boy and a girl," she informed us, while I grinned like an idiot and Connor held my hand and looked at me as if I'd just performed some sort of miracle.

To him, it was. No Wilcox *primus* had ever had a daughter since Nizhoni cast her curse, and he wasn't sure what to make of it. "So does this mean our son will be the next *primus*, and our daughter will be *prima* of the McAllisters?" he asked me, and I'd laughed and said,

"How about we let them choose what they want to be? It'll be a nice change of pace."

He'd looked thoughtful at that comment, and nodded slowly, saying, "I think that sounds like a great idea."

So now I held my own precious glass of champagne, determined to nurse it for as long as required, knowing I'd have to save some for the toasts. The guests milled around, segregating into their little McAllister and Wilcox clumps, just as I feared they would, although I noticed Sydney's parents seemed to be willing to talk to anyone who crossed their paths. I didn't know how much Syd had told them about Connor's and my respective families, and in that moment I didn't much care. I was just glad to see them treating all the wedding guests alike.

And then....

"Look at that," I whispered to Connor.

He followed my gaze to where Mason stood. A tall young man with brown hair was talking to her, gesturing with a glass of champagne in one hand, and I saw her laugh and flick a lock of long dark hair behind one shoulder.

Good deployment of the hair toss, Mason, I thought, unable to repress a smile.

"Is that…?"

"Yep, that's my cousin Adam. I guess his heart wasn't irretrievably broken after all."

"Wow."

"I think it's awesome," I said. "I hope they flirt all night and then go shack up in a hotel room somewhere."

"Seriously?"

I thought of how Mason had confessed she wasn't that thrilled about getting married, since she didn't want to marry a cousin and was worried that being with a civilian would be too complicated. That wasn't to say that hooking up with a McAllister might not have its own complications, but I thought it was a step in the right direction.

"Seriously," I told him. "Or do you want to be the only guy getting lucky in Sedona tonight?"

"Nah, I'm not that selfish," Connor replied with a grin.

"Glad to hear it," I said, and that was all the time we had to spend on our speculations, since a couple of his cousins came up to offer their congratulations.

And then it was time for dinner, and I just barely managed to make my glass of champagne last through the cinnamon-roasted duck breast so I would still have enough for the toasts. Even so, I ended up stealing a sip or two from Connor's glass, just because there were so many toasts—from Lucas, of course, and my father and Tobias and Anthony. Even Bryce McAllister stood up and quite unexpectedly gave us his blessing, which moved me much more than I thought it would. Somehow I hadn't thought any of the McAllister elders would unbend enough to recognize that Connor and I truly were meant to be together.

After that I kicked off my sandals and danced with my husband, alone on the dance floor, as the moon rose above the mesa to the east and "It Had to Be You" played through the loudspeakers cleverly concealed within the branches of the trees overhead. Once our first dance was over, everyone crowded in around us, the music picking up its tempo, Wilcoxes and McAllisters all moving together in a scene I was sure no one would have believed, if they'd seen it only six months earlier.

My feet were starting to give out on me, even minus the torture devices Sydney referred to as "sandals," so I went back to my chair and sat down, then put my feet up on the empty seat next to me, content to simply watch the happy crowd. Connor settled in beside me, then handed me a glass of ice water. "Don't poop out on me now," he said. "We've probably got at least another three hours to get through."

"I'm not pooping out," I replied, taking the water and drinking half of it down without stopping. After I let out a contented little sigh, I added, "I'm just waiting to get my second wind."

"I'm sure it'll miraculously appear as soon as it's time to cut the cake."

"Probably." I wasn't going to argue with him on that point; I'd been waiting for that spice cake with buttercream frosting all day.

But then I saw something that made me sit up straighter in my chair and drop my feet to the ground.

"I don't believe it," I murmured to him.

"What?"

Pointing would have been rude, so I settled for tilting my head over to the left, to a table a few yards away. Margot Emory had been sitting there alone, watching the dancing. Her expression was hard to read, but to me it almost looked...wistful? No, that was impossible. Margot wouldn't allow herself to be wistful.

But then Lucas Wilcox approached her. I couldn't hear what he was saying, of course, but it almost looked like he was asking her to dance. How many glasses of champagne had it taken him to work up the courage for that, realizing he was only going to get shot down?

I didn't know, of course.

The crazy thing was, it didn't *look* like she was shooting him down. She tilted her head back slightly to look at him, her hair, free at last from its eternal ponytail, slipping back over the shoulders of her turquoise sheath dress. Then she stood up, and even allowed him to take her by the hand and lead her to the dance floor. It was a slow dance, "The Way You Look Tonight," and yet she was allowing him to put his arm around her waist, hadn't tried to blast him into next week.

"Okay, now I truly believe world peace is possible," I said at last.

"After everything we've been through, I believe just about anything is possible," Connor told me, picking up my hand and pressing it to his lips.

The touch of his mouth against my skin made a delicious shiver run through me, and I halfway wished we could slip out now and start the wedding night early, spice cake or no. But I knew I would stay. I could do no less for my family…all of them, McAllister and Wilcox alike.

What a wonderful thought that was. So many wounds beginning to heal, so many old prejudices starting to fade away. It would take time, and I knew, people being who they were, that it wouldn't always be easy. But it would be worth it. For Connor, for me, for our children, and the children who were to come after them.

At long last, the unquiet ghosts of our past had been laid to rest.

The End

Made in the USA
Lexington, KY
05 August 2014